S0-AYW-486

7-07

Praise for

When Bobbie Sang the Blues

"*When Bobbie Sang the Blues* is a fun, mystery-filled read with endearing characters set in a coastal town that feels every bit as alive as the folks who live there. At the heart of the story is Christy Castleman, a level-headed and resourceful amateur sleuth whose persistence and kind-heartedness win the day. With just the right touch of romance and faith, the story provides a satisfying visit to a community and people you'll surely want to visit again."

—MINDY STARNS CLARK, author of the Smart Chick
mystery series and the Million Dollar Mysteries

"Peggy Darty gives us a charming romp through a delightful beach town, with romance and plot twists of intrigue."

—HANNAH ALEXANDER, author of *Death Benefits*

Praise for

When the Sandpiper Calls

"Forget that trip to the beach this year. Just escape into Peggy Darty's latest novel—and you'll be there. Mystery, romance, inspiration, and the authentic atmosphere of Florida's Emerald Coast will leap off the pages and into your heart."

—JOYCE HOLLAND, *Northwest Florida Daily News*

It's…an entertaining, appealing read with a surprising ending.
—PUBLISHER'S WEEKLY

"*When the Sandpiper Calls* by Peggy Darty is a story as intriguing as the author and her work. Peggy combines a unique mixture of cozy and crime in a masterful way, making *When the Sandpiper Calls* a page-turning must-read. Don't miss this intriguing story told by one of my favorite authors."
—YVONNE LEHMAN, author of *Coffee Rings,* director of Blue Ridge Mountains Christian Writers Conference

When
Bobbie Sang
the Blues

When Bobbie Sang the Blues

A Cozy Mystery by
Peggy Darty

WaterBrook
PRESS

WHEN BOBBIE SANG THE BLUES
PUBLISHED BY WATERBROOK PRESS
12265 Oracle Boulevard, Suite 200
Colorado Springs, Colorado 80921
A division of Random House Inc.

All Scripture quotations and paraphrases, unless otherwise indicated, are taken from the Holy Bible, New International Version®. NIV®. Copyright © 1973, 1978, 1984 by International Bible Society. Used by permission of Zondervan Publishing House. All rights reserved.

The characters and events in this book are fictional, and any resemblance to actual persons or events is coincidental.

ISBN 978-1-4000-7330-6

Copyright © 2007 by Peggy Darty

All rights reserved. No part of this book may be reproduced or transmitted in any form or by any means, electronic or mechanical, including photocopying and recording, or by any information storage and retrieval system, without permission in writing from the publisher.

WATERBROOK and its deer design logo are registered trademarks of WaterBrook Press, a division of Random House Inc.

Library of Congress Cataloging-in-Publication Data
Darty, Peggy.
    When Bobbie sang the blues : a cozy mystery / Peggy Darty. — 1st ed.
        p. cm.
    ISBN-13: 978-1-4000-7330-6
    1. Women authors—Fiction. 2. Detective and mystery stories—Authorship—
Fiction. 3. Florida—Fiction. I. Title.
    PS3554.A79W45 2007
    813'.54—dc22

                                        2006028477

Printed in the United States of America
2007—First Edition

10 9 8 7 6 5 4 3 2 1

For Steve and Lucy with love

one

Monday, September 18, 2006

The chime of the doorbell broke the bubble-drip-hiss rhythm of Christy Castleman's coffee machine. Early morning visitors at Christy's door were no surprise. A variety of people often appeared before or during breakfast, and Christy wasn't sure who to expect as she hopped down from the stool at the breakfast bar and headed to the back door.

Through the glass pane, a wide, fun-loving smile greeted her. Aunt Bobbie Bodine! Christy hadn't seen her aunt in years, but there was no mistaking the unique Bobbie. A bright smile highlighted dancing blue eyes in a delicate round face with enough laugh lines to sketch character. Short blond hair dipped and waved around her small face. A rebellious curl dangled on Bobbie's forehead, a symbol of her lively personality. Even at fifty-one, she was still a knockout by most male standards.

Christy smiled and waved as she turned the key in the lock. She opened the door and hugged her tiny aunt, all curves and lean muscle.

"Look at you." Bobbie stepped back and studied her. "Prettier than ever with those big blue eyes and golden brown hair. And you're slim as a rail. You must have guys chasing you all the time."

"All the time," Christy quipped.

Bobbie entered the kitchen, balancing herself gracefully on green cork wedges. "Am I interrupting your work?" she asked, glancing at the pen, journal, and open Bible on the counter.

"No, I read some scripture and write in my prayer journal every morning," Christy said. "It's the best way to start my day."

Bobbie made no comment, simply turning away.

Christy placed a mug in her aunt's hand, her eyes sweeping Bobbie's diminutive frame.

"Mmm...fresh coffee," Bobbie said as she filled her cup. "In case your mother hasn't called with the news, I hit town yesterday and went partying until late last night." She glanced over her shoulder and grinned, the blond curl bouncing with the movement. "My little sister went into shock, of course, being a prominent pastor's wife."

Christy laughed. "I'm sure she was glad to see you. And no, she hasn't called me. Welcome to Summer Breeze, Aunt Bobbie."

"Thanks, hon. It's good to see you. How long has it been?"

Christy frowned. "Three, four years, maybe?"

"No!"

"You came to visit after..."

"After one of my separations from Eddie. But this time it's permanent. I've just been through another divorce. Whoever said third time's a charm never met Eddie Bodine."

A ripple of laughter followed her remark. Bobbie had always been quick to point out her own mistakes. She enjoyed life and refused to be defeated by it.

"Bobbie, you always lift my spirits…and I think you affect others the same way."

"Oh, well…" She shrugged off Christy's affirmation and sipped her coffee. "There's nothing better than a good cup of coffee first thing in the morning." She winked. "Or second thing in the morning. I couldn't find a Starbucks."

"We don't have one yet," Christy said. "Nor do we have a Wal-Mart or Home Depot. This is Summer Breeze, remember?"

Bobbie made a face and looked at her watch. "What time does the garbage truck run?"

"Excuse me?"

"The garbage truck. Your mother said today is garbage day."

Christy glanced at the wall clock.

"Sometime around nine. But it's unpredictable."

"Well, we've got to beat the truck." Bobbie placed her coffee mug on the counter and headed for the door.

"Why do we have to beat the garbage truck?" Christy asked, following her.

"Don't you want to help your aunt make a little money? I've spotted one of those old pickle barrels—you know the kind you'd see in country stores? Stands about four feet high. It's been left curbside, three streets over."

Christy stared at her aunt for half a second, then rewound the rubber band on her ponytail, knowing it was useless to refuse.

Bobbie always got her way. Christy shoved her bare feet into flip-flops, then turned to the keys-n-things rack.

"We'll go in my truck," Bobbie said.

Christy trailed her through the kitchen door and across the sun porch. A red truck with a mangled chrome bumper sat parked at an angle in the driveway. Dented doors hinted at narrow escapes.

Christy climbed in the truck, pushing aside a cosmetic bag and a crumpled fast-food sack. A Dixie Cup of ice rattled in the cup holder as she slammed the door.

Bobbie hopped behind the wheel like a sixteen-year-old, then patted the cluttered dash affectionately. "Behave yourself. We're in a nice neighborhood. No ugly noises from the tailpipe." She turned the key, and the engine came to life.

Christy turned in the seat to peer through the back window. How could little Bobbie see over the hodgepodge of items piled in the bed of her truck?

"Thanks for coming along, sweetie. You're a good sport. Your mother has always been wound a notch too tight, so I have enough fun for both of us. I have a feeling your parents are a little anxious about how long I'll be a houseguest."

"Would you like to move in with me? I have a spare bed in my office."

"You're a dear to offer," Bobbie replied, "but I'll have my own place soon. Seth already told me about a cute bungalow for lease over at Sunnyside."

Christy turned and looked curiously at her. "You've seen Seth?"

"Seth dropped by your parents' house last night and mentioned a new blues club had opened up. We decided to check it out and had a marvelous time. I've been in Memphis for years, and Memphis is the home of blues music. I love it. Look, there's the pickle barrel."

They skidded to a halt before a rambling Spanish-style home. Christy recognized it and knew the owners collected antiques. She stared at the old oak barrel perched on the curb, apparently one of their castoffs. Three of the metal hoops had loosened and slid to the bottom of the barrel. To Christy, it just looked dirty and broken.

"What are you going to do with it?" she asked.

"Add it to my treasures," Bobbie said. "This baby will be valuable once I reposition the hoops and tighten the staves. I'm going to open a little shop here. Everyone in Memphis loved to shop with me, but..."

Christy waited for her to finish, but the words trailed in the air, the answer unfinished. Had the divorce prompted Bobbie's sudden appearance in Summer Breeze? The question nagged at Christy, but her instincts told her not to ask.

Bobbie parked the truck and looked at Christy. "Come on, honey." She hopped out the door and hurried to inspect the barrel.

Christy followed. She could hear the roar of the garbage truck grow closer. Helping her aunt, she tried to get a grip on the dirty barrel. As they lifted and tugged, the barrel seemed to fight back—an octopus with loose staves dangling like crazy arms. Finally, the barrel fell into the back of the truck, leaving Christy with an oak splinter in her palm.

The garbage truck heaved around the corner as Bobbie slammed the tailgate of the truck, and Christy ran around and jumped in the front seat.

When Bobbie got in, she pressed her hand to her chest and frowned. Christy watched as she opened her purse and removed a bottle of pills, twisting frantically on the cap. "I forgot to take my pill."

"Here, let me," Christy said. "I open Granny's pill bottles when I visit her. She has arthritis in her hands." She pressed down on the cap and twisted it hard. When the cap loosened, she handed the bottle back.

"Thanks." Bobbie popped a pill in her mouth and grabbed the Dixie Cup of melted ice, draining liquid from the bottom of the cup. With a flick of the wrist, she closed the bottle and dropped it into her purse.

"It's long-acting nitroglycerin. Keeps my heart from racing. A pill a day and I'm okay."

"Are you sure you're okay?" Christy asked, wondering about her aunt.

"Nothing I can't handle," Bobbie replied, pressing her dainty sandal against the accelerator. The truck shuddered and heaved like a tired old hound awakened to the chase.

Christy smiled at the absurdity of the entire morning. "I'm glad you're here," she said. "You'll add some much-needed spice to our lives."

"Don't you have a boyfriend for that?" Bobbie shot her a worried glance.

Christy hesitated. She and Dan had started their relationship in a romantic whirlwind of flowers and long talks over moonlit dinners, and everything had been fine for more than a year. But then problems began to creep in as they fell into the trap of taking each other for granted. Now she knew they both had work to do for the relationship to survive.

Christy's heart lurched as Bobbie headed straight for the lamp-post on the corner. "Aunt Bobbie, watch out!"

Bobbie maneuvered a sharp right, barely missing the pole.

"I have to rent a storage unit," Bobbie said, as though nothing out of the ordinary had occurred. "Where's the nearest storage facility?"

Eddie Bodine kept his distance, cruising along in his white Ford truck. Sitting close beside him, Roseann Cole studied the junk in the red pickup they were tailing. The two women in the cab seemed completely unaware they were being followed.

Roseann glanced at Eddie. His arms were wrapped around the steering wheel, and his eyes didn't leave the red truck. She sighed. This was getting boring.

She pulled down the visor mirror to reapply her Crimson Passion lip gloss. As she did, she studied her reflection. She was pleased with the new perm and the mass of dark curls it created around her face and neck, and her full lips were the rave in Hollywood. Still, she knew she wasn't a beauty. Her nose looked too thin for her face, and her brown eyes were small and close set. At thirty-four, she had learned how to make the most of her assets, however, and she liked the way her white tank top and designer jeans fit her curves. But— she glanced at Eddie—like Momma said, a girl had to have a plan.

Roseann recapped the lip gloss and snapped the visor mirror back in place. She looked at the red truck they were following. "Eddie, honey, why don't you just let it go?"

"Roseann, I told you. Bobbie made off with ten grand of my money, and I ain't gonna let that go, as you put it." His lips curled around the words, and his round face flushed beneath the black cowboy hat.

She reached over and trailed her fingers over his suntanned face, touching the edge of his close-cropped brown hair. She had insulted him when she suggested fewer haircuts. She'd never mentioned it again. Upsetting Eddie held consequences.

The dark eyes softened as he looked at her. "The thing is, I was her third husband. She got money off the first two, and she didn't need money from me."

She smiled and nodded, studying Eddie. At five feet nine, she sat three inches taller than he. His friend Freddy refused to date a woman he couldn't tower over, but Eddie liked the fact that she was tall and worked out to keep her body in shape.

"Roseann, you're the sweetest woman I've ever known, and I don't want to lose you. But if I don't get that money back from Bobbie, my creditors will string me up. With fuel prices what they are, my company's struggling." His black boot stomped the brake at the stoplight.

Roseann frowned. The fact that Eddie owned a trucking company and tossed money in her direction was the basis of her attraction to him.

"Honey, I don't wanna argue with you," Eddie said, his voice low and husky. "Now scoot over here and give me a kiss. I love the way you kiss."

Suppressing a sigh, Roseann scooted over to kiss him.

⟡

"This has to be the most beautiful place on earth," Bobbie said to Christy.

"I know. Sometimes I forget how lucky I am to live here."

On their way to the storage units, Bobbie drove the scenic route out of Summer Breeze, winding past long stretches of open beach. The emerald waves of the Gulf capped sugar white sands, inviting sunbathers to take advantage of the autumn sun. A purple umbrella protected a mother and her little boy as they gathered buckets of sand for their half-built sandcastle.

Christy looked across at her aunt. Bobbie's short blond curls billowed in the breeze coming through her open window. Christy remembered her aunt loved the ocean breeze; it never got too cold for her. She found herself hoping Bobbie would stay.

"Your shop might really catch on," Christy said, glancing through the back window to the pickle barrel lumbering around on its side in the bed of the truck. "It'll be something different."

"Wait'll you see my doors and windows!"

"Excuse me?"

Bobbie laughed. "I find old doors and windows and turn them into coffee tables, planters, and so forth. My pride and joy is my hall tree made from a picket fence. They were tearing down a picket fence from a yard a few blocks from me in Memphis. I grabbed the last two pieces just before they were tossed in the trash bin."

"Up ahead on the right," Christy pointed. "Those are the storage units."

"Great." Bobbie slowed down and turned into the graveled area, parking her red truck in front of the office.

⌒∞⌒

Their white truck cruised along, and Roseann turned to stare at the storage facility. "That sign says the gate opens at eight o'clock and closes at one in the morning."

"Thanks for the information," Eddie drawled. "Don't know what good it'll do me."

"They're standing in front of a unit with the door up. It looks empty. Think she's going to rent a unit? It's the one next to the office."

Eddie slowed the truck and glanced over his shoulder. "Maybe that's where she's gonna hide the money till she gets it all spent."

⌒∞⌒

It took less than twenty minutes for Bobbie to rent a unit from a man who introduced himself as Hornsby. "It's my last name, but I like it better than Leonard, my first name." He was tall and lanky with a long nose and tousled dark hair, and he wore a Hawaiian shirt and Bermuda shorts with a three-inch tear above the left knee. Christy couldn't tell if his brown eyes naturally protruded or if they had popped when Bobbie swayed into his office and asked if he had anything for rent.

"Happen to have a ten-by-twenty next to the office," he said, after an awkward moment.

Bobbie plopped her purse down on the counter, and they followed him to the adjoining unit. As he rolled up the metal door, a blast of stale, hot air greeted them.

"These metal units get pretty hot," he said. "But I'll leave it open for a little while, air it out."

"What about those stains on the concrete?" Bobbie pointed.

"Something from the previous owner. If you want, I've got some two-by-fours in an empty unit that I can lay down over the stain."

Bobbie nodded. "I only have a few boxes, but I'd like to protect them."

While Hornsby went after the wood, she turned to Christy. "What do you think?"

Christy shrugged. "I wouldn't want to stay in here long, but it's the middle of September. Soon the weather will cool down."

Hornsby returned, balancing several pieces of wood in his arms. He laid them over the stain.

"Okay, I'll take it," Bobbie said.

"Come back in the office, and we'll do the paperwork," Hornsby suggested.

Bobbie and Christy followed him back to his tiny office, where he opened a squeaky drawer and removed a file folder.

Bobbie didn't bother asking rates. She glanced carelessly over the contract he handed her, signed the forms, then pulled a wad of bills from her sequined shoulder bag. "I'll pay three months in advance," she said, slapping three one hundred dollar bills in Hornsby's sweaty palm. She turned to Christy. "I have a moving van set to bring my stuff as soon as I call them."

As they walked out of the office with Hornsby following, Bobbie turned to him. "Honey, you think you could help us put a couple of things in the unit?"

"I don't usually—," he began, following them to Bobbie's truck. His gaze slid over the boxes and settled on the sixty-gallon barrel.

"It'll only take a few minutes of your time." Bobbie laid a hand on his arm. "And I'm afraid we girls will throw our backs out." She turned to Christy. "I can't wait to work on that pickle barrel. I haven't seen anything like it at the flea markets or antique shops." She inspected the dusty barrel.

"Neither have I. But then I've never even heard of an antique pickle barrel," Christy said as Hornsby wrestled the barrel from the truck.

Bobbie slapped the dust from her hands and glanced at Hornsby as he set the last box on the storage unit's floor. "I'll call the moving van as soon as I get a place to live, and the rest of my stuff will be delivered. Thank you, Hornsby."

He nodded, looking from the women to the items in the unit.

"Is there anything in those boxes you'll need?" Christy asked.

"No. They're just decorating books and magazines that I packed up at the last minute."

"What's that?" Christy asked, pointing at an object protruding from one of the boxes.

"A jack handle. That box holds some things I had in my truck, but I'll leave them here so they don't rattle around anymore. I was ready to pull my hair out the next time something slammed across the bed of my truck."

"You ready to lock up here?" Hornsby asked.

"Yes, thanks."

He pulled down the sliding metal door, and Bobbie inserted a padlock on the handle and turned the key.

Christy nodded. "Then if we're done here, how about breakfast at Miz B's?"

"Great! I'm starved, aren't you?"

Bobbie waved to Hornsby as they got in the truck and slammed the doors.

"I'll bet you my line-dancing boots that Hornsby's the biggest gossip in town," Bobbie whispered as she started the truck.

Christy glanced through the back window. Hornsby leaned against Bobbie's locked unit, one bony foot slung carelessly over the other, staring after them. "Why do you say that?" she asked.

"Lesson in character, honey, since that's your trade as a writer. I never met a human with a real long nose like Hornsby, narrow suspicious eyes, and a mouthful of questions who wasn't nosy by nature."

"Reminds me of Roy Thornberry," Christy said. "A real thorn in my side. He's my former boss at the local newspaper. For almost two years, I wrote a weekly column, 'The Beach Buzz.' But after Labor Day, when tourist season ended, I resigned. I just couldn't put up with Roy anymore. He has to know everything that goes on in twelve counties. He claims it's his business to keep up, but he goes way beyond the call of duty and interferes in private lives." She recalled how he had pestered her endlessly about her relationship with Dan Brockman.

Bobbie turned back onto Front Beach Road and studied her reflection in the visor mirror. "Where did you say we're going for breakfast? Is it somewhere I can tuck my napkin into my collar? I'm awfully messy," she said, laughing at herself.

The white truck pulled into a service station with a view of the storage unit. Eddie stopped at a pump and put the hose on automatic. Then he climbed back behind the wheel and watched the road.

"Who's that with her?" Roseann asked. "She looks young enough to be her daughter."

"Bobbie can't have children," Eddie said. "She got pregnant when she was dating me, but a month after we got married, she lost the baby. The doctor said she couldn't have kids. That's when her personality changed."

"Yeah, well, I'm gonna get us something to drink and stake out that storage facility."

Ten minutes later, she left her look-out point near the phone booth at the edge of the service station and jogged back over to the truck.

"They're pulling out of the gate and are heading this way," she told Eddie. "They'll pass us in a minute."

"Get in!" he said. "Quick!" He bent toward the floor as though he were looking for something, and Roseann jumped in the seat and ducked her head. They heard the little red truck rumble past. Eddie had already paid for the gas, and he cranked up the engine and eased toward the road.

Roseann stared at him, thinking about what he had told her the night before. She cleared her throat. "Last night you said you signed your life insurance over to me last week. Why would you do that? You got a good thirty years left!"

A wide smile filled his round face. "You deserve it for putting up with me."

She smiled. Eager to help Eddie now, she leaned forward in the seat and peered at the truck.

"So who is that young woman?" Roseann asked again.

"I don't know, but if she's connected to Bobbie, we're sticking to her like a tick on a hound."

As they sped down the highway, Christy wondered how her wild aunt and her proper, perfectionist mother could be related. They grew up in rural Minnesota, but Bobbie had married young and moved away. She had spent most of her life in the South, and as a result, her southern accent sounded as pure as Georgia honey.

"Miz B's is my friend Bonnie's restaurant," Christy explained. "It used to be a steak and seafood house. Bonnie said there were enough of those up and down the coast, and what we needed was 'home cookin'.' Nobody does that better than Miz B—that's what we call her since she took over the restaurant.

"Bobbie, do you mind swinging by my place so I can pick up my car? After we eat breakfast, I need to get back home for a phone conference with my editor. I'm sure you have things to do as well."

"Sure," Bobbie replied good-naturedly. She slowed the truck and turned down Christy's street. "I'll follow you. By the way," she said as the truck whirled into Christy's driveway, "are there any sharp guys around? About my age? Maybe a little younger?"

"Did you see the bombshell that just left?" Hornsby asked Tony Panada as he sauntered through the back door of his office.

"I saw two bombshells. Which one are you talkin' about?" Tony was six-three, tall and bony, ears and nose dominating his face. He tried to be fashionably bald, but without a hairline to soften his ears, they stood out like doorknobs.

"The older one's Bobbie Bodine," Hornsby replied. "She just rented number 101. Pulled out a wad of hundreds that would choke a horse."

Tony thrust a Havana cigar in his mouth and flicked open a silver lighter.

"I told you! If you gotta smoke, at least stand in the door and blow the smoke out back," Hornsby snapped.

"Settle down, Hornsby. I need to have a little discussion with you." Tony blew smoke rings out the door, his back to Hornsby.

"I assume the discussion involves money."

"It does."

Hornsby chuckled. "Green's my favorite color. And the size always fits."

Tony stomped out his cigar and turned around. His eyes, a faded gray, studied Hornsby. "I could use another unit for my business. What about the one that backs up to Miz Bodine? Is it still empty?"

"Still empty," Hornsby replied. "But I don't want any little photography sessions going on back there."

"Hadn't thought of that, but it's a good suggestion. Actually, I have a personal interest in Miz Bodine and her ex-husband. If she's in Summer Breeze, I figure he'll be here soon."

Miz B's Family Restaurant hummed with life, as usual. White rocking chairs sat on the front porch of the stucco building, and hanging baskets of flowers and greenery added color and comfort. Miz B's felt like a big, happy home.

Christy opened the door for Bobbie, and they entered the wide foyer. A thick oak bookshelf stood against the wall and held a hundred cookbooks, well loved and well used.

"Nice touch," Bobbie said, admiring the cookbooks.

"What a friend we have in Jesus…" A rich soprano voice rolled through the open door of the kitchen. Suddenly the singing stopped, and a woman's voice yelled, "Junior, I ain't serving fried potato peelings. There are more potatoes than peelings in the garbage."

Christy laughed softly and tugged Bobbie's arm. "Come on," she said, leading her aunt across the restaurant. She peered around the kitchen door.

Miz B stood in the middle of the kitchen, wielding a paring knife she had obviously taken from Junior, who stared down at his lumpy potato skins.

"Don't be so hard on the poor guy," Christy called to her.

Miz B turned—all six feet, two hundred pounds of her. The worry wrinkles in her round, dark face relaxed into a wide smile as she looked at Christy, then Bobbie. She laid the knife on the counter and opened her arms to Christy. After an affectionate hug, she turned her attention to Bobbie, who lingered in the doorway.

"Woman, can you ever belt out the blues," Miz B said. "Why, you're a better singer than me."

"I guess Seth and I got a little loud last night," Bobbie said, looking embarrassed. "I just like to sing the blues. It's about all I can sing."

"Honey, you don't need to sing anything else." Miz B wiped her big hands on her purple apron appliquéd with red hats and looked at Christy. "Why didn't you come out to the Blues Club last night? Everybody was there. Even Dan." She bit her full lip. "I need to stop my babbling."

Christy knew the "babbling" referred to her mention of Dan. He had gone to the new club without her. But why not? She hadn't spoken with him since their breakup three weeks ago.

"Jamie, look who's here," Miz B called, leading Christy and Bobbie into the dining room. "You wanna get them something to drink? Coffee?"

Christy and Jamie Browning had become friends when Jamie and her young sons moved to Summer Breeze to escape an abusive husband. Beth, Christy's mom, had taken them under her wing, enrolling them in her Sunday school class and including the boys, ages six and eight, in activities with other kids their age.

"Let me tell you the best thing we got this morning," Miz B said, directing them toward a booth. "Country ham with red-eye gravy— not that white mess Shorty makes." Shorty's coffee shop had taken a hit since Miz B's opened. "And grits, of course. Forget the potatoes today. And I'll top you off with my special buttermilk biscuits."

"Sign me up," Bobbie said, rubbing her stomach.

"Me too!" Christy agreed.

Jamie appeared with two steaming mugs of coffee.

"Jamie, I'd like you to meet my aunt, Bobbie Bodine."

"Pleased to meet you," Jamie said, setting the mugs on the table. "Your niece has been a godsend for me. I moved here from Atlanta and didn't know a soul. Christy took me right in. And Miss Beth has done wonders for my sons through the church programs."

"It's nice to meet you," Bobbie said warmly. "I'm staying with Beth and Grant until I can find a place."

"What are the boys up to?" Christy asked.

"Getting ready for the retreat to Camp Honeywood," Jamie said. "They're so excited, I can hardly live with them. Is your mom going as one of the chaperons?"

Christy nodded. "Dad's going to run the gift shop on Saturday, and he's promised to eat out so he won't burn down the house."

Jamie laughed and hurried off to accommodate an older man waving an empty mug.

"Grant seems capable of taking care of himself," Bobbie said with a slight touch of sarcasm that had nothing to do with Christy's father and everything to do with her mother. Christy had given up trying to figure out the rivalry between them long ago.

"So you're Beth's sister?" Miz B asked, her dark eyes glowing as she appraised Bobbie.

Bobbie nodded. "You'd never know it, would you?"

"Well, you look a little bit alike, I reckon. Small build, small features."

"Yeah, but the similarity ends there," Bobbie replied. "Beth was the good girl who always said, did, and wore the right thing. I was the rebel. Still am." She winked at Christy.

Miz B chuckled, her chest heaving behind the purple apron bib. "Well, we're mighty glad to have you. Let me turn in those orders."

Jamie passed the table again, balancing several empty plates. "I see Miz B is personally taking care of you, so I'll stay out of the way." Her eyes strayed to Bobbie. "Will you be staying here long?"

Bobbie nodded. "I'm opening a shop called I Saw It First."

"What a cute name for a shop!"

"Oh, honey, it's just trash I find at flea markets and garage sales, but unlike most people, I look beyond the flaws and see the promise."

Christy smiled, impressed. "What a great way to put it."

Bobbie smiled back, obviously pleased by Christy's comment. "Yeah, I admit I get a lot of satisfaction out of working with things that have been thrown away, taking those objects and making them beautiful and useful again. That's especially important to families who don't know what to do with the junk in their attic or a broken dresser that belonged to Grandma."

"Well, I declare," Miz B said, having reappeared with two

plates piled with food. "That's just about the best idea I've heard in years. And that gives me an idea. Our Red Hat club meets here on Thursday. The girls would just love it if you could talk to them about restoring old things. We've all got stuff we don't know what to do with, but we don't want to throw it away."

"Great idea!" Christy looked across at Bobbie. "You could start drumming up business for your shop."

Bobbie laughed. "I like the way you think, honey."

"Eat and enjoy," Miz B said, placing their breakfast before them.

They ate in silence for a moment, and then Bobbie looked up at Christy. "I saw an old post lying in your parents' garage. Grant said it came from his mother's back porch and he hated to part with it." She stared into space as she munched on a crusty brown biscuit. "I can show the ladies how to turn that old post into a lovely coat tree." She looked at Christy and winked. "It would look real good."

Christy had seen the splintered old post and couldn't imagine it fitting anything but a garbage can, but she merely shrugged. "I just don't have that kind of imagination."

"You have a wonderful imagination. I love your mysteries. What are you working on now?"

"The third book in my pirate series. I have to do a ton of research."

A deep voice floated down from behind Christy's head. "I'll take a bite of that biscuit if you put a hunk of real butter on it."

Christy looked up at a grinning Jack Watson. He had on his usual jeans, and the blue polo shirt he wore emphasized his blue eyes, bracketed by lifelines. In his case, age only added to his charisma. Sometimes when Christy looked at him, she could see Chad, and her memory rolled back to the good times and hung onto the if-onlys.

"Care to join us?" she asked as his gaze swept Bobbie. "Jack, have you ever met my aunt, Bobbie Bodine?"

"No, he hasn't," Bobbie extended her hand. "I never forget a handsome face."

Jack chuckled and slid into the booth beside Christy. "Thank you, ma'am. I'm Jack Watson. I look out for your niece." He glanced at Christy and scowled as though remembering something. "Most of the time," he added.

Jamie paused at the table. "Hi, Mr. Watson. Would you like breakfast?"

"Nah, just coffee. Thanks."

"I assume you've already had your cold cereal," Christy said, handing him a buttered biscuit.

"She knows me pretty well," he said to Bobbie.

"I can see that," Bobbie replied, watching the two of them together. And then her eyes widened as though she had just thought of something. "You're Chad's father, aren't you?"

Fifty-four years beneath the Florida sun had sketched deep lines on Jack's forehead. Those lines deepened at the mention of his son's name. "Yeah." A halfhearted grin worked the corners of his mouth, and he turned to Christy, placing an arm around her shoulders and squeezing her gently. "Since we lost Chad, I've claimed this little gal as my daughter. So life hands out a few rewards, I guess."

Christy felt the warmth of his muscled arm around her shoulders, and she smiled into his eyes, once as blue as the deep water of the Gulf. Sun and age had paled the irises, and now Christy thought of the sky rather than the Gulf when she looked at him.

Bobbie cleared her throat. "Jack, I want to open a shop here. Maybe you'd have a suggestion on locations."

Jack turned to her. "What kind of shop?"

"I have a little hobby—make that an obsession—for turning trash into treasure."

"Oh?" Jack munched on the biscuit, studying her carefully. He looked back at Christy. "Maybe she can work on me."

"Stop it." Christy swatted his shoulder. "Aunt Bobbie is a very talented lady. She's won awards in magazines and craft shows."

"Just a few little awards here and there. I simply love restoring old things. I believe I see the treasure in a trashed object when most people only see the brokenness."

Jack stared at her. "Well, that's a real interesting concept. And this area is known for its treasures, especially the buried kind, like you say." He took a sip of coffee and looked from Bobbie to Christy. "Why don't we take a little ride and look around? I can think of a couple of places that might work."

"You two go right ahead," Christy said. "I'm expecting a call from my editor in"—she glanced at her watch—"exactly ten minutes. I'm stuck on a plot point and need her advice." She reached for her purse, and Jack stood up to let her out of the booth.

"I'm paying," Jack insisted, "so scoot."

"Hey, Christy, I'm singing at the Blues Club again tonight,"

Bobbie called after her. "Donna invited me to do a couple of sets. Why don't you stop by around nine?"

Christy hesitated, wondering if Dan would be there. Seeing him would be awkward. Still, she couldn't disappoint her aunt. "Sure. I'd love to hear you sing."

"Then I'll see you later, darlin'," Bobbie said.

Waving to Jamie and Miz B, Christy yelled, "I'm in a hurry—see you later!" She dashed out the door and down the steps.

And smack into the arms of Dan Brockman.

"Whoa," he said, holding on to her.

Even in jeans and a sweatshirt, Dan epitomized tall, dark, and handsome. But that wasn't the reason Christy had fallen in love with him. He possessed sound morals, depth of character, and a sense of humor that drew her to him like surf to the shore.

"Hi," she said, trying to read his expression through the dark sunglasses that protected his blue eyes.

"Hi to you. Don't you ever return phone calls?" He didn't sound angry, but he didn't sound friendly either.

Warm feelings rushed over Christy as they stood for a moment, staring into each other's faces. She'd met him in February of last year, and since then Dan had changed from the eager-to-please guy fresh out of Iraq with a military haircut and idealistic expectations of himself and others. These days he spoke his mind more quickly, immersed himself in his building projects, and seemed to avoid the subject of a future commitment.

"People are beginning to stare," he whispered. "But I don't have a problem with that."

Christy blinked and stepped back. His arms dropped to his sides. "Didn't we do this once before?" she asked.

"Yep. After I tried to persuade you to go out with me, and you swore you didn't have time for dinner. Then I caught you, literally, dashing out of the restaurant with that faraway look in your eyes. Like today."

"Panic might be a better word. My editor is calling in eight minutes." She hoped only a couple of minutes had passed. "I hear you met my aunt Bobbie at the Blues Club last night."

He removed his sunglasses and put them in his pocket. "Yeah, your aunt's got a terrific voice. You should have been there." He watched her face.

She hesitated, trying to gather her thoughts. *Why didn't you invite me?* she wanted to ask. But she forced herself to remain cool. "I'm going tonight," she said.

"Good. It's a pretty neat club. No smoking, nice crowd. People should support the place. The new owner just moved here from New Orleans. You should say hello tonight. Her name's Donna."

"Donna?" She hated the jealousy that flared inside her.

"Right. She's modeling this club after the one she and her father owned in New Orleans before Katrina hit."

"I see," Christy said, struggling to keep her voice even. Dan seemed to know a lot about Donna. He must have been making her feel welcome in Summer Breeze.

An awkward silence followed. Christy tried to force herself to leave, but her feet felt rooted to the spot.

"Well," Dan said, glancing toward the restaurant door, "guess I'd better grab a booth. Good luck on meeting that deadline."

"Thanks," she replied, trying to sound cheerful and light-hearted. By the time she reached her white convertible, her flip-flops hammered the pavement. Why did her heart jump every time she saw him? She knew Dan concealed his emotions well, but she had the feeling their meeting had rocked him too. Why couldn't she get it through her head that they needed to be "just friends"—how she hated those words—for a while to see if what they felt warranted making a long-term commitment? It felt that way for her, but Dan had begun to back up, shying away from taking the next step.

She hit the button on her car keys to unlock the door. *Well, good luck, Miz Donna,* she thought as she plopped into the front seat. *He's not an easy catch.*

As she turned the key in the ignition, she glanced at a couple sitting in a white truck two rows over. Then the sound of a child's laughter drew her attention. She waited to back out, watching a man gather up stray children and herd them into a car in front of her.

After she spoke with her editor, maybe she'd grab her tennis shoes and jog off her anger, now that her ankle had healed. Jogging had been her means of blowing off steam until she broke her right ankle on a ski trip with the church youth. She took a deep breath, feeling better. A jog would be the best way to put her encounter with Dan behind her.

Once the family was safely in their car, she let the top down on her convertible, relishing the cool breeze rippling her ponytail. She drove out of the parking lot, music floating from a CD, her determined face warmed in a splash of sunlight.

⌒∞⌒

As the couple in the white truck watched Christy hurrying to her car, Roseann asked, "Which one do we follow?" She studied the pretty woman in the convertible.

"We stay with Bobbie," Eddie said. "Quick! Write down the number of that plate."

Roseann grabbed her pen and copied down the number on a notepad. She looked across the parking lot at the red truck they'd been following all morning. "I'm gonna help you get that money back, Eddie," she said. "Maybe I can make friends with Bobbie, and you could stay in the background."

"Roseann, where that woman's concerned, it's hard for me to stay in the background."

Roseann chewed on the end of her pen, deep in thought. She looked across at Eddie. "The sign on that Blues Club we passed said, 'Bobbie Bodine, 9:00 Tonight.'"

Eddie threw his head back and laughed. "Yeah, she can sing, but she'll be singing the blues when I get through with her."

three

As Christy drove home, her frustrations began to melt into discouragement. She knew she must have been pushing Dan for a commitment. In retrospect, she had just wanted to marry and start a family. It had felt so good to love again. But the memory of Chad, who had died seven years ago, made her fear losing Dan and suffering another heartbreak. She became possessive and jealous, and those ugly feelings caused her fears to become a reality. She had driven Dan away.

After their last argument, she had stormed out of the restaurant where they were having dinner. Then for a week, Dan had been too stubborn—or perhaps too angry—to call her. When she finally saw his number on the caller ID, she refused to answer. And she couldn't bring herself to return his other calls. Then he had quit calling.

Christy turned down her street of pastel houses set in neat squares of green grass. As she turned into the driveway that ran alongside her pale pink house, she recalled how folks in Summer Breeze had once left their doors unlocked. Not anymore. Not since a prominent resident turned out to be a vicious killer.

She unlocked her front door and hurried up the hallway, bypassing the kitchen and turning into the second bedroom that served as her office. She cut across to the desk and tried to force her thoughts toward the questions she needed to ask her editor. She took the handset of the phone into the living room and sank onto the blue chenille sofa.

While she waited for the phone call, her gaze roamed around the living-dining area that was her haven. Beside the matching love seat, glass end tables held fashion magazines and a couple of new mystery novels. After kicking off her shoes, Christy put her bare feet on the glass coffee table and glanced at the entertainment center. She considered checking out the news and weather but dismissed the idea. She didn't need any distractions.

The phone rang, and she picked up the handset.

After the conversation with her editor, Christy changed into a jogging shirt and shorts. As she hurried back to the kitchen, grabbing a bottle of water, car keys, and billfold, she heard the slam of a door followed by an enthusiastic bark.

She rushed to the back door and yelled, "Tell him to water the grass and leave the corner of my house alone!" Her younger brother, Seth, stood in her backyard, and she looked meaningfully at Atticus, his beloved black and tan bloodhound.

"What?" Seth frowned. "No 'Hey, how are you'? Just get your—"

"And no swearing. It upsets Atticus." She walked over to pet

Atticus, who stood waist high. "See your ball over there?" She pointed toward a corner of the yard. "Go for it."

He did.

She straightened and looked at Seth. "Who but you would name a dog after a fictional character?"

"How come you're the only one who gets it?" he asked, grinning at her.

"Maybe it had something to do with the way you kept raiding my bookcase. How many times did you read *To Kill a Mockingbird*?"

"I raided your bookcase, and you stole my favorite T-shirts."

She pretended to be horrified. "Surely not. We were the two most perfect children in town."

They both laughed. As she looked at him, Christy wondered why they had spent their early years killing themselves to please everyone, only to hit their teenage years like two hand grenades disguised as Easter eggs. Her rebellion had culminated in the accidental death of Chad, the man she'd loved and planned to marry. Heartbroken and considering the tragedy punishment from God, she had left Summer Breeze for four years, finding answers at last in a small mountain church in Colorado.

Seth's rebellion had struck like a thief in the night, stealing his last resolve to "fit in." He had run off to Australia to put space between himself and his frustrations in Summer Breeze. Christy knew he needed to test his wings, find out who he really was, but the guy who returned hardly resembled her beloved younger brother. This guy partied every night, chased girls all over the

Emerald Coast, and remained absent from the family pew. He had worked hard to escape the image of the kind and vulnerable preacher's kid.

Atticus trotted up with the ball in his mouth and looked at her with soulful brown eyes.

"Thanks." She leaned down to hug him. "You're a sweetie."

"Guess you have to be a dog to get a hug around here," Seth remarked.

Christy laughed and walked over to hug her tall, slim brother, who towered over her at six feet. His pale brown hair rolled over his collar, shining and smelling of something exotic. He sported his uniform: faded T-shirt and jeans worn soft as butter. Christy smiled at him, studying the boyish face, the freckled nose, the soft brown eyes, the sensitive smile.

"I love you," she said, making him start with surprise.

"Could have fooled me with your warm hello, mate." The word *mate* kept cropping up in his vocabulary, along with a few others Christy had never heard.

Her gaze dropped to his Birkenstocks, covered in teeth marks. She grinned, glancing across the yard, where Atticus was in a stand-off with a cardinal. The bird flew away, and Atticus ambled toward them with innocent confidence.

Christy bent to scratch behind the hound's ears and looked up at Seth. "I'm thinking about taking a drive over to Shipwreck Island for a jog. Would you two like to come along? Is he car trained?"

Seth laughed. "The chewing is the problem. Maybe we'll just follow you over."

Christy laughed again, guessing the inside of his old red El Camino must bear a hundred teeth marks on the seat covers.

They had run the length of the beach when Seth laid a hand on her arm. "Hold up," he said. "We're not in a contest here."

"You need to get back in shape. All your late-night partying is turning you into a couch potato," Christy said through gasps. But she stopped running and placed her hands on her knees, lowering her head to catch her breath. She turned her head to study her brother, then grimaced. "The fumes from last night's party are pouring out, little brother."

Ignoring her comment, Seth plopped down on the warm sand, looking around. "Remember when we used to picnic here? You and I spent hours back there," he said, indicating the woods behind them, "certain we'd find buried treasure from that old Spanish ship that got demolished in a hurricane."

She nodded, glancing over her shoulder. "I did find buried treasure in a different way, writing about pirate ships and gold."

"And you're good at it." He studied her from a sideways glance, his hair draping half of his face. "So are you going to tell me what's wrong?"

She looked away, fighting tears. Denying her feelings to Seth would be a waste of time for both of them. "It's Dan," she said. "I just ran into him coming out of Miz B's, and my heart started doing somersaults. I hate myself for it."

"You hate being human?"

"I hate being vulnerable."

"I thought you walked out on him."

"After he started backing up."

Seth tugged on her hand, pulling her down to the sand next to him. "Listen," he said. "I know I'm the last guy that should be giving relationship advice, but every time I've seen you and Dan together, I just feel you two are right for each other. You're both intelligent, ambitious, enjoy the same things, have similar views, and yet are different enough to make it interesting."

Christy sighed. "I thought so too."

"The way he looks at you, the way you look at him." He swore under his breath. "Maybe if a girl I liked looked at me that way, I'd change for her. But Dan's a serious guy. When he's ready, he'll commit. Are you willing to wait? You know, slowing down is not a bad thing, Christy."

"Yeah..." Her voice trailed off as her mind moved to the woman Dan had mentioned. "Did you meet Donna at the Blues Club when you and Aunt Bobbie were there?"

He chuckled. "Is that what's got you riled? Well, relax. *Miz* Donna's a pretty woman, but I don't think Dan's interested." He searched her face. "Don't tell me you—"

"Dan has made it quite clear how important his freedom is to him, so why should I care who he's with?"

"That's a silly question. Of course you care who he's with, and he's just as worried about you."

Christy lifted the corner of her shirt to wipe her face. "How do you know?"

"I ran into him late the other night. We had a drink and hung out for a while. All he talked about was you."

She lifted her head. "What'd he say?"

Seth shrugged. "That he'd called you several times, and you never called him back. He thinks you're upset because after a year and a half, he hasn't made a commitment."

"Well, he's right."

"He said for eight years he was tied down with the military, and before that his old man pushed him to get through college. He wants some free time before being responsible for someone else, to be sure of what he's doing."

Seth watched a sea gull cross the sky; then his brown eyes drifted back to Christy. He draped a long arm around her shoulder. "Then he admitted he missed you like crazy."

Her breath caught and she stiffened, instantly on the defensive. If she believed that, she would start to hurt again. "He's working on the missing me part in the company of other women, apparently," she said, not bothering to hide the bitterness in her voice.

"You know this for a fact?"

She sighed. "Seth, why do I have such bad luck with guys?"

Seth thought for a minute, never one to give quick, easy answers like some people. "I don't know how to answer that. Chad checked out competing in car races. You couldn't stop him from doing what he loved. I think Dan just needs a little time and space. If he really loves you, it'll work out." He looked out at the water. "I keep thinking about Ingrid, the girl I met in Sydney. When she drove me to the airport, I felt like I was leaving something important behind. We

were supposed to be free spirits, she and I, and yet…being free did-
n't feel so cool anymore."

"Maybe that's why you're wearing yourself out on the party cir-
cuit," Christy said. "You're trying to prove you've forgotten her."

He raked his hair back from his face, reached into his jeans for
a rubber band, and secured the long ends in a ponytail.

"Do you love her?" she asked softly.

He frowned. "Nah, I just liked her a lot. I do know one thing."
His brown eyes held an intensity Christy hadn't seen in months. "I
want to finish college and do something useful with my life."

She reached for his hand. "You said you went to Australia to
find yourself. I think you did."

The sun was slipping behind the horizon when Eddie pulled into
the parking lot of the Blues Club. Roseann turned in the seat and
looked at him. "What's your plan? I know you have one."

He angled his truck next to Bobbie's red one, and they got out.
"We'll go inside, pretend to be friendly. I'll say I have to go to the
rest room, so when I leave the table, she'll probably drop her guard.
You watch her purse. Grab it if you get a chance."

"Eddie, I doubt I'll get a chance to steal her purse. Besides, I
don't think she's packing ten grand in her billfold."

He swung his leg back and planted his black boot squarely on
the door of Bobbie's red truck, the heel leaving its mark. "That
helps," he said. "Now I won't feel like kicking her when I see her."

"I think she's put the money in that storage unit," Roseann said, trying to offer some encouragement and settle him down. "Somehow we just missed it."

He put an arm around her waist and grinned up at her. "That's what I like about you. You use your head. If you can make friends with her, do it."

Roseann reached up to fluff her curls. "Yeah, I can see how it would be to our advantage. But Eddie," she warned, "you behave yourself tonight."

He squared his shoulders and thrust his chest out as they walked toward the front door.

Christy pulled into the packed parking lot of the Blues Club at twenty minutes after nine. She had changed clothes twice, then taken two phone calls, which made her run late. She circled the concrete block building decorated with blue neon musical notes running around the front and sides of the club. She parked in the only empty space and hopped out, locking her car. As she hurried across the parking lot, music drifted through a side window. Blues music. Then she heard a woman's voice, clear and rich, floating on the soft September evening, and almost stopped in her tracks. She remembered her aunt always humming a tune, usually a sad one, but hadn't realized her voice was so beautiful. What had happened to Bobbie to bring out the sad songs?

Christy had asked her mother once, but Beth had shaken her

head and said, "I don't know. When we were growing up, she sang all the time, and it was fun, lighthearted music."

Christy climbed the steps, glancing up at the words "Blues Club" in blue neon script over the front door. She entered and looked around. More elegant inside, the club's walls were covered with framed photographs of blues singers from Memphis and New Orleans. A bar ran along the left wall, and on the right a row of booths stretched to the rest rooms. A narrow aisle led straight to the back, where a raised stage enclosed in a brass rail held the band.

From the ceiling, three spotlights beamed down on Bobbie, dressed in a black pantsuit, elegant in its simplicity. Her blond hair shone silver in the circle of dusty white light. She held the microphone in her hand, staring off as though the song had taken her to a special world. "When I hear the blu-es call my name…" Her voice drifted away, leaving only silence and the low wail of a trombone.

Everyone in the club stood, applauding wildly, and Bobbie bowed low. "Thank you so much. Enjoy yourselves," she said, smiling across the crowd. "I need to take a break." She turned and thanked the band behind her as they picked up their instruments and filled the room with music. Feet shuffled, chairs scooted back in place, and people began to talk among themselves.

Christy's gaze followed Bobbie to a round table directly in front of the stage, where Jack pulled out her chair. Christy blinked through the low light, her eyes widening. On the other side of the table, Dan sat beside a striking brunette she had never seen.

Her heart plummeted. How could Dan humiliate her like this? Why had he and his date chosen to join her aunt and Jack?

Furious, she turned and bumped into a woman in a sequined denim shirt.

"Hi, I'm Donna," the woman said. She was pretty, in her early thirties with a friendly smile. Was this Christy's new competition? If so, she didn't seem to mind that she had been replaced as Dan's date tonight.

Christy remembered her manners and extended her hand. "Christy Castleman."

Donna smiled warmly. "Christy! I've heard a lot about you. Your aunt is very popular with everyone, and I can see why. She has a terrific voice, and she's a very sweet person. Come on, I'll take you to her table."

Christy hesitated. Donna seemed nice, as Dan had said. And he did have a right to see anyone he wished. But who was that with him tonight, if it wasn't Donna? She glanced over her shoulder. At this point, she couldn't sneak out the door, and she wasn't about to let Dan and his date stop her from saying hello to Bobbie and Jack.

She forced a smile. "Thank you."

Gripping her handbag tightly, she squared her shoulders and told herself she could do this. She could be so polite that Dan would see she was indifferent to his dating.

"Look who's here," Donna said as they reached the table.

"Christy!" Bobbie called, pleased to see her, but a tense expression strained her face.

Christy hugged Jack, then turned with a casual "Hello, Dan."

He had stood as she approached, smiling at her. She tried not to notice how handsome he looked in his white, button-down shirt and dark pants. Her eyes swung to the tall woman with long curly hair. Christy gave her a friendly smile.

"Christy, this is Roseann Cole," Dan said.

The woman's brown eyes took in every detail of Christy's appearance as she said, "Hi, Christy. Nice to meet you." She spoke with an anxious, high-pitched voice and wore a bright orange shirt that glowed like a hunter's vest. Her lipstick matched the blouse. Christy tried to conceal her dismay over Dan's date as Jack pulled out a chair beside him.

"Your aunt has the sweetest voice this side of heaven," Jack said, an unmistakable glow in his blue eyes. It was good to see Jack looking so pert and actually out on the town. He tended to hole up at Rainbow Bay, a clover-shaped inlet six miles east of Summer Breeze. Following an afternoon rain, beautiful rainbows arched the sky over Jack's gray bungalow, where he lived with memories of the wife and son he had lost. Yet he loved the place, and he lived to fish.

"You were wonderful," Christy said, smiling at Bobbie.

This time there was no mistaking the fear in Bobbie's eyes as she looked at someone across the room. "Thanks, honey. Seth was here earlier, but he was expected somewhere else."

Christy nodded. "He's a very busy guy these days."

"I'm so impressed that you're a writer," Roseann said. "I'm not much of a reader, but I so admire anyone smart enough to write books that get published."

Christy studied the woman, trying to understand what Dan saw in her. However, she had to admit that Roseann seemed like a sweet person who wanted to be friends.

A deep voice boomed from behind Christy. "Well, Bobbie, maybe you'll make enough money singing to pay me what you stole."

Christy whirled and stared at the short man who stood behind her. He wore a black ten-gallon hat and a white shirt with pearl buttons. A huge belt buckle advertised a famous beer.

"Eddie," Roseann said, reaching for his hand, "sit down and be nice. Bobbie invited us to sit here. You heard her yourself before you took off for the bar, so don't say things like that to her."

"Eddie, you've been drinking," Bobbie said, "and I know how you get after a few drinks. You think you're six foot five instead of five foot six. You start looking for a fight. So why don't you leave before you get your rear end whipped again?"

"Not until I get what I came for," he said, glaring back at her.

Christy realized this man was Eddie Bodine and that Roseann must be his girlfriend.

"Where's the money?" Eddie demanded. "Better yet, where's the vacuum cleaner?" His voice rose, and a hush swept over the crowd.

"The vacuum cleaner?" Bobbie cried. "Don't tell me you drove all the way from Memphis to Florida because the vacuum cleaner wasn't written up in the divorce papers!"

Eddie leaned forward, his dark eyes narrowed beneath the cowboy hat. "Don't play dumb with me. I know you too well. And you knew what was hidden in the vacuum cleaner."

"You're crazy," Bobbie said, reaching for her purse and pulling out the bottle of pills.

"What is it?" Jack leaned over to her. "Are you sick?"

"Forgot to take my medicine." She twisted the top of the bottle, but the cap wouldn't come off. Christy could see Bobbie's hands shaking, and she jumped out of her chair to help. Before she could, however, white pills exploded across the table and floor.

Christy and Jack scrambled to pick them up as Roseann stood and grabbed Eddie by the hand. "You oughta be ashamed of yourself, Eddie."

An older man appeared with a broom and dustpan and began to sweep up the pills.

"Wait!" Bobbie hollered, stopping him. "I don't want them thrown away. They're too expensive. I'll wipe them off when I get home."

The little man looked startled, then turned and disappeared through the kitchen door.

Bobbie grabbed a nitroglycerin pill while Jack continued picking them up off the floor and putting them back in the medicine bottle. Christy glanced back at Eddie and Roseann and saw Dan had Eddie by the arm.

"You can leave quietly, or I can take you down right now," Dan said, his face set in a firm line. No one who heard him could doubt he meant it, even though he spoke in a low, controlled voice. He towered over Eddie, who visibly backed down.

"We're going." Eddie said. He jerked his arm free from Dan's grip.

"I'll just come along with you," Dan said. "I want to see the taillights of your vehicle so we know you're gone."

Eddie's face flushed with anger, but Roseann tugged his hand. "Eddie, please. You're embarrassing me."

At her high-pitched plea, Eddie looked at her, took a deep breath, and nodded. In his tight jeans, he looked slightly bow-legged as he walked up the aisle. Dan, good as his word, followed them through the front door.

Christy knelt beside Bobbie. "Are you okay?"

Pale and trembling, Bobbie nodded and took another sip of water.

Jack was busy replacing pills in the bottle, then handed it to her. "Now that you have your medicine, I'm going after that bozo."

Bobbie grabbed his arm. "No, Jack. Let him go. He's caused enough trouble."

"Well, I'm going to be sure he doesn't cause any more." He patted her hand, then turned and hurried toward the door.

Tony Panada sat at a table in a darkened corner, quietly enjoying the scene. His eyes lingered on the small blonde whose songs seemed to mesmerize the crowd. Bobbie Bodine had become a woman of interest. She'd stolen the idiot's money and run off, and now the hot-tempered Eddie had caught up with her.

Oh well. She should have known better than to get involved with that character.

Tony ignored the talk around him, tilting his head back to

study the ceiling as he tried to remember something. Had there been a vacuum cleaner in that unit?

⸎

Christy watched Bobbie strain to hold back the tears and regain control. "Come on," she said. "Let's go home."

Bobbie shook her head. "I'm going to the rest room to freshen up. I promised to sing again after the break. I'll forget about him once I start singing." She grabbed her handbag and rushed to the ladies' room.

The people at the adjoining tables began talking again, relaxing as the band struck up a happy tune. Christy stared after her aunt, torn between following Bobbie or going outside to be sure there was no trouble. She reached in her purse and removed her cell phone, holding it by her side as she walked quickly toward the door. She would call Deputy Arnold if Eddie hadn't left.

When she stepped outside, Dan stood at the bottom of the steps. Jack ran alongside Eddie's white truck, yelling, "You stay away from her or I'll kill you!"

Christy gasped. She had never seen Jack in such a rage. His face was blood red, and his hands were balled in fists. "Jack! Come back!" she hollered.

Two couples crossing the parking lot heard Jack's threat and stopped to stare at him as the white truck roared into the street and headed west.

"Come on, Jack." Dan walked over to clamp a hand on the older man's shoulder. "They're gone for good. I let him know he'd be very sorry if he ever came near Bobbie again. Or Christy," he added, looking across at her.

As her eyes locked with his, she felt the tension of the evening begin to dissolve. "Thanks for helping out," she said to him.

"No problem."

She looked at Jack, who had begun to calm down.

"Bobbie told me he used to get rough with her," he explained. "She's afraid of him, but I told her not to worry. I'd see to it that little punk got run out of town."

A soft, bluesy song broke the tension, and Bobbie's voice filled the night. Jack listened for a moment, then shook his head. "Christy, your aunt's the most amazing woman I've ever met."

Christy gave him a hug. "I believe you're smitten, Jack Watson."

He grinned and headed for the door. "You guys coming?" he called over his shoulder.

They followed Jack inside the club and quietly took seats at the table. Watching Bobbie sing, Christy felt as though her aunt escaped to her own private world when she sang the blues, shutting everyone and everything out. Even now, she sang as though nothing had happened. Christy had never imagined her aunt was so talented. Why hadn't her mother ever mentioned this?

Dan leaned toward her. "She's quite a lady."

Christy nodded, still watching her sing. "Yes, she is."

The music faded into the night as Bobbie completed her last

song and took a bow to thunderous applause. Christy, Dan, and Jack were still clapping as Bobbie reached the table. They all began talking at once, complimenting her, but she waved the words aside.

"If you don't mind, I'd like to leave now," she said, looking at Jack. Her eyes swung to Christy and Dan. "What about you two?"

Dan turned to Christy. "Want to go for a late-night snack?"

"Sure. Care to join us?" Christy asked Jack and Bobbie.

"No, thanks. Go have fun," Bobbie said.

Christy thought her aunt seemed exhausted and on the verge of tears. She put her hand on her arm. "Everything will be all right," she said.

"I hope so," Bobbie replied, but she looked unconvinced.

"Okay, you kids run along," Jack said, his good mood restored. "Christy, I'll see your aunt home. Don't worry."

"Thanks, Jack."

Christy's hand slid into Dan's with surprising ease as they walked out of the club and crossed the parking lot.

"You look very pretty tonight," he said, his blue eyes sweeping down her black blazer and jeans. Her new black high heels clipped over the concrete as she fell in step with him. "Nice shoes," he added and grinned at her, knowing her penchant for shoes.

"Thank you." She smiled, pleased he had noticed and relieved he was alone tonight. She had jumped to wrong conclusions twice now, and she told herself she could change. She could give him time and space without seeming insecure. He was a good man, and she didn't want to lose him. They owed each other a second chance, and this time she was determined not to rush things.

four

Tuesday

C hristy rolled over in bed and reached up to open the drapes. A clear blue sky sent golden rays of sunshine through her window. She stretched lazily as a wonderful contentment eased over her. Glancing across at the chair that still held the clothes she had worn last night, she merely smiled. It had been late when she came in, and all she'd wanted to do was put on her pajamas and crawl into bed…and dream of Dan.

They had spent a wonderful evening together at a cozy oceanside restaurant near Destin. They left Dan's SUV in the parking lot of the Blues Club and drove in her convertible so they could feel the crisp breeze blow over them.

As they dined on shrimp cocktails and peach tea and then sharing a rich chocolate dessert, they enjoyed light, easy conversation. Christy explained that Eddie was Bobbie's ex-husband, but she must have married him in his better days. Then she quickly moved on to another topic, hoping they could put the unpleasant scene with Eddie behind them.

When they returned for Dan's car, there were only a few hangers-on at the club. Christy saw that Jack's black SUV was gone, as well as Bobbie's red truck. She didn't worry about Bobbie anymore that night.

⸎

After a shower and a mug of coffee, Christy decided to go by her parents' home to check on Bobbie. She wheeled into the wide driveway of the brick ranch-style home. Palm trees and shrubs dotted a long, grassy yard, and flower beds circled the house. Her parents enjoyed working in the yard, and they were proud of their picture-perfect home.

As Christy climbed the back steps to the kitchen door, she heard her mother's voice.

"How dare you come here and disgrace us, Bobbie! You were out till midnight the first night, and last night it was at least one o'clock."

Christy glanced at the garage. The door was open, and her dad's car was gone. If the sisters were going to get into one of their rows, she suspected her mother had waited until they were alone.

"I've done nothing to disgrace you," Bobbie rallied back. "Christy and Seth are glad to see me, even if you're not."

"I *was* glad to see you, but I hoped this time it would be different. I've already had three phone calls this morning to tell me about the scene you and Eddie made in that lounge. He said you stole money from him."

"Beth," Bobbie yelled, "you're still so goody-goody you refuse to hear my side of a story. You were always Momma's pet!"

"And you were always the black sheep."

Christy shook her head, wondering why so many arguments went back to the last century, bringing up old grievances.

"At least I didn't run off and get married when I was sixteen!" Her mother scored a hit.

"Marrying Joe Henry was the smartest thing I ever did," Bobbie snapped. "I got a free ticket out of the Minnesota icebox to good ol' Atlanta. But I know you never liked him."

"I tried to like Joe Henry," her mother said in self-defense.

"You thought that because he came from a rich family, he believed he was too good for us."

"That's not what I thought! I disliked the way he left you at home alone every night while he hung out at the bars. You told me yourself, remember? You called me late one night crying, saying he was having an affair with a cocktail waitress."

"Beth, it's useless to reason with you," Bobbie said, the fight gone from her voice. "You've always believed I was nothing more than a gold digger."

Christy listened, reluctant to intrude on a private argument, hoping they would settle their disagreement. But the argument had escalated, getting uglier by the minute, and she reached for the door handle.

"Whoa," Christy interrupted, entering the kitchen. "You two are all that's left of your original family. You should be grateful to have each other, not catfighting whenever you get together."

"We aren't catfighting," Beth said, obviously trying to calm down at the sight of Christy. She stood in the center of the kitchen, her hands on the hips of her white jeans. "I respect the fact that you're an adult who chooses where she goes and with whom, Christy, but—"

"You leave her out of this!" Bobbie cried, tears cascading down her cheeks. Her hair hadn't seen a brush, and she was still in her wrinkled silk pajamas. "She and Seth are your best gifts to the world. I wish I could have been so lucky! She came to hear me sing."

"Sing?" Beth echoed, obviously absorbing another shock. "Was that before or after you strewed pills all over the place?"

Bobbie whirled and left the room, and almost immediately Christy could hear drawers slamming shut. She was packing.

Christy faced her mother, eyes narrowed. "Mom, I think you're much too concerned with wanting everything to look perfect. You need to show more empathy for your sister."

"I try, but..." Beth sank into a chair, looking defeated.

"By the way," Christy added coldly, "Eddie was the one who caused the scene with his crazy allegations. The pills some gossip told you about are nitroglycerin. She takes one daily for accelerated heartbeat. Her heart raced, and she tried to get the bottle open when they spilled. Guess she forgot her daily dose."

Christy had never heard her voice sound so unfeeling, but she had finally lost it with her mother. Oddly, she felt relieved.

Beth stared, her mouth open. Christy wondered if the stunned expression on her face resulted from learning of Bobbie's heart condition or hearing Christy's tone of voice and sharp words.

Bobbie appeared in the kitchen doorway, dressed in jeans and a T-shirt, her suitcase in hand. She marched toward the back door, ignoring her sister.

Christy hurried after her. "You're coming home with me."

Bobbie straightened. The tears had been wiped from her cheeks, and the determined expression on her face made Christy feel even worse. "No, thanks. I'll just…"

Christy hugged her. "Please." She spoke softly. "Come home with me, at least for a while. We need to talk."

Bobbie turned sad eyes to Christy. She looked older in the morning light. Her sparkling personality had lost its sparkle.

"Okay," she said. She walked out the door to her truck.

Christy went to the garage and found the long post from Granny's farm lying on a back shelf. She hefted it and lugged it to her car, thinking about the project Bobbie had promised for the Red Hat luncheon.

"You missed an interesting scene at the Blues Club last night," Tony Panada said as he entered Hornsby's office.

"Aw, I don't care about them clubs. I'd rather go home to my woman." Hornsby swatted at a fly buzzing around the office. "I've seen more flies this morning than all week."

"It's still hot weather, man. What do you expect? Listen, I'll be out of town for the rest of the week. Keep an eye on my units. Especially the prize one."

Hornsby shrugged. "Sure. Business or pleasure?"

Tony looked grim as he ran a hand over his bald head. "Business. Last night was pleasure." His lips moved, but there was no smile, only a slight curl above his chin.

On their way to Christy's house, she and Bobbie stopped at the local hardware store. The items Bobbie needed to turn the old post into a coatrack were in storage back in Memphis.

As they entered the store, Bobbie looked at her. "The Red Hat club uses red and purple colors, don't they?"

Christy nodded. "Red hats, purple dresses."

Her aunt went up one aisle and down the other, grabbing cans of spray paint, corbels, screws, wooden pegs, and sandpaper. "If only I had my power drill. Christy," she called across the aisle, "do you have a toolbox?"

"A small one with the basics."

Bobbie nodded, mulling over different size nails, finally picking up an assorted box. She paused at the end of the aisle to study some wood stacked in a large box. She selected a long piece and then two more that looked one-third the size of the first. Studying the items in her basket, she nodded to herself and guided her full cart to the checkout counter.

She pulled out more bills and paid for her purchases, then

followed Christy back to the parking lot. "Okay, I'll have something special to show the ladies on Thursday," she announced.

After they devoured a ham sandwich, chips, and iced tea, Christy helped her aunt set up for her project in the backyard. As Bobbie laid out her assorted supplies, Christy frowned at the purple spray paint and glanced questioningly at her aunt.

Bobbie grinned. "Don't pass judgment until you see the finished product."

"Fair enough. I'll leave you to your work," Christy said, heading back to the house. As she did, her mind replayed the argument between her mother and her aunt. She felt saddened for both of them, for in her heart she knew neither meant the cruel words they had hurled at each other.

She sat at the eating bar and picked up her pen to write in her journal. Then she paused, thinking about the words she had spoken to her mother. She didn't regret what she had said, although she wished it had not been necessary.

Her mother was a wonderful person, really, helping wherever there was a crisis, reaching out to those in the community who needed food or clothes. She had spent hours preparing and delivering meals.

Christy tried to focus on her journal, but her thoughts still centered on her mother and her aunt. It seemed to Christy that life had come easily for her mom. Beth earned a scholarship in interior

design at the University of Alabama, where she met Grant Castleman. They married when he graduated, and she helped support
them while he attended seminary.

Sure, they'd moved around the country some, and she'd had to
pinch pennies in the beginning, like most young wives. Then they
had agreed on Florida as a permanent home, and her mother had
settled into a contented world. Her father's congregation loved him,
and there was no doubt in anyone's mind that Beth and Grant's marriage was as solid as bedrock. Yet, through the process, Beth seemed
determined to make everything perfect for everyone. Christy shook
her head. One person couldn't make the world perfect.

Christy tightened her grip on the pen and studied the column
before her. "Praise Report." *Dan!* Christy's heart lifted as she wrote
about the wonderful evening she and Dan had shared. Despite
their past conflicts, they had been relaxed with one another, talked
easily, and had fun being together.

The kitchen phone rang, and Christy laid down her pen and
answered. The voice on the other end was shrill and tense.

"Christy, this is Roseann Cole. I'm awfully sorry to bother you,
but I don't know who else to call. I thought about calling your
aunt, but I don't know how to reach her."

Christy frowned. "What's wrong?"

"Eddie's missing."

His angry face lurched into Christy's memory. "What happened after you two left last night?"

"We stopped at a bar, and he started tossing down rum and

Cokes. After a while, I finally persuaded him to go back to the motel. When we got back, he sat down in a chair and started working his way through the minibar, and I went to take a shower. When I came out, he was gone."

She paused for a moment. Christy waited.

"I watched a TV program for an hour, then called the Blues Club. I spoke with Donna, and she said Eddie hadn't come back, but if he did, she'd call me. She took my number down, but I never heard from her.

"Then around two this morning, I called the jail to see if he had been arrested. And I've just called the hospital. He's not either place." Her voice broke, and she began to sob. "I don't know anyone here, and I don't have a car..."

Christy felt sorry for her but didn't know how to respond. "My aunt is here at my house. If you'll hold on, I'll go ask if she's seen him."

"Thank you."

Clutching the cordless phone, Christy hurried to the backyard. Bobbie was singing in a low voice as she worked the sandpaper up and down the old wooden post.

"Bobbie, Roseann Cole is on the phone—"

"Who?" Bobbie looked up in confusion.

"Eddie's girlfriend." Christy repeated the telephone conversation, and Bobbie frowned and stood up, dusting off her jeans.

"He never came back to the club, and he wasn't hanging around the parking lot when Jack and I left. We were both looking too." She shrugged. "I have no idea. If I had to make a guess,

I'd say he went to a bar and got himself in a card game. Probably hates to go back and tell her he lost all his money."

Christy nodded and repeated the conversation into the phone as she walked back to the house.

"I don't know," Roseann said, now in control of her voice. "I reckon that's possible. I just wish he'd come back, even if he did lose his money."

Christy tried to think of something to say but failed.

"Sorry to bother you," Roseann added.

"No bother. Give me your phone number, and if I hear anything, I'll call."

"We're staying at the Starlight Motel. And here's my cell." Roseann recited the number. "That's another thing," she said. "He hasn't called me."

Christy took down the cell phone number, then had another thought. "Does Eddie have a cell phone?"

"He lost it."

Christy rolled her eyes, feeling even sorrier for this poor woman who seemed too naive to deal with a man like Eddie. "He'll probably return soon," she said, trying to offer some encouragement, and hung up.

She had a bad feeling about hotheaded Eddie. If the man had an ounce of sense, he would have stayed away from the Blues Club after being threatened. However, she wouldn't put it past him to wait in the parking lot, hoping to get even with Bobbie or Jack.

With a start, she remembered Jack's awful threat. *If you come near her again, I'll kill you.*

Christy swallowed, trying to fight off the ugly fear slithering through her. She ran out the door to the backyard. "Bobbie, what time did Jack take you home?"

Bobbie stopped working on the post and glanced off in the distance. "Let's see. We left the club right after my last number, a few minutes after eleven. We must have gotten to Beth's in ten or fifteen minutes."

"So he left you at eleven fifteen?"

Bobbie grinned. "No. We sat in the driveway and talked for a little while."

Judging by the twinkle in Bobbie's eye, Christy figured they'd made out right under her parents' bedroom window. She had a better understanding of her parents' feelings about having Bobbie in their house. What had her mother said during her argument with Bobbie? *The second night in a row you've come home late…last night it was at least one o'clock…*"

"Now why are you looking at me like that?" Bobbie asked. "Jack kissed me good night. Is that a crime?"

Christy looked away, shaking her head. "I'm just working on the time frame here. If Jack left you at, say, eleven thirty and went home, he had to drive past the Starlight." She looked at Bobbie.

"What are you thinking? That he might have run into Eddie along the way?" Bobbie fidgeted, obviously concerned.

"Bobbie, why was Eddie babbling about a vacuum cleaner?"

Bobbie sighed. "When we were married, he once hid money in a vacuum cleaner bag. That was a long time ago, and I'd forgotten it. On Saturday, I went back to the house to get some pots and pans, a box of pictures, and my vacuum cleaner. I heard from a friend that he and his girlfriend had left Friday to go to a UT football game in Knoxville. I waited until Saturday morning and then went in, got my things, and left. It never entered my mind to check the vacuum cleaner for money."

Christy hadn't forgotten the way her aunt kept pulling big bills out of her purse. "From his ranting at the club, I think he hid something in the vacuum cleaner, don't you?"

"Well, that vacuum cleaner is in my storage unit in Memphis. If he hid something in it, he should be looking there, not here."

"But why would he hide money in a vacuum cleaner if he knew at some point you would be coming to pick up your things?"

Bobbie reached for a fresh sheet of sandpaper. "He didn't know I was coming Saturday. Or that I have a spare key. I'm no dummy. I wanted to be able to come and go when he wasn't there. As for what he hid or why, it's football season, and he calls the bookies and bets on games. He bets on everything. But I wouldn't have figured him to put it in that old vacuum cleaner again." She shook her head and began sanding the post.

Christy lowered her eyes to the post, pretending an interest in her aunt's project. She didn't want Bobbie to see the worry—and the suspicion—in her eyes. It sounded like Bobbie knew a lot about Eddie's habits. And why drag along an old vacuum cleaner when she appeared to have plenty of money for a new one?

"I think I hear the phone," Christy said, aware her aunt was watching her closely. She turned and hurried to the house.

Once inside, she paced the kitchen floor. She had to talk to someone about this. Her first inclination would have been to call her mother, but that was out of the question after the morning confrontation. Her dad? No, he would side with her mother. Dan?

She frowned, thinking it over. Not yet.

Jack. She had another reason to talk to him. She needed to know if he had seen Eddie on his way home. She grabbed the phone and dialed his number. After several rings, a lazy hello came over the wires.

"Good morning, Jack. It's Christy."

"I know my favorite girl's voice."

"I think I've been replaced as your favorite girl."

A husky laugh followed her comment. "That aunt of yours is really something."

"Yeah," Christy replied, suddenly feeling irritated and not sure why. "Jack, did you happen to run into Eddie Bodine on your way home last night?"

"If I'd run into him, as you put it, you'd have heard about it already."

Christy winced. "Well, I've heard that he's missing. His girlfriend just called and said he left the motel last night and never returned or called."

Jack was silent a moment. "Aw, he's off in some bar in a card game, probably. Bobbie told me how he gambles."

"No, Jack, I don't think so. He hasn't even called her."

"Maybe he left town without the girlfriend."

Christy considered that. "Maybe he did. But why would he?

She appeared attentive and tolerant of him, although I can't imagine why. I don't think he'd take off without her."

"Who knows what he would do? From what I saw of him last night, I wouldn't put anything past him."

Christy wanted to say that she wished Jack hadn't threatened him, but she held her tongue. Instead, she said, "Well, I'll let you go. Incidentally, Bobbie is staying with me. She's out back working on a project she'll be presenting at the Red Hat meeting on Thursday."

"Tell her I said hello," he replied, his voice mellowing.

"I will." She said good-bye and hung up, thinking that Jack Watson sounded ten years younger. Maybe his burgeoning relationship with Bobbie would prove to be a good thing. And he hadn't encountered Eddie on his way home. Another good thing.

Through the kitchen window, Christy watched Bobbie sand the post. She had to believe her aunt was innocent in taking money from her ex-husband, even though she may have deserved it. Maybe Eddie, with empty pockets and a hangover, would return to the motel and to Roscann today.

In the meantime, Christy had other things to worry about. With a houseguest, she needed to restock the refrigerator. She picked up her purse and keys and stuck her head out the back door to tell Bobbie where she was going.

On her way to the market, she spotted Roseann Cole wandering down the sidewalk. She looked lost and confused.

Christy pulled to the curb beside her. "Hi, Roseann. Have you heard from Eddie?"

Roseann shook her head, and the mass of dark curls drooped. "No, I been asking up and down through here"—she gestured at the shops—"but no one has seen him."

Looking at Roseann's forlorn face, Christy felt the call to be a good Samaritan. Her father's words were rooted deep in her soul: *"Always help someone in distress."* This woman was obviously in distress.

"Why don't you get in the car?" she said. "I'll drive you around town, and we'll make a few more inquiries. Then I can drive you back to the motel."

Roseann seemed surprised by her offer, but she quickly opened the door and got in. Very quickly, in fact. She all but jumped in and slammed the door. "This is awfully nice of you," she said.

It was a hot September day, and Christy could see the perspiration on Roseann's face and arms. "How long have you been walking?" she asked.

"For an hour or so. First, I went to the service station back there to see if Eddie had stopped for gas. The man said he hadn't. Since then, I've just been walking around, looking and asking."

Christy nodded. "No one has seen his white truck parked anywhere?"

"No. But I guess white is a pretty common color for a truck."

Christy pulled away from the curb. Traffic was light and slow since it was a weekday, and the tourist season had slacked off after Labor Day. "Are you from Memphis?" Christy asked, trying to divert Roseann's worried thoughts.

"From Forest, Mississippi, which isn't far from Memphis. I was born and raised in Forest. Then Momma and I moved to West Memphis when I was in high school. I met Eddie in West Memphis about six months ago. I was working a day job as a waitress in a restaurant that happened to be a favorite of his."

"You were working a day job? Are you in school to learn another trade?"

Roseann twisted one of her curls around her finger. "I'm taking some metaphysical courses in the evening."

"Oh? I don't know much about that."

"Do you believe in psychics? Momma's a psychic."

Christy glanced at her. "Really?"

Roseann nodded. "She told me I'd meet a man, shorter than me, but that it wouldn't matter. She said he owned his own company and would make me rich. She said we'd fall in love right away." She sighed. "Two weeks later Eddie walked into the restaurant and stared at me until I went over to wait his table." Her brown eyes turned to Christy. "Momma was right."

Roseann lowered her head. "She saw death in the cards, and I refused to listen. She called back this morning, but I wouldn't answer. I just won't accept that something like that has happened to Eddie."

Christy merely nodded. It was hard to see why Roseann, much younger than Eddie, had been attracted to him. But her aunt had once claimed to be in love with the man, so apparently he had charm and could be nice when he wasn't in a rage.

Christy glanced at her watch. It was three thirty. Where had the day gone? She silently agreed with Roseann. Something was terribly wrong. Or else Eddie was a complete jerk to leave her stranded this way.

"I've been thinking about going to the sheriff," Roseann said. "Do you know where the police station is?"

"The sheriff's office is in Panama City, but Deputy Bob Arnold is the authority for Summer Breeze and reports to the sheriff. Folks here have lots of respect for him." She glanced at Roseann and smiled. "He's the tallest, broadest man around, so everybody called him Big Bob until this summer, when his boss told him to be more formal with the community. So out of respect now, we try to call him Deputy Arnold, but sometimes I slip up and forget. We're only a few blocks from the station. Why don't I take you over and see if he's in? It wouldn't hurt to tell him what you've told me."

Roseann agreed, and Christy parked in front of the small concrete building that housed the only official law enforcement office for Summer Breeze. Deputy Arnold's SUV sat in the driveway.

"Come on," Christy said to Roseann. "You're about to meet a man who takes his work very seriously. If Eddie is missing, Deputy Arnold will do his best to find him."

Roseann smiled for the first time, her red lipstick slightly smeared under the corner of her lip. "I sure hope so."

Deputy Bob Arnold was seated behind his large, cluttered desk when they entered, but upon seeing them, he rose to his feet.

"Good morning, Christy." His eyes moved to Roseann, and she stared back in wide-eyed amazement.

Deputy Arnold stood six-five with a broad body and a face to fit. Beneath a thick crop of silver hair, the face was big and round with a large nose that flared on the end and a wide mouth with lips that could close so tightly they looked zipped. His eyes were clear gray, and their expression brooked no nonsense.

"Deputy Arnold, this is Roseann Cole," Christy said. Roseann quickly stepped forward to shake his hand and mumble a "pleased to meet you."

Christy gave him the rundown of what had taken place, leaving nothing out, including the argument with Bobbie the night before. *I might as well tell him, so he'll know I'm not holding back.*

"What makes you think he's missing?" Deputy Arnold asked, looking doubtfully at Roseann.

She twisted the strap on her gold handbag. "After he got in that argument with Bobbie, and then when those guys—"

"What guys?" He frowned at her.

She glanced from Deputy Arnold to Christy and back.

"Dan and Jack were there and asked him to leave," Christy supplied.

"I imagine if Jack Watson was in on it, he did more than ask him to leave," the big deputy shot back.

Roseann dropped her head, nodding. "He did. He threatened to kill him if he didn't stay away from Bobbie. But I'm sure he didn't mean it like that," she added quickly.

Deputy Arnold's gaze shifted to Christy as a frown gathered on his thick forehead. He raked a big hand through his silver hair. "And what about Dan Brockman? What did he say to him?"

"Well," Roseann continued, "he walked us out, and he told Eddie he wanted to see the taillights of his truck leaving town. He was pretty angry too, so that's why I don't think Eddie would have gone back over there or approached either one of them again. Unless he ran into them somewhere when he left the motel," she added meekly. "He'd been drinking, and he does things he wouldn't normally do when he's drunk."

Deputy Arnold nodded, looking Roseann over carefully as he spoke. "Tell me again about that argument. I've heard Christy's version, so let's hear yours."

Roseann hesitated, looking at Christy. "Well, Eddie believed Bobbie had stolen ten thousand dollars in cash from him."

"Ten thousand dollars?" Christy gasped.

"And where did this guy get that much cash?" Deputy Arnold boomed.

Roseann sank deeper into the chair, lack of sleep showing in her face now. "He gambles. He won big on some football games, and when the bookie paid him, he put the money in a Ziploc bag and hid it. I don't know where, but he claimed Bobbie ran off with the vacuum cleaner, so I reckon the money was hidden there."

Deputy Arnold leaned forward, his gray eyes filled with questions. "A vacuum cleaner?"

"Bobbie says Eddie once hid money in the bag of the vacuum cleaner," Christy said, "and I guess he thought no one would look there."

"Bobbie seems to know a lot about his hiding places," Bob said, looking at Christy with his piercing stare.

"Well, she was married to him for several years, Deputy

Arnold. I guess a wife knows these things." Christy knew her tone sounded defensive, but she could see that he was already forming conclusions based on Bobbie's actions.

"And where is this vacuum cleaner now?" He looked from Christy to Roseann.

"In a storage unit back in Memphis with Bobbie's furniture and the items for her shop," Christy answered.

"But Bobbie is here, so that doesn't mean the money is still in this vacuum cleaner bag." He wagged his silver head. "Never heard of a hiding place like that, and I thought I'd heard everything."

Christy's mouth felt dry, and her heart began to hammer. "Deputy Arnold, I don't think my aunt knows anything about this. She went to the house to pick up some pictures and the vacuum cleaner and loaded both on the moving van. She thought Eddie was flat broke, or he was when she left, so I don't think she'd be rummaging around in the vacuum cleaner bag when she had a hundred other things on her mind."

"There's something else," Roseann said, leaning forward in her chair. "Bobbie was right about him being broke—until last week, that is, when he won on the football games. Anyway, he'd promised to pay off a couple of bookies with the ten thousand. They've threatened him, and for all I know, they could have followed us here. I've been worrying that maybe they caught up with him…" Her eyes filled with tears, and she lowered her head and began winding the straps of her shoulder bag around her fingers.

"Now, that makes more sense to me than anything else you

gals have told me," Deputy Arnold said. He folded his broad arms across a pile of papers. "Have you seen anyone following you? Did he say at any time that someone might be watching you two?"

She looked up, staring over Deputy Arnold's head, as though reflecting back over the past days. "He never said anything, but he got real jumpy when we got here. He kept looking in the rearview mirror." She shook her head. "I'm sorry. I'm not very observant.

"Oh, one other thing. I forgot to tell you this," she said to Christy. "After we left the Blues Club and stopped at that bar, he kept looking across the room. It was dark and I couldn't see what he was staring at, but then he suddenly got anxious to leave. I just thought he was jumpy about what Mr. Watson had said to him, but since then I've thought maybe he spotted one of those bookies who was after him."

Deputy Arnold pursed his lips. "If that was the case, I'd be in that motel room with the door locked and no inclination to be going out. If you had the water running in the shower, is it possible someone could have knocked on the door and you didn't hear?"

"Oh, yeah," Roseann said, nodding. "I had the shower going full blast, and though I can't sing like Bobbie, I like to sing in the shower. Country songs. Sometimes I get a little loud."

As Christy watched and listened, she began to understand how easily Eddie could have fooled Roseann about many things. She was obviously devoted to him, and Bobbie had always claimed that Eddie liked to be with people who made him feel important. Roseann fit the bill.

Deputy Arnold picked up a notebook. "Give me times, here. What time did you leave the club, go to the bar, and get back to the motel?"

"We left the club sometime after ten, I think. Eddie wanted to stop off at that Last Chance Bar near the motel. I guess we stayed about an hour. I'm not sure what time we got back to the motel. He flopped down in a chair to watch TV, and I went to take a shower."

"And what time did you come out of the shower and find him gone?"

She frowned. "I remember that part. I looked at the clock. It was eleven thirty."

"Describe him to me. And the truck." He scribbled as Roseann gave him the details. Then he stood. "Tell you what. You go back to the Starlight and wait in case he tries to contact you, or in the event that he returns. I'll cruise around town, check out a few areas, and give you a call tonight."

Roseann nodded. "Thank you."

Christy stood, knowing their conversation had concluded. Roseann looked from Deputy Arnold to Christy, finally caught on and stood up, hooking her shoulder bag over her arm.

"Thank you, sir," she said again, turning to follow Christy out of the building and back to the car. "He seems like a nice man," she said as she got in on the passenger side.

"He has a loud bark and a soft bite," Christy laughed, remembering how he had scolded her for interfering in his investigation of Marty McAllister's death. But in the end, when Christy uncovered a clue that had been overlooked, leading her to the killer, Deputy Arnold had hurried to the hospital to see her. To her surprise, he had been emotional and apologetic. "He's a very competent deputy," Christy added, wanting to leave that thought with Roseann.

"I hope he can find Eddie," Roseann said, her mind obviously locked on the mystery of his disappearance.

Christy pulled into the Starlight Motel, and Roseann directed her to the room where they were staying. Both women searched the parking lot for Eddie's truck, but it had not reappeared.

Roseann turned to Christy. "I sure appreciate all you've done."

"You're welcome. Do you still have my phone number?"

Roseann nodded. "On the bedside table."

"Then call if you need anything."

"I will. And tell Miss Bobbie if she hears from Eddie to please tell him to call me."

Christy shook her head. "I don't think she'll be hearing from him, but I'll tell her to call if she does."

"Thanks, Christy." Roseann stared at her for a moment, her brown eyes changing. Christy thought of two brown marbles, cold and hard.

Christy felt a chill, wondering what Roseann was thinking as she slammed the door and sprinted to her room. *She suspects that Jack, or even Bobbie, may have something to do with his disappearance,* she thought. As she drove to the market, she kept an eye out for Eddie and his white truck.

❦

That evening Bobbie and Jack decided to grill out at his place, but when invited, Christy declined. "I have to work on my novel," she said. "But you two have fun."

They roared off in Jack's SUV, Bobbie sitting close beside him.

Christy went back inside, smiling to herself. They looked like two teenagers falling in love for the first time. She hoped things worked out for them.

Wednesday

Christy didn't hear her alarm for several minutes, and as she fumbled toward consciousness, she realized she'd never heard Bobbie come home either. She rolled over on the pillow, stretched, and eyed the clock. Three minutes after nine. The aroma of coffee drifted from the kitchen, and she tossed back the covers and headed to the bathroom to freshen up.

When she reached the kitchen, she found a note on the eating bar. "Gone to the hardware store to get more supplies. And Donna wants to know when I can sing again."

"Good," Christy said, pouring herself a cup of coffee. She had been worried about the scene in the club Monday night. Bobbie had a wonderful voice, and it would be a shame for Eddie to ruin her chance to sing. Christy poured cream and stirred her coffee, thinking about Donna. Her invitation to Bobbie to sing again proved she wasn't ruled by gossip or speculation. Anyone who witnessed the scene should realize Eddie was nuts. At least, he seemed that way to Christy.

Glancing at the phone, she fought the urge to call Roseann and find out if Eddie had returned to the motel. Maybe she'd just drive by later.

She walked out onto the sun porch to enjoy her coffee. Bobbie had spread newspapers across the floor and left her painted post there to dry. Christy admired the glossy purple post with its new red base. *Amazing,* she thought.

A little red truck roared into the driveway, and Christy watched her aunt hop out like a sixteen-year-old. A brown sack bulged in her small arms.

"Good morning," Bobbie called, her blond curls bobbing as she hurried up the walk.

"Morning," Christy called back, walking over to open the screen door for her. Beaded earrings dangled from Bobbie's ears, a turquoise circle that matched the beads on her T-shirt. She wore crisp white jeans and a pair of wedge sandals.

"Like your outfit," Christy said.

"I've always loved clothes." Bobbie sidestepped the post to enter the kitchen and deposit her load on the counter. "The corbels I bought yesterday didn't fit..." She paused, noting Christy's confusion. "I have to insert little racks if it's going to be a coatrack," she explained.

Christy smiled. "You and Jack must have had fun last night. You look radiant this morning."

Bobbie clasped her hands and looked at Christy with an expression of joy. "He's a wonderful man. We grilled steaks, and I whipped up some of my creamy mashed potatoes. We baked peanut butter cookies at midnight." She laughed and turned to unload her purchases.

Christy's eyes swept her aunt's diminutive frame. "Well, I guess you're just one of those lucky people who can eat anything she wants and never pack on a pound."

Bobbie didn't seem to hear her. A frown had appeared on her forehead, and she turned back to Christy. "Eddie's truck wasn't at the motel when I passed it this morning. Maybe he came back and they left. I hope I've seen him for the last time."

Christy breathed a deep sigh. Maybe everything had turned out okay after all. "I hope you're right. Well, I have to get dressed and make a dash into town to get office supplies. I ran out of computer paper last night, and my printer needs a new ink cartridge. Can I get you anything?"

"One more chance," Bobbie said, her eyes hopeful.

"Excuse me?"

"One more chance at happiness. At love. Oh Christy, it feels like it's possible now."

Christy reached out and patted her arm. "Yes, I believe it is."

❧

Later in the morning, as Christy stood in line to pay for her purchases, she thought about Bobbie and Jack and Dan. And Seth. After a terrible scare, everything seemed to be slipping back to normal in everyone's lives. The cashier totaled her purchases, and she slid her credit card through the machine.

As the machine processed her card and the store clerk handed her the receipt, Christy remembered the day she had rushed in and bought a shredder while fighting tears. It had been her way of dealing with rejection slips before she found the right publisher.

"Have a good day," the clerk said to her.

"You too." Christy smiled and walked out into a lovely September morning.

As she drove down Main Street, humming with the radio, she glanced at the sidewalk fronting the shops, then did a double take. Roseann Cole, wearing tight jeans and a purple T-shirt, stood at the corner, waiting to cross the street.

The light turned red, and Christy braked, sticking her head out the window. "Roseann! Since I hadn't heard from you, I thought you'd left town."

She shook her head. "No. Eddie hasn't come back."

Roseann waved and crossed the street, and Christy stared after her, trying to absorb the fact that Eddie had abandoned Roseann. Or that he had truly gone missing.

A horn beeped behind her, and Christy realized she was holding up traffic. She accelerated, her thoughts jumbled. She fought an impulse to stop by the deputy's office to see what he really thought. Maybe Jack was right. Maybe Eddie had run out on Roseann.

When she turned into her driveway, Bobbie came dashing from the backyard. "Deputy Arnold called here asking about Eddie again. He said they found his truck parked on a side street near the Blues Club."

Christy stared at her. "Oh no."

Bobbie followed her into the house, frowning. "That scares me. I'm afraid the bookies caught up with him. Right before I walked out for good, he got a threatening phone call. When he hung up, he said he had to pay a debt fast or they were gonna beat the—" She broke off, rephrasing her thought. "He put a lien on his mother's house and paid them off, but I haven't forgotten how scared he looked."

Christy sighed. "Well, I just saw Roseann Cole. She told me Eddie hasn't come back."

Bobbie sank into a chair. She had put an apron over her clothes to catch a few red streaks. A tiny dab of paint sat on the end of her nose.

"Hey, it's twelve thirty, and we haven't eaten lunch," Christy said, thinking they needed a change of subject.

Bobbie blinked and her expression brightened. "I forgot to tell you. Last night Jack cooked an extra rib eye for you, and I brought it home with some potatoes. All you have to do is warm it up. I already made myself a sandwich. Good thing I did." She sighed. "I think I just lost my appetite for a while."

"Try not to worry," Christy said. "Just get back to your project, and we'll stay busy with our work. If anything happens, I'm sure we'll hear about it."

Bobbie nodded, saying nothing. She sauntered out the door to the sun porch to study the purple post.

Christy reached into the fridge and pulled out a plate wrapped in aluminum foil. When she uncovered her lunch, she swallowed, thinking her appetite had not been affected. She settled down to her food and a glass of iced tea.

Later, as she washed dishes, the steak seemed to swell in her stomach as her mind replayed the tape of Eddie, Roseann, and the scene in the Blues Club. Eddie's raging accusations against Bobbie, Jack's bold threats, and Dan's anger cast a dark cloud over them.

Christy looked through her kitchen window to the backyard, studying her aunt as she measured the post, which now was looking more like a coatrack.

Bobbie was such a tiny woman, scarcely five feet tall. It amazed Christy to think about all Bobbie had endured in her lifetime. She was singing again—a sad, low wail about a broken heart. *A little woman with a big voice,* Christy thought, wondering how many times Bobbie's heart had been broken.

She tried to push morbid thoughts from her mind as she went to her computer and unloaded her supplies. Her writing had always been her escape, but she worked best in solitude. Since she had converted the room into a half office–half guest room for Bobbie, she had given up some solitude. The sofa had become a pullout bed, and she had tucked in a small nightstand and reading lamp.

Still, Bobbie had been gone last night, and now she was in the yard, so Christy had no excuse not to focus on her mystery novel. She forced herself to sit down at the desk and turn on the computer. She reread the chapter she'd written last night and frowned. It needed work. Reaching for her thesaurus, she started thinking about words.

To her amazement, the afternoon passed quietly and productively. When she got up from her desk, stretched, and went out to see what Bobbie had done, she caught her breath.

The splintered old post had been transformed into a glossy purple coatrack with a sturdy red base and gold corbels to hold jackets and caps. Or hats.

"It's stunning," Christy said. "The ladies will love it."

"Oh, I'm not through. Do you have a button box?"

"Me? No, sorry."

"What about old jewelry you don't want?"

"Ah, I get it. You're looking for decorations in keeping with the red hat theme? Something red or purple?"

Bobbie nodded. "Is there a dollar store anywhere near?"

"No, but I have a better idea. Joy McCall, Queen Mother of the Red Hats—that's their term for leader—just returned from a Red Hat Society convention, and she must have brought back a hundred miniature red hats that flash when you fix the button right. She was wearing one last week."

"Great," Bobbie said, staring at her handiwork. "Tomorrow when we go to the luncheon, we'll wrap a couple of garbage bags around the coatrack so we can surprise the ladies."

"I'll call Joy now. They're going to love meeting you tomorrow and hearing you talk about your work and your shop."

Pleased with their accomplishments, the subject of Eddie Bodine was not mentioned again.

seven

Thursday

The next day, at five minutes till twelve, Christy and Bobbie climbed the steps to Miz B's carrying a strange object covered in two huge, black garbage bags. Bobbie wore a purple silk pantsuit and red tam. Christy, in a flowing skirt and matching shirt, followed.

Joy McCall met them at the door of the party room, a welcoming smile on her face. Joy was a blonde with lively blue eyes and a friendly smile. Christy couldn't remember ever seeing her frown. She wore a purple jersey dress decorated with red hat memorabilia and a sassy red hat complete with sequins and feathers.

"Good morning, you two," she said, a twinkle in her eyes. They hadn't told her how they were using the pins when she had delivered them to Christy's house the previous evening. "Welcome to our Sassy Snowbird luncheon."

"Sassy Snowbird?" Bobbie asked.

Joy explained. "The chapter was founded when some of the snowbirds who wintered on the Emerald Coast wanted to meet other women. Two belonged to Red Hat chapters in other states and decided to form a chapter in Summer Breeze, drawing in the locals as well."

She led them into the party room. "We can't wait to hear how you create this magic. And we'll be your best customers when you get your shop open."

Christy's Aunt Dianna came up to greet them. "Bobbie! Welcome to Summer Breeze. I'm sorry I haven't called you, but my hubby and I just got back from Gulf Shores." Dianna was tall with short auburn hair, vivid green eyes, and a nice figure. She put the spark in the club with jokes and fun. She turned to Christy. "Hey, cutie."

"Hey, fashion queen," Christy teased back. It was a secret joke between the two that they both could shop until they dropped— literally.

Other ladies stepped forward to welcome Bobbie and Christy, all dressed in various types of decorative red hats and purple outfits.

"Okay, girls," Joy called out, "give the server your orders. And don't forget, today Miz B made blackberry cobbler. Then I'll introduce you to a very nice, very creative lady."

Bobbie and Christy placed the disguised object in the corner of the party room and took a seat at the table. Christy smiled across the table at her aunt Dianna, whose eyes glowed with curiosity.

Joy tapped her water glass with a spoon. "Okay, ladies, quiet down. What do you say we leave business until later and let our distinguished guest show us how she made whatever that mysterious thing is in the corner." She gestured over her shoulder. "And to add a little mystery to her charm, let me tell you that Bobbie can sing the blues like you wouldn't believe."

Upon hearing this, Miz B stuck her head through the doorway and yelled to the crowd, "Can that lady ever sing the blues! I've heard her, and she'll put goose bumps on your skin and tears in your eyes! Now go on with your introduction, Joy."

The questions flew as the Red Hats stared with glee at the mysterious black-shrouded object.

Joy looked at Christy. "Would you like to introduce your other aunt?"

"My pleasure," she said, standing. "This is my mother's sister, Bobbie Bodine, and she has an amazing talent for restoring old things. She's just moved to Summer Breeze and soon will be opening a shop where she'll carry all sorts of interesting treasures. I think she plans to offer classes as well."

"Hear! Hear!" a new arrival from England called out.

Christy watched the ladies squirm, whisper to one another, and stare at the black object as though something live might burst through the packaging. She didn't want to keep them guessing.

"Please welcome Bobbie Bodine, a lady of many talents!" she said.

A round of applause followed as Bobbie stepped to the podium, looked around the room, and flashed a million-dollar smile. Her big blue eyes glowed with a passion for people as she began to speak.

"Hello, everyone. Thank you for inviting me to talk about my favorite subject: finding treasures. I have an obsession for restoring the beauty in old objects or family heirlooms that have been cast aside. I call it looking beyond the flaws and finding the promise.

"For example, I found an old post from the Castleman farm in Beth and Grant's garage. It was sentimental to Grant, so he kept it, although Beth kept saying, 'What do you plan to do with that splintered old post?'"

Bobbie motioned to Christy, and she stepped forward to help. They carried the black object to the center of the room where everyone could see. Christy peeled away the garbage bags, and a purple coatrack appeared. The gold pegs held four red hats, varying in size and shape. Bobbie turned on the buttons, and dozens of tiny red hats attached up and down the post began to twinkle.

"That's the neatest thing I've ever seen!" a woman named Valerie said, standing up so quickly her red cowboy hat slid over her forehead.

Everyone was talking at once—"How did you do that" and "Tell us what to do" and "What made you think of it"—when a door slammed behind them and Deputy Arnold entered the room. He did not appear to be in a party mood.

"Hey, Deputy Arnold," Joy called out. "Are you going to join us?"

Everyone laughed at first, but the laughter died away as a grim Deputy Arnold looked back. He marched down the side of the room and approached Christy. "Which one's Mrs. Bodine?"

Christy felt her heart sink, like the ball dropping on New Year's Eve in Times Square. She grabbed a breath and tried to smile as she looped her arm through Bobbie's. She made the introduction, and Bobbie turned on the charm, but it didn't work on the big deputy.

"Well, Mrs. Bodine," he said, his voice booming, "I thought you'd like to know there's something ripe in your pickle barrel— and it ain't pickles! I need to speak with you in private."

He led Bobbie out of the room, and Christy quickly followed, barely clearing the door before he slammed it.

Outside the door, Bobbie spoke in a low voice. "My pickle barrel is in storage," she said, looking confused.

"Yeah, I know. Hornsby called me out there this morning. He'd been smelling something foul coming out of your unit and couldn't reach you on your cell phone. He went inside, and what he found prompted him to call me."

Christy could hear movement on the other side of the door. She could even hear whispers. She imagined all the ladies pressed against the door, their red hats askew.

"Wh-what did you find?" Bobbie asked. She honestly seemed to have no idea what he was talking about. Christy suspected where this was going, and Deputy Arnold's next sentence confirmed her fears.

"We found the man who has been missing since Monday night, your ex-husband, Eddie Bodine. He was struck in the back of the head and shoved into the barrel. The medical examiner is doing an autopsy now. What do you know about this?"

Bobbie swallowed. "I don't know anything about it! We learned he was missing when his girlfriend called Christy."

Deputy Arnold's gray eyes swung toward the closed door of the party room, where voices rose in protest. "Well, I think you have a fan club working in there, so before they come after me with hat pins and steak knives, we need to leave."

"Where are we going?" Bobbie asked, rooted to the spot.

"You're gonna need to come down to headquarters and answer some questions." He turned and walked toward the restaurant exit. Bobbie lowered her head and followed.

"Big Bob, you don't have to be so dramatic," Christy whispered as the three of them entered the foyer.

Miz B, a mass of purple and red, met them holding a huge platter of fried chicken. "Bob, what do you think you're doing?"

"Save me some chicken," he said, hurrying Bobbie out the door. Once they reached the parking lot, he turned to Christy. "I don't recall inviting you to come along."

"She's my aunt. She doesn't know anyone here, and besides, *Dep-u-ty* Arnold, she hasn't done anything wrong."

The big man sized up the tiny blond woman for the first time. She opened her purse and reached for her bottle of pills, her face pale.

"What are you doing?" he demanded, peering at the pill bottle.

"Taking my medication," Bobbie answered.

Christy glared at him. "Why are you being so mean and unreasonable? My aunt would never murder anyone. You're putting too much emphasis on the fact that they had a disagreement in a public place."

"I have to ask this little lady if she stole ten thousand dollars from

Eddie Bodine, which he came here to retrieve. But before he could do that, he wound up dead in his prime suspect's pickle barrel. In her locked storage unit." He leaned toward Christy. "Now do you think I'm being unreasonable?" He turned back to Bobbie. "Who else has a key to that unit?"

Bobbie shook her head as she continued to wrestle with the bottle cap.

Automatically, Christy took the bottle from her, pushed down hard and twisted, and then handed it back. "I'll get a bottle of water from the car," she added.

"Thanks," Bobbie said.

When Christy returned with the water, Bobbie swallowed the pill and then turned to Deputy Arnold. "About the storage unit, that guy Hornsby probably keeps a spare key to every unit."

"Did you loan your key to anyone else?"

Bobbie opened her purse and looked inside. Christy and Deputy Arnold watched as she fished out a key ring and lifted one of the keys. "Here it is, but I haven't been back to that unit since Christy and I were there on Monday."

Christy stepped in. "Can't you see she isn't strong enough to overpower Eddie?"

"Maybe she had help."

Christy thought of Jack and the threats he had made in the parking lot of the Blues Club. Jack wouldn't have killed Eddie Bodine, and neither would Bobbie. But had someone framed them?

Her thoughts whirled like sand in a storm as they walked toward the deputy's big SUV.

"Look," Deputy Arnold said, softening a bit, "I'm just following orders. We need to ask you some questions." He opened the back door and gestured for Bobbie to get in.

"Just a minute." Christy tugged at Bobbie's sleeve. "I'd like to speak with her privately."

Deputy Arnold scowled.

"Just remember who solved your last murder case for you," Christy reminded him.

He said nothing, just walked around the back of the car to the driver's side.

Christy led Bobbie away from Big Bob, finding privacy on the other side of a parked car. "Bobbie," she whispered, "if you had anything to do with this, tell me now. It's the only way I can help you."

Bobbie shook her head. "I had nothing to do with it."

"Do you have any idea who would try to frame you?"

Bobbie looked off in the distance and hesitated. Then she shook her head. "I don't know, Christy. I can't think. My mind's muddled."

"I understand." Christy sighed. "I'll follow you down to the station. Just answer them truthfully and try to relax."

Bobbie nodded and walked to the deputy's car. As soon as she'd climbed into the backseat and shut the door, Deputy Arnold drove off. Christy raced toward her car.

She was driving out of the parking lot when Miz B waved her down.

"What can we do to help?" she asked, her plump hands clasping and unclasping.

Christy sighed. "Just pray. It's all a mistake."

eight

Bobbie sat in the interrogation room facing a serious-looking detective, young and sharp, who introduced himself as Mike Johanson. She knew she had to get a grip on her emotions. She had cried all the way to Panama City.

Christy had been forced to wait outside the interrogation room. Bobbie had waived her right to a lawyer; however, Christy told her to answer only the basic questions, then ask for a lawyer or call for Christy the minute she felt pressed.

"I want to hear your version of that night at the Blues Club," Detective Johanson said.

Bobbie leaned forward in her chair, looking him straight in the eye. "I haven't seen Eddie since Monday night at the club. And I have no idea who killed him or how he got in my storage unit."

"What time did you leave the club?"

"I left with Jack Watson just after eleven. I was staying with my sister and brother-in-law, Beth and Grant Castleman, and we got to their house about ten minutes later. I believe I entered the house around eleven thirty."

"Did your sister or her husband see you when you came in?"

"No, they had gone to bed. But Beth may have heard me. She's a light sleeper."

He scribbled something in his notebook, then looked at her. "So you're saying Jack Watson left you around eleven fifteen."

"That's right." Bobbie studied this man and his poker face. He showed no reaction to anything she said.

"What is your reaction to the deceased's reference to the vacuum cleaner the night of your quarrel at the Blues Club?" he asked. "Roseann Cole claims Eddie told her you knew he hid money in the vacuum cleaner."

"That's right. I did know that. But when I went back to the house to pick up pots and pans, pictures, and the vacuum cleaner, I took them straight over to my apartment where the moving van was waiting."

He looked up from his notes. "What would keep me from thinking you looked in the vacuum cleaner bag either at his house or on the way to your apartment?"

"Because I was paying those moving guys by the hour when they loaded from my shop and home. Looking in the vacuum cleaner was the last thing on my mind. Last I heard, Eddie was flat broke."

"Could you give me the name of a contact with the moving company?"

She reached in her purse for her billfold and shuffled through dozens of business cards until she found the one for the moving company. "There's the name and phone number of the manager in the Memphis area. He can give you the names of the men who loaded my stuff. And on the back of that card, you'll see the phone number for my storage unit in Memphis." She snapped her bill-fold closed and returned it to her purse.

Johanson studied the card for a moment, then laid it on the desk. "All right. Let's talk about your storage unit here. Who else has a key?"

"The manager of the facility."

"Did you loan your key out to anyone at any time?"

She shook her head. "No. I haven't had the unit that long."

"When was the last time you were out there?"

Bobbie thought for a minute. "I was there Monday morning with my niece to unload some items from my truck."

"Like what? Besides that barrel, I mean."

"Some boxes, an extra can of oil, a flashlight, and a jack and jack handle for my tires."

"How long was that jack handle?" he asked, looking more intense.

She instantly went on guard, suspicious about where he was leading but determined to be calm. She spread her hands in front of her. "About this long."

"Say, twenty to twenty-four inches?" he pressed. For the first time, a sly grin curled his lips. "Let's talk about that jack and jack handle. Why wouldn't you leave those items in your truck?"

"For the same reason I decided to remove the other things. My truck was loaded down, and I didn't have room behind the seat. I didn't want to listen to that jack and handle slam around in the bed of my truck anymore."

"Where did you leave the jack handle in your unit?"

Bobbie was thinking as quickly as the detective. Deputy Arnold said someone smashed in Eddie's head and dumped him in the pickle barrel. That someone must have used the jack. She took her time answering, trying to be exact. "I placed those items on the floor just inside the door."

"That made it convenient, having that jack handle close to a sixty-gallon barrel, didn't it?"

"It's a pickle barrel," she said, lifting her chin and cutting him up and down with her eyes. "I believe I may want to get a lawyer now. These questions seem to have gone from basic to sarcastic."

"I'm not trying to be sarcastic, Mrs. Bodine, but you can see our dilemma. We find your ex-husband—with whom you've had words the night before—in your locked unit, stuffed in a barrel. I'm sure you can understand why we would want to question you."

"Of course I can," she snapped. "But I have no idea how he got inside that unit…" She paused, thinking.

Johanson watched her.

"You know," Bobbie said, staring over his head, trying to remember, "I was in a hurry and thought I'd be coming back with more stuff. I could have left it unlocked." She nodded, hoping she was right as she studied his face, watching for some clue. There was none. His dark eyes bored through her. *This guy never lets up,* she thought, taking a deep breath. "That's all I know to tell you."

He flipped back a few pages, and she could tell he was reviewing other notes he had taken. Then he looked back at her.

"All right, you're free to go. But don't go far. We'll need to talk with you again."

She stood. "Thank you."

Turning, she did her best to walk gracefully out of the room, but she felt about as solid as Jell-O.

Deputy Arnold waited with Christy while two detectives conferred quietly at the end of the hall. One of the detectives walked up to shake hands with Deputy Arnold, then turned to Christy.

"I'm going to need everybody's alibi for Monday night and Tuesday. We'll start with you."

"I left the club around ten thirty, ten forty-five, with Dan Brockman," Christy said.

"This was after Dan threw Eddie and his girlfriend out of the club and threatened them?" the detective pressed.

"He didn't threaten them." Christy tried to keep her tone level. "He just said he would wait until he saw their taillights leaving the parking lot."

"So you were outside and heard this?"

Christy hesitated. "I came outside just afterward."

"Then I'll stick with the statements of the three people who were actually there." He flipped a page in his notebook and studied a few names.

Christy's hands tightened on her purse. "But this man, Eddie, made a terrible scene, and he was half-drunk."

The detective clicked his pen twice. "It's not my job to judge his character, Miz Castleman. My job is to find out who killed him."

Christy swallowed, her thoughts returning to Dan. "Mr. Bodine was in a drunken rage. Dan and Jack were only trying to protect Bobbie."

Deputy Arnold and the detective exchanged glances, and the detective looked as though he already knew what Jack had said… or done. Whatever that was.

"What time did you say good night to Dan?" he asked, studying a page of scribbles in the notebook in his hand.

Christy tried to think. She could see now why people seemed to have trouble remembering exact times when faced with a serious interrogation. She took a deep breath. "After midnight. Between twelve thirty and one, I think."

The door to the interrogation room opened, and Bobbie stepped out with Detective Johanson. Her eyes darted around the group and came to rest on Christy. She hurried toward her.

"You're free to go, Mrs. Bodine," Detective Johanson said, falling in step with her. "But as they say, don't leave town."

"She'll be staying with me." Christy gave her address and phone number and linked her arm through her aunt's. "Are you okay?" she asked.

Bobbie nodded. "I just need something cold to drink."

On their way out of the station, they stopped at a drink machine, and Christy bought two bottles of soda. She handed one to Bobbie, and they hurried out to the parking lot.

"Thanks so much for coming along," Bobbie said, sipping her drink. "I've had about as much of these people as I can handle for one day."

Christy nodded, unlocking the passenger door. Bobbie slid in and laid her head back against the headrest. Christy closed the door and quickly moved to the driver's side. As she slid behind the wheel, her head spun. She started the engine, anxious to get out of the Panama City traffic and onto the highway that led to Summer Breeze.

"I can't believe Eddie's dead," Bobbie said. A tear slipped beneath her lashes and slid down her cheek. "We were together for a long time," she sobbed. Christy handed her a Kleenex. "In the beginning, we were happy, and then...things changed. He changed. And I guess I changed too."

Bobbie dabbed her eyes with the Kleenex. "Eddie had an awful temper. I used to call him Banty when he got mad because he flared up like a banty rooster and went into a strut." A tiny grin hovered on her pale lips, then faded. "He started gambling, and that brought on the drinking, and...he started to get abusive with me. One night we had the mother of all fights, and that's when I got the terrible pain in my chest."

Christy gasped. "We didn't know that. Why didn't you call us? Mom would have—"

"Would have what? Dropped everything and rushed to my side, forsaking all her church and wifely duties?"

"I would have come, Bobbie."

Bobbie reached over and patted Christy's arm. "Bless you. The truth is, I didn't want to upset anyone's life because I'd made such a mess of my own. I had friends in Memphis who helped me, but friends don't replace family. After being with you guys, I realize the importance of family more than I ever did before."

"Mom loves you, Bobbie," Christy said firmly. "I'm sure you two will overcome your differences and realize how important family is—particularly at a time like this."

Bobbie nodded, twisting the Kleenex in her hands.

As Christy replayed the events in her mind, one aspect of Bobbie's story troubled her. Christy tried to phrase her words as gently as possible. "If only Eddie hadn't been yelling about money he claimed you stole from him."

"That's a lie." Bobbie straightened, her features pinched. "How was I supposed to know there was money in that vacuum cleaner?"

"They'll be asking you this question over and over, so get ready. You seem to know something about his money-hiding habits."

Bobbie nodded, the anger on her face melting into weariness. "One Sunday last year, he told me not to use the vacuum cleaner for a couple of days. Said he needed to repair it. I knew it wasn't broken, so I looked inside. In the vacuum cleaner bag, I found a Ziploc bag with some hundreds in it. So I didn't use the vacuum cleaner. And I didn't take his money. Not then, not now."

Bobbie turned in the seat, dabbing at her wet cheeks. "Christy, you couldn't possibly believe—"

"Of course not. I'm just trying to prepare you." She frowned. "I'm afraid Roseann's conversation made your actions sound a bit suspicious; also, she reiterated the part about Jack and Dan being angry. I honestly don't think she realized she was incriminating anyone. She just wanted to reveal her limited knowledge."

"Yeah, well, her knowledge may not be so limited. It's hard not to know what's going on with Eddie. He isn't...wasn't real smart, but then neither is she. Sorry." Bobbie sighed. "I shouldn't have said that." She stared at the road, and neither spoke for a few minutes. Christy exited the highway and entered Summer Breeze.

"Well," Bobbie said, turning away from the window, "it's obvious I've been framed. The question is who and why."

"To Roseann's credit, she did say something that should make the inspectors look in another direction," Christy said. "She claimed Eddie owed some bookies money and was afraid they were following him. After the two left the Blues Club, they stopped at a bar, and apparently Eddie got real jumpy. Roseann said he kept looking over his shoulder. When they went back to the motel, she went to take a shower and left him in the chair watching TV.

"When she came back into the room, he was gone. Deputy Arnold doesn't think he'd have gone out if he knew the bookies were looking for him. Roseann said she was singing in the shower and wouldn't have heard a knock on the door."

Bobbie rolled her eyes. "Those guys don't knock. They grab the desk clerk by the throat, get a key, and go in."

"Then maybe that's what happened. When they found out he didn't have the money..." Christy let her statement hang in the air.

Bobbie nodded. "Yeah, and I can see Eddie giving them a story about the money being in my storage unit—if he knew I had one. He'd probably found out from Hornsby. I mean, that's the only storage facility close by, right?"

"Right."

"Maybe he'd been over there snooping around, thinking I stashed the vacuum cleaner in my unit. Maybe he bribed Hornsby with his story and he let him in my unit."

"Even though that's illegal, I could see Hornsby doing it," Christy said. "He didn't ask you what you wanted to store or give you any rules when you began pulling out bills." Christy turned into her driveway and cut the engine.

Bobbie was looking at her, eyes wide. "I just thought of something! Even if I didn't forget to lock the unit, Eddie could have picked the lock. He worked for a locksmith as a second job when we first married. He used to brag about how he could get into any place he needed to."

Those words brought Christy's first ray of hope. "Then he could have taken whoever was after him to your storage unit, thinking the money was there. When there was no vacuum cleaner, they got fed up with his stalling."

Bobbie didn't share her enthusiasm. "But why bother framing me? I thought bookies made an example out of guys who didn't pay their debts. Blood and gore is more their style."

Christy frowned. *She's right,* she thought. It had begun to make sense, like pieces fitting together in a puzzle, but Bobbie had just pointed out something that rescrambled the puzzle.

She tried to hide her discouragement as they walked into the house. "Come on, Bobbie. Let's get something to eat."

Bobbie shook her head. "I just want to lie down."

"Good idea. I'll turn off the phones so you won't be disturbed. And while you're resting, I have a couple of errands."

Bobbie didn't seem to hear what Christy was saying as she dragged herself into the guest room and sank onto the bed.

Would she be able to sleep? Christy wondered, watching Bobbie snuggle into the pillow. Or would she, like Christy, be tormented by fear and worry?

And the horrid image of Eddie's body in the pickle barrel.

The errands Christy had mentioned to Bobbie consisted of two things: going out to the storage unit, then trying to find Jack to warn him to get ready to be questioned.

Christy cut across the side streets and hit the back highway leading to Hornsby's units. At the gates, she found a parking spot amid the jumble of parked cars. She recognized Joy McCall's green Jeep Wrangler, and as she approached, she could see Joy behind the wheel, Valerie in the passenger seat, and Aunt Dianna in the back.

Joy thrust her head out the window. "Christy, we have some things to tell you."

"What?"

Valerie leaned forward. "The dead guy's girlfriend—I don't remember her name—came in my salon yesterday to see if I had time to trim her hair. I was booked, but I told her to come back. She said she was looking for her boyfriend and went into the story of how he left the motel room and all. I had Jane in the chair doing a color, and she happened to be at the Blues Club that night. She noticed two strange guys sitting at the table next to her. After Eddie and his girlfriend left, the two guys put their heads together whispering, and then they left. Jane and her friend were ready to leave too, so they paid their tab, and just as they were getting in their car, they spotted those strange guys getting into a black Mercedes."

Joy grabbed Christy's sleeve. "I nearly got hit by a black Mercedes as I was pulling out of Carrie's Crafts. It came around the corner so fast it went over the curb. It had tinted windows, so I couldn't see how many people were in it. I tried to get the numbers on the plate, but all I got was Tennessee before it whirled around the next corner. I almost called Deputy Arnold. I wish now that I had."

"Well, it's not too late," Dianna spoke up from the backseat. "I heard this guy Eddie is a gambler. There's no telling who else may have had reason to kill him. How is Bobbie?"

Christy shook her head. "Not good. She's resting now."

"They won't let anyone inside the gate up there," Joy said.

Christy gazed at the deputy from Panama City who stood guard at the closed gate. Her eyes moved slowly to Bobbie's unit and the yellow crime-scene tape stretched across it. One didn't often see that in Summer Breeze, and the sight cast a mood of horrid fascination.

A man in a truck with a Joe's Plumbing sign on the door pulled up and leaned out his window. "I need to get to my unit," he yelled.

The deputy shook his head. "No one is allowed in," he said, loud and clear.

"Do you think he's still there?" someone in the crowd asked.

"Who?" asked another voice.

"You know. The...guy in the pickle barrel."

"All right folks," the deputy shouted to the crowd. "There's nothing to see. The white van has come and gone and 'he' is no longer inside the unit."

Sick at heart, Christy turned and walked back to her car. As she drove off, a tear slid down her cheek. The day that began with fun and happiness had turned into a nightmare—a nightmare, she feared, that had just begun.

The most important thing on her mind, at the moment, was talking to Jack. His involvement in the investigation would be crucial. She had to talk with him privately before Deputy Arnold and the detectives got to him.

At the service station, she turned onto the narrow sand road that led out to Rainbow Bay and Jack's place. As always, her gaze wandered to the ten acres of towering live oaks Jack had given Chad to build their dream home. Dan had bought those ten acres from Jack, but his plans for building there had stalled.

Jack's gray bungalow came into view, and Christy slowed down, spotting two other vehicles parked in the driveway. Neither belonged to Deputy Arnold. Pulling to a stop a few yards back from a truck she didn't recognize, she noticed J. T. Elmore's old beat-up truck farther ahead.

Bobbie. The awful day rolled over Christy like a tropical wind, tugging at the roots of her beliefs. Remembering Jack's threat, Christy feared he scored high on the suspect list. She cut the engine and hopped out.

Around back, she spotted Jack and J.T. indulging in their

favorite beverage while Jack grilled three king-size hamburgers. In a deck chair nearby sat Buster Greenwood, who usually holed up in his digs at Shipwreck Island in the hermit lifestyle he preferred. Jack and J.T. occasionally provided him with a social life. Buster was overweight with a round head the size of a dinner plate, partially covered by a stained baseball cap. He overhung Jack's narrow deck chair and almost tipped it when he looked over his shoulder to see who had arrived.

Jack laid down the burger flipper, and placed a hand on his heart. "Ah, at last an angel has come to save us."

J.T.'s arthritic knees prevented swift movement, but he hobbled toward her with a wide smile, showing off a missing tooth. "And this angel's real."

Christy noticed his clothes were clean and freshly pressed, and he wore a new baseball cap.

"J.T., you're looking fit," she said, giving him a quick hug.

Jack smirked. "Aw, he's sweet on Cora Lee Wilson, Buster's cousin."

Buster chuckled, looking pleased with the idea.

J.T.'s knobby little face turned red as a snapper. He whirled on Jack. "You got a right to talk. You haven't shut up all day 'bout Christy's aunt."

"Speaking of Bobbie," Christy said, looking grimly at Jack, "I've got to talk to you right away." She grabbed his arm and led him around the house to the driveway. "They found Eddie Bodine dead in Bobbie's pickle barrel this morning. In her locked storage unit. What do you know about it?"

He jerked his arm free. "Me? I haven't talked to that drunken bum since Dan bounced his butt across the Blues Club parking lot. And it's a good thing I haven't."

"That's exactly the kind of thing you mustn't say," she snapped. "This man is dead. Half a dozen people in the parking lot heard you threaten to kill him."

"Aw, come on, Christy—"

The sound of tires spitting gravel interrupted his words as Deputy Arnold's SUV swerved into the drive, skidding to a halt mere inches from Christy's bumper. Detective Johanson sat in the passenger seat.

Both rolled out of the car. Johanson glared at Christy while Deputy Arnold shook his silver head and frowned his disapproval. "Christy, you have to stay out of this investigation. We need to talk to Jack privately."

"How can I leave with you blocking the drive?" Christy asked, pointing.

"Just go around him in the side yard," Jack said under his breath.

Buster and J.T. strolled around the side of the house, then froze, staring wide-eyed and slack-jawed at the scene before them. J.T. shoved a half-empty bottle deeper in his pocket while Buster whirled and slid, catching himself against the corner of the house, before disappearing into the backyard.

"You boys go back to your mischief," Deputy Arnold called. "We're not here to talk to you. Jack, Detective Johanson has some questions."

Jack sighed. "All right. I got nothing to hide."

Christy searched his eyes. He met her gaze briefly, then looked away. She kissed him on the cheek, then headed back to her car. A peek in her visor mirror showed wild blue eyes and flushed cheeks.

As she drove home, she glanced across at the service station on the corner. She spotted a woman deep in conversation, unaware that gas was flowing out of her tank.

That's how I feel, she thought, *like fear is rolling up and spilling over.* Fear pumped by frustration and worry. She knew Jack well—so well, in fact, that it would have been out of character for him to leave Bobbie that night, his emotions churning, and drive straight home and go to bed. Either he would have wanted to talk about his big evening with J.T., who might have been at Cora Lee's house, or he would have stopped off at some late-night gathering place to have a relaxer and ponder his evening.

What if he had seen Eddie either coming out of the motel or going into it? He might have wanted to hurt him, but the last thing he would do is kill him and leave him in Bobbie's storage unit. What if they hadn't planned to leave him there? What if he was merely stashed there until he could be moved to a better place?

Christy massaged her forehead. Why was she thinking such crazy thoughts? She couldn't believe that her brain was actually concocting such a theory. She felt ashamed of herself, as though she had betrayed both her aunt and the man she loved like a father.

And speaking of fathers…she was approaching the community church, its tall bell steeple inviting all who were weary or heavy laden to come for rest. A lighthouse had once dominated the narrow strip of land that jutted into the Gulf, but several years ago a tornado had swept through, destroying most of the lighthouse. The remnants were then torn down, and the stretch of land cleaned up. The community decided they needed a church and worked together to build one. A simple white clapboard church now offered a beacon of hope to replace the lighthouse.

She turned on her left blinker and swung into the driveway. She spotted her dad's car, along with Martha Ann's gray compact. Martha Ann had to be the most dependable church secretary on the face of the earth. She never missed work, although she suffered from allergies and arthritis. Her devotion to Pastor Grant Castleman lined up directly behind her husband of thirty-six years.

"Hi," Christy said as she breezed past Martha Ann. "Is anyone with him?"

"No. Mr. Hayward just left. You know his wife…" Martha Ann's voice faded, her eyes sadly conveying the condition of Mrs. Hayward.

Christy nodded and hurried on.

Grant Castleman hung up the phone just as she entered, and he turned worried eyes to her. "Where have you been? Your mother has called your house, your cell phone, Bobbie's cell phone—" He picked up his phone and punched an extension. "Martha Ann, hold my calls, please."

Before Christy could answer, he continued. "Earlier, I got a phone call from Ed Bailey—you know Ed, one of our deacons. He has a unit out at Hornsby's and was unloading a chest when the police arrived. He heard that Bobbie's ex—Eddie Bodine—was found in Bobbie's unit." His forehead rumpled in a worried frown. "I assume that's why you're here."

"One of the reasons." She sank into the chair opposite his desk. "Bobbie was giving a demonstration at the Red Hat meeting when Deputy Arnold interrupted and called us outside. He took her down to headquarters for questioning in the death of Eddie Bodine. I followed them downtown and then brought her back to my house. She's lying down now."

A lump that felt as big as a fist clogged her throat. She fought tears. "She didn't do it, Dad. We just don't know why someone is trying to frame her. But we have a theory." She told him about Eddie's missing money, the vacuum cleaner, and the bookies.

Her dad listened carefully, his brow furrowed, his dark eyes intent. When Christy finished, he nodded. "That's a strong theory. You could be right. Can your mother and I visit Bobbie this evening? We want to help."

Relief seeped through Christy's body. She'd been carrying a heavy burden all day, and she needed help. "Please do. She needs you and Mom. We both do," she added. "You want to come over after work? I'll order pizza."

"Sure." He smiled at her, his eyes filled with concern. "Cheer up, honey. I think the authorities will find out who did this horrible thing."

Christy studied her hands for a minute, thinking about the other reason she had stopped by his office. "Dad, I don't know if Mom told you, but she and Bobbie had a terrible fight."

He nodded and lowered his gaze to a legal pad of notes resting beside his commentary. "I heard something about it," he replied, tactful as always.

She looked back at him, appraising him thoughtfully for a moment. Even though he was her father, she had always thought him handsome, with dark hair and eyes and a trim, lanky build. If she had to name one trait about him that always came to mind, it was "fair." He always tried to be fair with his children and his congregation and anyone who came to him with a problem. Grant Castleman believed in the benefit of the doubt. He also believed that all people should be treated with respect, and in his agreeable manner, he did that.

She smiled at him.

"For such a serious day, why the smile?" he asked.

"I'm just thinking how blessed I am to have you as my dad."

This clearly took him by surprise. He leaned back in his chair and smiled back at her. "Well, I have no idea what prompted that compliment, but I'll take it."

Christy's smiled faded. "Did Mom tell you that in addition to her squabble with her sister, she felt I sided against her?"

"Something like that. Let's hear your version."

"My version. Well, I stopped by the house and heard them from the back porch. Mom was laying into Bobbie about creating a scene, which she didn't. It was Eddie who created the scene. Then she flipped when she heard Bobbie had been singing—and by the way, that club is a nice place. Nice people, no smoking."

"It doesn't sound like everyone was nice or that the evening ended up so nicely, as you put it."

"I get your point. Bobbie's heart races and flutters. Apparently, she didn't take her daily pill, because she got upset with Eddie and tried to open her bottle and spilled the pills. Mom as much as called her a druggie, saying she heard how she dumped pills all over the place." Christy leaned forward in her chair. "That wasn't fair, Dad, and you know it."

He nodded. "I know it's been a long time since I've seen your mother as upset as she is now. She feels awful about what she said. She's also deeply hurt by your words."

Christy sighed and shrugged. "I just told the truth, Dad. Mom has always seemed so perfect—"

"Or you've chosen to see her that way," he said. "She doesn't feel that way about herself at all."

"Well, when it comes to her sister, she is very judgmental." Christy paused, realizing she had to be fair here as well. "I admit I see a tension or resentment between them. I can't remember ever seeing them laughing together or even looking like they enjoy each other's company the way Seth and I do."

"Your mother felt Bobbie got all the social attention, so she tried to be the smart one who pleased her parents. Unfortunately, that drove the sisters farther apart."

Christy nodded, seeing the logic in his explanation. "The other thing is," she said, turning their conversation back to the investigation, "Bobbie seems to have quite a bit of money on her, with no explanation of where she got it or why she suddenly decided to move here. When Eddie made that scene, he said she knew where he had stashed ten thousand dollars and that she stole the money and took off. That's his story. But…Bobbie does seem to have a lot of cash on hand."

"Well," her father said, "at dinner that first night, she told us that she had sold her shop in Memphis. That would account for the money."

"When you sell a business, I suppose you sell your list of clientele and some of the inventory."

"And the building. I think she owned the building."

Christy brightened. "Oh, I didn't know that."

"Well, I don't know that to be a fact," he said, "but I assumed from the way she described how she had to paint and paper and fix up her shop that she owned it. Not many people invest that much in a rental."

Christy nodded. "That's true. Some of the things that used to be in her shop are in storage in Memphis. She's planning to move everything here for her new shop."

"So she's definitely going to open a shop here?"

"Didn't you get that impression?"

He hesitated, reaching for his pen and turning it up and down over the pad in a gesture she recognized as stalling.

"What?" she asked.

"Honey, your aunt has never been too…reliable in what she does. I haven't been around her that much over the years, but I've seen her change overnight. Once she came to visit years ago and told us she planned to move back to Minnesota and marry a boyfriend from high school. She seemed completely serious, but Beth told me that night that Bobbie wouldn't go back to Minnesota. She hated the cold weather. Sure enough, by the next afternoon, she had completely changed her mind and decided to stay in Atlanta. This was right after her divorce from Joe Henry."

"I think she's serious about it this time, Dad."

"Well then, we'll pray for the best for her."

Christy hugged her dad and left, feeling hopeful for the first time in hours. He always made her feel better. In August, when she had broken up with Dan, her father had reminded her to use her faith, to believe God had a plan for her life and that if Dan were part of that plan, things would work out.

She drove home, humming to herself as she pulled into the drive. The humming stopped when she realized Bobbie's red truck was gone. She hurried inside, frowning at the unlocked door. When she reached the room where she had left Bobbie, the bed was empty.

B efore she went looking for Bobbie, Christy decided to turn the phones on and check her messages. Dan had called four times.

"*Hi, Christy. I heard the bad news. How can I help?*"

"*Christy, it's me again. Call me.*"

"*Hey, I don't want to keep bugging you, but I'm worried. Call me anytime, night or day. You know I care about you,*" he added softly.

Christy drew a ragged breath. "I care about you too," she said. They had both avoided the word *love* in their phone messages, and yet they had often spoken of their love over the past eighteen months. She sank into the chair at her desk, feeling as though the day had drained all emotion from her. Now, hearing Dan's voice evoked another emotion, sharp and strong. She missed him. And she needed him. If they hadn't argued, if she hadn't walked out, if they hadn't both been stubborn, he would be with her now. He would wrap his strong arms around her and press her head against his shoulder, and she would feel safe in a world turned upside down.

"*Christy, I finally reached Deputy Arnold and told him about the black Mercedes. I reminded him he owed it to his community to look for it.*"

Christy dialed Dan's number but got only voice mail. "Hi, Dan. Thanks for calling. Yes, I need you. And I care about you too."

As she hung up, her thoughts swung to Bobbie. Had she gone to Jack's house?

The phone rang. Christy glanced at the caller ID and read Miz B's number.

"Hi, Miz B."

"I had a talk with Hornsby," Miz B said without preamble. "He and his girlfriend came in for a late lunch. I guess he's closed down his office with so much going on."

"What did he have to say?"

"I bribed him with my special meatloaf—his favorite—and my strawberry cheesecake—her favorite. It worked. He told me the police asked him to keep quiet, but with all the officers and the medical examiner's team, it's no secret what happened. Said when the coroner and his men tried to get Eddie out of the barrel, it was like trying to untangle a pretzel." Miz B's voice sharpened. "Hornsby got a little amused over his pretzel joke. I told him I didn't think it was funny. Then he looked nervous, started glancing over his shoulder. Muttered something about pushy Yankee types, and that didn't make sense to me. Christy, that guy's either scared or hiding something. Or seems that way to me."

Christy considered that. "You could be right."

"Now my theory," Miz B continued, "is that those bookies killed him and hauled him out to Bobbie's storage unit. Those guys know how to get in padlocks. They dumped him in the barrel so it would look like his ex-wife took his money and killed him."

"You could be right about that as well," Christy said.

"Honey, I gotta run. I'm needed in the kitchen. Junior's goofing off again."

"Bye. And thanks for helping."

Christy hung up and looked at the wall clock. Three o'clock! She had been so caught up in her phone messages and conversations that she hadn't realized how much time she had lost.

Or how long Bobbie had been gone.

Her heart raced as she reached for the phone and dialed Bobbie's cell. Her aunt's lilting voice answered, inviting her to leave a message.

She had to find out where Bobbie had gone. *Now.*

She punched in Jack's number. She was about to hang up, thinking he wasn't home, when he breathed a weary hello into the phone.

"Hi, Jack. How'd it go with that detective?"

"Like I expected. Grilled me for an hour." He sighed. "He's just doing his job. I want the killer caught as much as anyone. Otherwise, it makes Bobbie look…well, you know. I don't want people thinking the wrong thing. I know she wouldn't kill anyone. Besides, she was with me."

"Did they ask you about the time you took her home, when you left, where you went, and those kinds of things?"

"Of course they did. Over and over. By the way, I'd like to speak with her."

Christy's hopes sank. She couldn't admit she had called in search of her aunt. She didn't want to worry him more now. She might have to worry him later, however, if she didn't find Bobbie soon. "She isn't here, Jack. Want me to have her call when she comes in?"

"Yeah. She needs friends now, Christy. Thank God she's staying with you."

"I know. Hey, I'd better go. Talk to you later, Jack." They said good-bye and hung up.

Christy tried to fight the panic rising within her. She grabbed her car keys and purse just as the sound of a vehicle turning into her driveway reached her.

She rushed outside, hoping Bobbie had returned. It was Seth, however, who jogged up to her door. Atticus trotted toward the backyard.

Her first thought, as she watched Seth approach the porch, was that he resembled their father, despite his attempts not to. Her second thought was that he looked as upset as she felt.

"I've been in Pensacola visiting friends," he said as he hugged her. "I just got back in town and heard Bobbie's ex was found dead in her storage unit. What's going on?"

She told him about everything that had happened, beginning with Deputy Arnold storming into the Red Hat meeting and ending with the questioning downtown. "When we returned, Bobbie wanted to lie down. I left for an hour or so. When I came back, she was gone."

"Did she leave a note?"

She slapped her forehead. "Hadn't even thought of that." She rushed back into the kitchen and looked at the message pad on the counter. "Nothing."

Seth swore.

She frowned at him. "Now listen. I've tried her cell phone, and she's not at Jack's place. He asked to speak to Bobbie, and I said she wasn't home. I didn't want to worry him." She felt miserable. "Oh Seth, today has been a nightmare."

He paced the kitchen floor, raking a hand through his long hair. "Tell you what. We'll both look for her," he said. He stopped pacing and faced Christy.

She touched his arm. "I'm so glad you're here. The idea that those guys from Memphis got to her—"

"Don't think like that," Seth said. "I'm sure she just went out someplace."

He reached into the fridge for two bottles of water and handed one to her. She took the water, then shoved her cell phone in her purse.

"You call me, or I'll call you," he said, striding out the door ahead of her. "I'll drive by the Blues Club. You check out Miz B's restaurant." He called to Atticus, and they jumped into his car.

Christy hurried toward hers, praying Bobbie was all right.

Christy and Seth took different routes, staying in touch by

phone. As her eyes searched the streets of Summer Breeze, her nerves pricked her skin like hot sand.

Calm down. Maybe she just wanted to be alone, went for a cup of coffee or something. You're overreacting.

She sped toward Miz B's restaurant. As she swung into the parking lot, her gaze swept the vehicles, but Bobbie's red truck was not there. She parked and hopped out, trying to calm herself. She entered the restaurant at a run and looked around.

Jamie waved from a table, where she stood refilling salt and pepper shakers.

"Has Bobbie been in?" Christy called to her.

"No, I haven't seen her. Listen, I'm sorry—"

"Thanks, Jamie. Gotta run."

Out the door and back down the steps, she ran to her car. Just as she hopped in, Seth's car sped into the parking lot and screeched to a halt beside her.

"She's not at the Blues Club, and Donna hasn't seen her," he reported.

"And she hasn't been in Miz B's. Seth, do you think it's possible she took off?"

"I'm more freaked that those bookies didn't find the money on Eddie, and now they're after Bobbie."

Christy agreed, but she struggled not to let it take over now. If she allowed herself to dwell on the horror of what the bookies might do, she'd start hyperventilating and be useless in looking for Bobbie.

"Maybe I should call Big Bob," she said, her voice shaking.

"First, let's take another swing around town," Seth said. "Think she went to see Mom?"

"Maybe. They weren't on speaking terms, but—"

"I'll drive by," Seth said, already backing up.

"Don't go in and alarm her," Christy called, starting her car and following him out of the parking lot.

Maybe she's gone back to the house, Christy thought. *Oh God, please let her be there; let us find her.*

The ugly memory of Eddie's murder jumped full force into her head, and she swerved to miss a car. She remembered a true crime story on television about a victim who had been tortured. Was there a chance that Bobbie, like the victim in the story, was hanging upside down in a meat locker?

"Stop it!" she yelled at herself.

She drove past the Starlight on her way home to see if Bobbie had gone to talk to Roseann. Another disappointment. No red truck.

Traffic slowed as old Mrs. Fentress ambled across the street with her walker, heading for the ice cream shop. Christy turned onto a side street and wound around the block to avoid the bottleneck. Something pulled her gaze to a parking lot across the street. Bobbie's red truck! Or at least she thought it was.

Swerving into the crowded parking lot, she pulled up beside Bobbie's truck. She cut the engine and slumped over the wheel, weak with relief. Beyond the parking lot, she could see people entering a square concrete building.

She jumped out of her car and ran up the sidewalk. Through

the open door, she could see a group assembled in straight-back chairs. Just before she stepped inside, she heard her aunt's voice and came to a halt.

"Hi, my name's Bobbie, and I'm an alcoholic."

Christy quickly backed up, edging around to the side of the building. She took a deep breath, trying to absorb the situation and feeling a new respect for her aunt. While she had been out looking for Bobbie, her thoughts alternating between a kidnapping and a runaway, her aunt had gone to an Alcoholics Anonymous meeting, where she could find help among others like herself.

She dialed Seth's number. "Seth, I found her. She's at an AA meeting. I'll park at a distance and wait until she comes out. Hopefully she'll go back to my house."

Seth sighed. "Good. Hey, when I swung by the folks' house, Mom was backing out of the driveway. She said Mrs. Hayward died, and she's meeting Dad at the Hayward home to help out. I guess the family is pretty broken up. She wanted me to tell you they couldn't come over tonight, but she'd call first thing in the morning. I didn't tell her we were looking for Bobbie."

"Well," Christy said, rubbing her forehead, "I'm sorry about Mrs. Hayward, but I'm relieved Mom and Dad will be occupied tonight. I'm drained."

"Yeah, me too. I'm going home now. If Aunt Bobbie doesn't come home, call me. And tell her I came by to see her and that I'll call tomorrow."

"Right. I love you, brother."

"Same here."

Christy closed her cell phone and returned to her car. She drove across the street and parked in the driveway of a house listed with a For Sale sign.

Ten minutes later, the meeting ended, and Christy watched her aunt hurry to her truck. She waited until the little red truck had disappeared around the corner. Then she backed out of the driveway and followed. When Bobbie turned into the market, Christy parked at a distance.

Fifteen minutes later, Bobbie hurried out with a bulging sack and hopped in her truck. As Bobbie turned down the next block, Christy could see she was headed back home.

She found Bobbie in the kitchen, unloading a grocery bag. "I bought a few staples for us."

"Thanks, Bobbie. Are you hungry?"

"Yeah, but I think I'll call Jack first. It'd be good to talk with him."

"Good idea," Christy said, smiling at her.

Relief flooded through every pore of her being. The crisis had been imagined, and yet…she had reason for concern. There were bad guys out there, probably looking for Bobbie. Tonight, though, Bobbie was safely out of the path of the enigmatic black Mercedes.

eleven

Friday

Christy stepped out of the shower and dressed in jeans and a pink T-shirt. The house was quiet, and she didn't know if that meant Bobbie had left or was still asleep. Concern for her aunt still dominated her thoughts, and she tiptoed down the hall and peeped in at Bobbie's bed.

Bobbie lay huddled beneath the quilt, only the top of her golden curls showing. Christy breathed a sigh of relief and went into the kitchen. She flipped the switch on the coffee maker, then sat at the eating bar and opened her journal.

"Prayer Requests." She could fill two pages. Instead of writing, she opened her Bible to the verse her Dad had instilled in them as children whenever they were afraid. Turning to Isaiah 41:10, she decided to copy the passage in her journal. This verse had been her lifeline over the years. "So do not fear, for I am with you; do not be dismayed, for I am your God. I will strengthen you and help you." She laid down the pen and read on, stopping on a couple of verses that added power to the first promise. "For I am the LORD, your God, who takes hold of your right hand and says to you, Do not fear; I will help you."

Christy closed her eyes and began to pray, asking God to help her and all of her family, especially Bobbie.

"Hi."

Christy jumped, unaccustomed to having someone in the house. Her back was toward Bobbie, so of course her aunt wouldn't realize she was interrupting anything. Turning on the stool to face Bobbie, she smiled. "Hi."

Her aunt stood in the doorway in her silk pajamas, her curls tousled. She looked at the open Bible and the journal but said nothing. She crossed the kitchen and opened the cupboard, reaching for a mug.

"Thank you for helping me," Bobbie said. When she glanced over her shoulder, Christy could see tears filling her huge blue eyes. "I pride myself on being strong, but lately, all I want to do is cry."

"That's normal, given what you've been through."

Bobbie poured coffee into her mug. "Ready for yours?"

Christy nodded, handing her Mystery Lady mug to Bobbie to fill.

Bobbie studied the sassy lady on the cup. "Cute mug. Where'd you get it?"

"A friend bought it for me after I sold my first mystery novel."

Bobbie nodded. "Very appropriate."

Christy went to the refrigerator to retrieve a half pint of cream. "Dad and Mom were coming over to see you last night, but Mrs. Hayward, our former organist, died."

"I'm sorry to hear that." Bobbie sipped her coffee, study. Christy over the rim of her mug. "What do Beth and Grant thin. about…Eddie? And about me?"

"They believe in you, Bobbie."

The telephone rang, and Christy turned, dreading the day's barrage of calls. Her parents' number showed up on the caller ID.

When she answered, her mother's voice sounded small yet determined. "Hi, honey. How are you?"

"I'm okay. You?"

"Worried. Concerned. I'm so sorry for all that has happened. Poor Bobbie. I wish I could come by your house this morning, but I've promised to drive some kids to Camp Honeywood first thing. Before I leave, though, I'd like to speak with Bobbie."

"Sure, Mom." She handed the phone to Bobbie, huddled over her coffee. "Mom would like to speak to you."

Bobbie seemed to shrink deeper into her pajamas. She hesitated a moment, then took the phone. "Hi, Beth," she said, her voice shaky.

Christy could hear her mother's voice on the other end, and the tears that earlier had filled Bobbie's eyes now coursed down her cheeks. Christy handed her a napkin and left the kitchen.

Mug in hand, she returned to her bathroom and looked at h face in the mirror. She looked tired. She applied some lip gloss smoothed the edges of her long hair. Then she hurried dow^e hall and out to the sun porch. She had finally reached ^py phone last night, and he had asked if he could stop by o^ay to work.

She took a seat in a wicker chair just as his truck swung into the driveway. Dressed in work clothes, Dan looked neat and handsome, but an expression of worry sat squarely on his face.

"Hi," he said as he stepped into the sun porch. He leaned down to kiss her.

"Oops." Christy pulled back and looked down. Her mug had tipped, and coffee ran down her T-shirt.

"I'm sorry," Dan said.

"No problem. I'm clumsy, as you know." Christy brushed at the stain. "Would you like coffee?"

"Can't. We're running behind on that project at Sunnyside, but I had to see you. How're you doing?" His warm fingers caressed her arm.

"I'm okay." She gave him a quick rundown of what had happened yesterday. When she told him about Deputy Arnold showing up at the Red Hat meeting, he shook his head.

"Knowing Deputy Arnold, he didn't bother to be tactful," he said.

Christy shook her head in disgust. "In the presence of all the Red Hat ladies, he informed Bobbie that something was ripe in her pickle barrel and, to quote him, 'It ain't pickles.'"

"Was he trying to be funny?" Dan asked, anger edging his voice.

She sighed. "No, I think he was just trying to get her out of the room so he could drive her over to Panama City. She was questioned by a detective—"

"Named Johanson. He stopped by my house right after I got home from work."

"You didn't mention that when we talked last night."

"Figured you had enough to think about. How did Bobbie hold up?"

"I wasn't in the interrogation room, but she must have kept her cool because they let her go. But they used that worn-out phrase, 'Don't leave town.'" She frowned. "Tell me about your experience."

He crossed his arms and scowled. "Johanson and his men have talked to everyone in town. With every so-called eyewitness, I got rougher with Eddie. The last account has me picking him up and throwing him out the front door."

"Dan, I'm sorry."

"Don't be. I didn't throw him out, but I felt like it. Johanson kept asking what time I took you home, what time I went home, and didn't I have any witnesses about the time I arrived home." He sighed. "I don't. I had too much on my mind to sleep, so I walked down the hill to the beach. I just sat there, watching the waves roll in. I didn't see anyone, and I doubt anyone saw me at that hour."

She placed a hand on his arm. "I wish you hadn't been dragged into this. You were just trying to help my aunt."

"Don't worry about it. Bodine was bullying Bobbie, and I have a problem with bullies. Anyway...I think we should discuss something more pleasant. Like dinner this evening."

"Dinner would be great."

"Then why don't we drive down the beach and find a quiet

place where we can talk? We'll have more privacy if we get out of Summer Breeze."

"Good idea," she said, smiling into his eyes.

For a moment, neither spoke. She felt love for him swelling in her heart, and from the way he looked at her, she knew he loved her too.

"Seven o'clock?"

She nodded. "I'll be ready."

She put the mug down, and he took her in his arms. When they pulled apart, he seemed reluctant to leave. He glanced at his watch.

"Have a good day, Dan," she said.

"You too. Or rather, *try* to have a good day."

She watched him jog back to his truck. Then she sighed and touched her lips, thinking about his kiss. When she entered the kitchen, Bobbie was sitting at the eating bar, grinning at her.

"You'd better hang on to him," she said with a wink.

Christy smiled. "He's pretty special. Did you and Mom patch things up?"

"Yes. She apologized for what she said. And I apologized to her. She said she'll come back early from Camp Honeywood to spend time with me." A glow of happiness had replaced the tears, and for the first time in twenty-four hours, Bobbie had found her smile.

The phone rang again. Christy threw up her hands and grinned at Bobbie as she answered.

"Christy, this is Roseann Cole. I'm trying to make plans for getting Eddie back to Memphis, but they won't release his body."

Christy digested that information. "In a murder case like this one, the body will be held until the autopsy is completed." She sighed. "I'm sorry to say that may take a while. Since he's from out of state, though, the process may move faster. There's a lot of pressure to put a rush on this case."

Christy heard a heavy sniff on the other end of the line. "I wanted you to ask your aunt who I should call," Roseann said. "Eddie never talked about his family." She repeated the number of her cell and said she was still staying at the Starlight.

"I'll find out for you," Christy said. "Did you have to go down to the station in Panama City for questioning?"

"Yeah. Deputy Arnold took me down there, and I told them everything I know. But I don't think I was very helpful. They didn't keep me long, and I reckon they were pretty nice about it."

Christy wanted to press her about what she'd told them, but she knew that would be inappropriate.

"Another thing," Roseann continued. "They're holding Eddie's truck, going over it for evidence."

"You said Deputy Arnold found it near the Blues Club?"

"A couple of blocks away or something like that. I guess Eddie went back there after all."

There was a moment of silence.

"I'll get back to you with the information you need about Eddie's relatives," Christy said.

"Thanks," Roseann mumbled and hung up.

Bobbie stood at the counter, buttering toast. She looked at Christy with a question in her eyes.

"That was Roseann Cole," Christy said.

Bobbie laid down the butter knife. "What did she want?"

"She wants to contact Eddie's family and thought you would know who to call."

Bobbie sank down on a stool. "Both of his parents died years ago, but he has a brother in Hendersonville, Tennessee—Mitford Bodine. I only met him a couple of times, but I'd bet anything he still lives there. He wasn't like Eddie. He was the type who puts down roots, stays in one place. He owned a service station. Bet he still does."

"Mitford is a very unusual name. He should be easy to locate. Anyone else?"

"No. There were just the two brothers." All the joy had drained from Bobbie's face, and Christy thought it was time for a change of subject.

"Okay. I'll tell Roseann. Hey, are you fixing us breakfast?"

Bobbie stared at the toast. "Sort of."

"Great. What did Jack have to say last night?"

"He asked me to meet him for lunch today. He insists we keep looking for locations for my shop, but that may be out of the question now."

Christy gave Bobbie a hug. "No, I think it's more important than ever that you go on with your plans. In fact, I'll help you get the shop going once you nail down a location."

Bobbie came back to life, her eyes filled with hope. "You'll help?"

"Of course I will. I'm excited about I Saw It First."

Bobbie looked as though a light had been turned on behind her eyes. "That's great, honey."

Christy noticed her Bible had been moved, and she caught Bobbie glancing at a highlighted passage. "That's my favorite verse," she said. "I find strength—"

"I don't mean to sound rude, Christy, but those words just haven't worked for me." Bobbie closed the Bible and handed it to her. "Want me to scramble some eggs?"

Christy put the Bible, journal, and pen in their drawer. "No, thanks. I need to dash out and pick up a sympathy card for the Haywards. And maybe I'll stop by the Starlight and deliver that information to Roseann Cole. She's stranded," she added. She watched Bobbie pour more cream into her coffee. Bobbie didn't comment or show any sympathy for Roseann. A spark of annoyance singed Christy's good mood, but she resolved not to take Bobbie's actions personally. She was in a crisis, but Roseann was in a crisis too.

Christy rummaged through a drawer and found a spare key. "Here you go," she said, laying it on the eating bar. "We need to keep the doors locked."

Bobbie nodded, munching on her toast. "See you later."

"Later." Christy grabbed her shoulder bag and keys from the rack and dashed out the back door. As she started the car and backed out, she wondered what Bobbie thought about her intention to visit Roseann. She just wanted to observe her again and find out if she knew anything that could help clear Bobbie's name. But did Bobbie see it as a betrayal?

Christy turned into the Starlight Motel and parked in front of

Roseann's room. She knocked on the door and called, "Roseann, it's Christy."

The door opened, and Roseann stood before her, dressed in white capris and a matching shirt. Her dark hair had been styled, and she seemed to have pulled herself together quite well. She stared curiously at Christy.

"I have the information you need about Eddie's family," Christy said, suddenly feeling awkward.

"Just a minute." Roseann left the door and returned with pen and pad. "Thanks for stopping by, but you could have just called." She didn't bother to invite Christy in.

Christy repeated what Bobbie had told her, and Roseann wrote down the brother's name.

"He did talk about his brother some," Roseann said, looking up from her notes. "Said they must have had different dads because his brother turned out good. All he ever said about his old man was that they hated each other."

Christy winced, thinking Eddie's upbringing may have had something to do with the way he turned out.

"So I'll call his brother, Mitford," Roseann continued, sounding weary. "I've already made arrangements with a funeral home to take him back to Memphis. I'm just waitin' on Eddie's truck. They're hanging on to it longer than I would have thought."

"Have you considered a rental car?"

"I'll wait on the truck. Everything that belonged to Eddie needs to go back to Memphis when he does."

"I understand," Christy said. "Dale, the owner of the funeral home, is a nice guy. I'm sure he'll work with you on the expenses of getting Eddie to Memphis." She held her breath, hoping Roseann would take the bait.

Roseann's gaze swept Christy before she responded. "Well, I don't have much money, but Eddie gave me a credit card. I think there's enough credit left to get him home."

"And once you're there," Christy pressed, "I'm sure he has a life insurance policy that will cover the rest of the expense."

Silence followed, one that Roseann did not bother to fill. She stared at her notes. "I don't know," she said at last.

Christy suppressed a sigh. She had hoped Roseann would volunteer information regarding a life insurance policy, if it existed, and its beneficiary. She knew it wasn't Bobbie. But getting information from Roseann proved to be tougher than she had expected. After all, Roseann wasn't sure that Bobbie, and maybe Jack, hadn't killed her boyfriend, and Christy was Bobbie's niece.

"Roseann, I'm sorry for what's happened," Christy said gently. "But you understand I'm not responsible for other people's actions. If I can help you, I will."

"Why would you want to help me?" Roseann's eyes narrowed behind the heavy black mascara.

"You don't know anyone here."

"Thanks," Roseann replied halfheartedly. Christy doubted that Roseann would accept her offer of help. But then, she couldn't really blame her.

"Well, I'd better run." She didn't know what else to say, and apparently Roseann didn't either. Her wary gaze lingered on

Christy. "Good luck," Christy added lamely, then turned back to her car. Roseann's door slammed behind her.

Christy glanced at her watch. Ten thirty.

Recalling her conversation with Miz B, she decided to drive out to the storage facility. If Hornsby was there today, maybe he'd talk to her.

⌒∽⊗∾⌒

Hornsby's storage units still hosted a beehive of activity. The yellow crime-scene tape seemed iridescent in the morning sunlight, calling attention to the fated unit. The gate was open, however, and no deputy was stationed to stop people from entering. Cars and trucks were parked in front of units as people checked to make sure they hadn't been robbed during the Monday night tragedy.

Christy circled the facility and spotted a deputy with one of the detectives she had seen in Panama City. They stood in front of the unit that backed up to Bobbie's. Why were they looking at that unit? Who owned it?

She found a parking space away from the activity and hurried to the office.

Hornsby's desk looked as though someone had aimed a fan at it and blown papers in all directions. That same fan had tousled Hornsby's hair into a black tumbleweed. She could tell from the way he kept shoving a hand through his hair that he had been the fan. He had his mouth pressed against the phone, but his voice reached her.

"I've stalled about not having a combination to that fancy dial lock on your unit, but they've got search warrants to go through every unit. They've worked their way down to yours—" He looked up at Christy standing in the doorway and jerked back in his chair. "Someone's here. Gotta go. Yeah, you better hurry back and check on things." He hung up and looked at Christy. "What do you want?"

She pretended to be shocked. "That's not a very friendly greeting, Hornsby. My aunt just wanted to know when to tell the moving van to bring the rest of her stuff."

Hornsby shook his head. "She won't be able to put anything in that unit for weeks. And I don't have another unit. She'd better check elsewhere."

"If you don't have another unit, then I believe she's due a refund. I saw her pay you three months in advance, and it hasn't been a week."

"Well, it ain't my fault her ex-husband ended up in there or that she's the number-one suspect. It'll probably cost me what she already paid to get the place deodorized. And I've got to have a load of gravel hauled in to replace all that's been scattered from vans and police cars coming in and out."

"I'm sorry about that."

His protruding brown eyes were streaked with red, as though he hadn't slept much. Dark circles underlined his eyes. "That unit was locked. Nobody else had a key. And I didn't use mine," he emphasized, "until that foul smell came through the walls. Then it was my duty to see what was wrong."

Christy nodded, pretending sympathy. "I know this has been awful for you. I imagine the police and the press are hounding you to death."

His shoulders slumped, and he let go of the heavy sigh he had been holding. "Phone's ringing off the hook. I've been tempted to lock up and go home, but I can't with them detectives—" He broke off, busying himself with his papers.

"Yeah, I can imagine."

His head jerked back up, his eyes glittering with suspicion. "So what's going on with your aunt?"

"She's upset, naturally." Christy remembered what her aunt had said as they drove away after renting the unit. *I'll bet you my line-dancing boots that Hornsby's the biggest gossip in town. Never met a man like him who wasn't nosy...* " Christy searched her mind for the best way to manipulate him. Manipulation was not a good thing, she knew, but she had to protect her aunt.

"The thing that bothers us most is the black Mercedes," she said.

Hornsby's dark eyes bulged. "What black Mercedes?"

"The one from Tennessee that everybody's been seeing around town. I'm sure you must have noticed it circling the units. In fact"—she studied him closely—"someone thought they saw it parked in front of your office, like maybe they were looking for a storage unit."

His gaze shot out to the parking lot, then back to her. "I ain't seen a black Mercedes from Tennessee. I'd have remembered it. And nobody's asked for a unit since your aunt rented that one." He wagged his head to indicate the scene of the crime. "Deputy didn't mention it."

"No, he wouldn't," she said, shrugging. "They can't talk about the investigation to anyone." She decided to get bold. "Those guys who were after Eddie Bodine were bookies. Word is, they followed him here."

She could practically see his heart pumping beneath his thin white shirt. "I haven't heard anything about that," he said, coming to his feet. He peered out the window. "But I'll keep an eye out."

"Thanks, Hornsby. I'd better run. Oh, one more thing. The guy who owns that unit that backs up to Bobbie?"

Anxiety leapt onto Hornsby's face and pulled at his features. "What about him?" he asked hoarsely. She heard the fear in his voice.

"He's kind of strange, isn't he?"

"What do you mean, strange?"

"Who is he? I mean, he looks a little suspicious to me."

"Suspicious? I wouldn't have suspicious people renting units," he said, obviously angry. "Or rather, I didn't until your aunt—"

"Be careful, Hornsby."

"You know I'm not allowed to give the identity of my tenants. But I don't like you implying Tony Panada is suspicious. For your information, he's a respectable businessman. He owns a printing company downtown."

She nodded. "Then I guess I was mistaken. See you later."

As she started her car, Christy reached under her seat for the extra phone directory she kept with her. She placed it on the seat beside her until she reached the service station farther down. She steered into the parking area and cut the engine. Flipping through the phone book, she found Tony Panada's name with a Panama City home address. TP Printing Company was located there as well. She dialed the number.

A professional-sounding receptionist answered.

"I'd like to get some information, please," Christy said. "Exactly what type of printing do you do?"

"We do a variety of things. Brochures for businesses, invitations for parties, business cards… What did you need?"

"I'm interested in party fliers," Christy replied.

"Oh, that's one of our specialties. I suggest you come down and look at some of our samples, or you can make up one of your own."

Christy thanked her and hung up. She was definitely on the wrong trail with this one. Tony Panada probably kept the storage unit for extra paper and supplies. She replaced the phone book under her seat and shoved her cell in her pocket.

Then something occurred to her. Why would Panada choose a small storage facility more than twenty miles from his home and business? There were several storage units closer. She doubted Hornsby's prices justified the drive.

Everyone had a reason for what they did. What was Tony Panada's reason for going so far out of his way to keep a unit? The only answer that made sense to Christy was that he had something to hide.

As she drove back into Summer Breeze, she decided to go by Miz B's to chat with her. She always lifted Christy's spirits. She'd probably find Bobbie and Jack there as well.

But first, she needed some fuel. She turned into the town's most popular service station and pulled up to a pump. Just in front of her, she saw J. T. Elmore gassing up his old truck.

"Hey, J.T.," she called. She set the pump on automatic, then walked up to him.

"I can't afford to do that," he said, nodding toward the fuel pump in her car. "I have to buy ten dollars at a time, with the price of gas and all."

"Well, I have a tendency to run out before I know it," she said, looking him over. He seemed out of sorts and had reverted back to wearing his old jeans and frayed shirt. Something wasn't quite right.

"Are you okay?" she asked, placing a hand on his bony shoulder. "You look a little pale."

J.T. kicked at a pebble with his worn tennis shoes. "Aw, I didn't sleep last night. I went over to Cora Lee's house, and we had a fight and busted up."

"What happened?"

He shoved the hose back into its stand and capped his tank. He straightened and looked at her. "I just messed up, that's all."

"Now, J.T.," she said, looking affectionately at him, "if you just messed up, I'm sure there's a way to straighten it out. From what I've heard of Cora Lee, she's a pretty forgiving person."

"Till it comes to me going to a bar. She don't rare up too much about me socializing with the boys out at Jack's place, but she's a real religious woman, hates that Last Chance Bar down the street." He wagged his head, almost toppling his stained baseball cap.

"But you don't go there, so why should she be upset?"

The end of his nose turned red, a signal that his blood pressure was rising. His gaze shot away from her, focusing on a dent on his truck. "Ah, never mind. It's just a misunderstanding."

She placed a hand on his arm as he reached forward to open his door. "Did Jack get you in trouble?"

He nodded. "But I knew better."

"What did he do, J.T.? You can tell me."

He turned, his eyes watering. "Never thought I'd care that much about a woman again. I hate to lose her."

"J.T., you aren't going to lose her over going to that bar with Jack," Christy soothed. "I can talk with her. I'll tell her Jack insisted. That you would never have gone if he hadn't needed a favor."

"The only reason I went was to keep him out of trouble," he shot back. "But Cora Lee had got wind of it by the time I got to her house last night. I gotta go, Christy."

"Wait, J.T." She decided to bluff. If she was wrong, he would straighten her out. "I know Jack was upset Monday night and threatened Eddie Bodine. If you hadn't been with him, he might have done something he would have regretted."

J.T. whirled, looking around the station to see who had heard her. "All we did was watch Bodine and that woman," he said. "We didn't do nothing wrong. And Jack never talked to him. Then Cora

Lee's cousin Hank—wild as a buck—came in to buy cigarettes and saw me. He told his wife, and she told Cora Lee while they were at a quilting bee yesterday. As soon as Hank went out the door, I followed him to the truck, tried to explain I never went to bars anymore. Didn't do any good," he said, heaving a sigh. "Cora Lee still got the word.

"Anyway, I went back inside and told Jack I was leaving. I knew I was in trouble with Cora Lee, and I wanted to go back home. The only reason I was there is Jack saw me coming back from Cora Lee's house and waved me over. Told me he wanted me to go with him to that bar."

He seemed to have run out of words, so he just stood by his truck, miserably shaking his head.

Christy tried not to show the disappointment she felt. She forced her tone to remain cheerful, although it was difficult. "Did Jack leave when you did?"

"Naw, but he said he was leaving in a minute."

She nodded. "Well, J.T., I'm going to talk to Cora Lee. Maybe I can help you out." She winked at him.

"Miss Christy, if you said something to her, it'd go a long way toward her forgiving me." New hope glowed on his face. "I think she does her grocery shopping around ten o'clock on Saturdays."

"I'll talk to her." She smiled. "Bye, J.T."

She headed back to her car to replace the hose on the gas pump, then went inside to pay. When she heard J.T.'s truck roar off, the pleasant expression disappeared from her face. Jack had lied to her. Even worse, he had lied to the police by saying he went straight home. How could he possibly think no one in that bar would admit he was there when questioned?

Everyone around Summer Breeze knew Jack Watson, and rarely was he seen in a bar. What, she wondered, had happened after J.T. left?

twelve

As soon as Christy drove into Miz B's lot, she saw Jack's black SUV parked beside Bobbie's red truck. Too furious to be reasonable now, she charged into the dining room and spotted the two of them huddled together like lovebirds. Both looked up with wide, surprised smiles as she approached the table.

"Oh, Christy, I have the best news," Bobbie began, excitement rising in her voice. "We've found the perfect location for my shop. I should have waited for you to see it, but I was afraid someone else might grab it."

Jack studied Christy's face, reading the signals, but he tried to keep up a cheerful countenance. "It's that shop that was just vacated last week—one of those fancy boutiques that didn't make it after tourist season."

"There's a large storage area in the back where I can rebuild and refinish furniture." Bobbie spoke quickly, obviously thrilled about the shop. "The front is a bit small, but I can…" She stopped, suddenly aware Christy wasn't paying attention. "Honey, is something wrong?"

Christy stared at Jack. "I just spoke with J.T. down at the service station. He looked rotten, and when I pressed him as to why, he admitted he and Cora Lee broke up last night."

"Oh, what a shame," Bobbie said, looking from Christy to Jack.

"Jack, you did go back to that bar Monday night, and you took J.T. with you!"

Jack snarled. "Aw, I didn't force him to go. Fact is, he kinda liked the idea, no matter what he let on to Cora Lee."

Christy glanced around the restaurant, then lowered her voice. "You lied about going straight home Monday night."

"Jack," Bobbie said, putting a hand on his arm. "What happened?"

Jack's face darkened. He heaved a sigh and lowered his gaze. "I've done nothing wrong."

Except get J.T. in a heap of trouble, Christy wanted to say. "Didn't you know someone would see you there?" she asked. "Don't you think that hotshot detective will question every person in the bar that night? Jack, he won't believe you about anything else now!"

"Oh dear," Bobbie moaned, her blue eyes clouding with worry.

"It's beginning to sound like you're the one who doesn't believe me," he said, a muscle clenching in his jaw. "I stayed there for half an hour, back in the shadows. When Bodine and his airhead girlfriend left, him drunk as a baboon, they never saw me. I knew, by then, he was too far gone to do any harm. Matter of fact, she drove them back to the motel. When I passed the Starlight, the truck was parked there. I have no idea what happened after that."

"So, see," Bobbie said, looking at Christy, "he was just trying to help. And this proves Eddie went back to the motel."

"I'm afraid it doesn't prove anything once the authorities begin to doubt what Jack tells them." Christy sighed. "Maybe I'm over-reacting. I don't know. I think I'll go home and cool off."

She got up and left the booth without a good-bye, as she was confused and angry and wanted to leave before she said something she would later regret. Maybe Bobbie could talk Jack into recanting the statement he'd made earlier. But she wasn't sure that was the right thing to do either. By lying to everyone, thinking he was protecting Bobbie, Jack had just dug a deeper hole for himself.

As she drove home, Christy spotted Seth's red El Camino in front of the video rental store. Atticus dominated the front seat, keeping watch. She parked in the first vacant space at the curb and hopped out of the car. Seth ambled out of the store and saw her hurrying in his direction.

"I need to talk to you," she said.

"Man, you get right to it every time. What's up?"

"Got a minute?"

"Do I look like I'm in a hurry?" He grinned. "Have you had lunch?"

She wasn't hungry, but at least they could sit down and talk. "No. Where do you want to go?"

"On the rare occasions that I'm not spending my money on a

girl, I dine on bologna or peanut butter and jelly. But for you, I'll squeeze my budget. How about a hamburger?" He nodded toward the café across the street.

"Fine. I might even treat you so you don't have to squeeze your budget." She reached through the open window of Seth's car to scratch Atticus behind his long ears. "Hey, sweetie. Is this guy treating you right?"

Atticus's warm tongue swiped her arm.

"I know. You're the best-loved guy in town."

Seth put the videos in the car and looked at Atticus. "You look comfortable, so stay put and I'll bring you a treat."

An enthusiastic bark followed them as they crossed the street.

Just walking beside Seth lifted Christy's spirits. She cast a sidelong glance at him as he held open the door for her. His T-shirt advertised a bar in Australia, and his jeans were as worn as ever, but his brown hair gleamed, and clean soap smells wafted to her. *I hadn't noticed how handsome he's become,* she thought. She could see why there was a different girl every night.

They entered the café, and she led the way to a booth in the back. The lunch crowd had dispersed, and now only a half-dozen diners lingered.

"Hey, Seth and Christy." Mrs. Smitherman, slim and fifty-something, spread menus before them. "Seth, my Todd in Atlanta always asks about you when he calls home."

Seth grinned up at her. "How's my old buddy?"

"Doing great. Graduates from Georgia Tech this month. He already has a job with an important company in Atlanta."

Christy watched Seth as he tried to keep the smile in place, but his eyes drifted down to the menu and back. "Super! Todd was always at the top of the class."

"What about you? Heard you'd been in Australia."

"I worked over there for a while." He sat up straighter in the booth. "I'm going back to Florida State next semester, working toward a degree in marine science."

"That's good to hear." Her eyes moved to Christy. "And how's our celebrity writer? We're all so proud of you."

"Thank you. I'm fine, but we're starved." She glanced back at Seth. Most of their lives, people had raved over cute little Christy and stared at shy Seth. It made Christy uncomfortable when she got compliments and Seth was bypassed or merely glanced at curiously.

"A hamburger all the way for me," Seth said. "And"—he looked at Christy, teasing her with his pause—"a glass of milk."

Christy's lips twitched as she studied the menu. Although she tried to resurrect an appetite, it was hopeless. "Just a cup of your famous clam chowder and iced tea."

As Mrs. Smitherman hurried off, Seth leaned forward. "Petite, precocious Christy." This time he smiled, and the old sarcasm disappeared.

"Jack lied about going straight home Monday night," she said, lowering her voice. "After he dropped Bobbie off, he went to the bar where Bodine and his girlfriend were."

Seth's eyebrows shot up. "Whoa."

"Yeah. He met up with J.T. outside the bar, asked him to join him, and now Cora Lee is furious and has broken up with J.T."

"What? Who?"

She shook her head. "The important thing is that Jack lied to the police, and they're going to find out he followed Bodine there. This is going to damage his credibility."

Mrs. Smitherman returned with their drinks and silverware.

"Thank you," Christy said.

"So what'd he find out when he stalked Bodine?" Seth asked once Mrs. Smitherman was gone.

"Just that he got more drunk and left with Roseann. He watched them get in the truck and drive across to the Starlight Motel. That agrees with Roseann's story."

"Then what? Did he and J.T. go over and call him out?"

"No. He says he went home."

"Yeah, well, he may have to prove that," Seth said. He took a big gulp of milk.

For the first time all day, Christy laughed. "You look like a commercial featuring the milk mustache."

He touched a napkin to his mouth. "I'm kind of crude."

"Yeah, you are. But it's good to have my adventurous Seth home."

She tilted her head to study him. "You're a budding Russell Crowe."

Seth laughed. "I don't think so, but thank you."

Their food arrived, and Seth dug in. Christy lifted her soup spoon and dipped it into the chowder. "I've got a date with Dan tonight," she said lightly.

Seth gave her a thumbs-up as his jaws worked the hamburger.

⌒≫∽

When Christy got home, she took an aspirin and went to her bedroom, hoping for a nap to settle her down before her date with Dan. Sleep eluded her, though, as she kept trying to piece together all she had learned today. Eventually she gave up and climbed out of bed.

By six thirty, she had showered and was slathering lotion on her skin when she heard Bobbie's truck. Since Dan was due to pick her up soon, she wanted to avoid revisiting the conversation at Miz B's and the tide of emotions from the afternoon.

She turned on her blow-dryer and began to style her damp hair with a round brush, smoothing it into loose waves around her shoulders. She hoped the noise would keep Bobbie from knocking on her door. Apparently, it did.

When Christy finished with her hair and turned off the dryer, she listened. She could hear noise from the kitchen—a cabinet door slamming, the creak of the refrigerator door. Then she thought she heard Bobbie's voice in conversation. Christy walked around the bedside table and noted the phone line was lit up.

Refusing to eavesdrop, she glanced at the clock, relieved to see that time was working in her favor. She still had half an hour before Dan would pick her up.

She opened her closet door and pulled down the new outfit she had bought during her latest shopping excursion: a green floral skirt with a white camisole and sheer cardigan. As a final touch, she dabbed on the perfume Dan had given her for her birthday.

She did a once-over in the dresser mirror. Looking at her reflection, she thought of Bobbie. She had the same round blue eyes, only her aunt's eyes were larger. The natural Norwegian blond in her genetics had been passed on to her in gold streaks around the sides of her face and across her bangs, which brightened her countenance. Otherwise, her hair was light brown.

Now that Christy had spent time with Bobbie, she realized she resembled Bobbie more than Beth. Maybe her natural sense of adventure—her gypsy nature, she called it—totally foreign to her mother, had come from her aunt.

As she hooked gold earrings in her ears and snapped on a gold bracelet, she heard the doorbell ring. *Perfect timing,* she thought, hurrying out of her bedroom, a small clutch tucked under her arm.

Bobbie greeted Dan at the door, staring with admiration into his handsome face.

"Hi, Dan," Christy called as she entered the room.

Both turned to look at her, and Bobbie gasped with approval. "You look absolutely gorgeous," she said, looking back at Dan.

"I agree." His eyes took in every detail as Christy approached.

Christy turned to her aunt. "Are you staying home tonight?"

"I'm going to be busy with plans," Bobbie said, waving an arm toward the dining table covered in tablets and papers. "I'm so excited about my shop," she added, her eyes glowing. She didn't seem at all angry about Christy's confrontation with Jack.

"Sounds wonderful," Christy replied. "We won't be late," she said, looking at Dan.

"But don't wait up," he added.

Bobbie looked from Christy to Dan. "Have a wonderful evening. You two make a beautiful couple."

"Careful, Bobbie," Christy teased. "You'll run him off, and I won't get dinner."

Everyone laughed as Dan reached for Christy's hand, tucking it in his. They walked to his car, and he leaned forward to kiss her cheek as he opened the passenger door. "You look lovely tonight," he said.

"Thanks. You clean up real well," she teased. He wore a blue pinstriped shirt and navy pants.

He closed her door gently, came around the front of the SUV, and got in. "Your aunt seems awfully excited," he said, backing out of the drive.

She made an effort to forget the bad news she'd heard this afternoon and focus instead on being with Dan. "Yeah, she has a passion for the work she does. And I think she really needs to get that shop going in order to move on with her life. I don't want her sitting here, worrying herself to death about this investigation. Where are we going?" she asked pleasantly, eager to divert the subject.

He named the restaurant, a quaint little place near Seaside that was off the beaten path. Having been there with him once before, Christy nodded and smiled. "Perfect."

He reached for her hand as they drove along, his other hand gripping the steering wheel. "Some people fall in love, or think they are, but in the end they discover they never really *liked* the person." He glanced at her. "But if we were just meeting for the first time, I'd already want to spend more time with you."

"Maybe we could think of our relationship that way."

"Excuse me?"

Christy hadn't planned to say this, but the words came easily, and she wanted to make her point. "I think you were wise in suggesting we slow down the relationship. You don't want to be rushed or feel threatened, and I've come to realize that I don't want to do that either."

His blue eyes deepened. "The thing is, I feel we're right together. But we got going like a runaway freight train and—"

"I know. So let's just start over as friends meeting for dinner, discussing the events of the day. Well"—she grinned at him—"maybe it would be more fun if we discussed the events of a different day."

"I could tell you about my new project."

"Great. I'd love to hear about it."

He told her his idea for some small garden homes just beyond Sunnyside. "There's a strip of land that hasn't been snatched up by developers, and I've put some money down to hold it."

"Sounds like a great idea. I get tired of looking at all the high-rise condos and apartment buildings strung out along the Gulf."

As Dan explained the floor plan of the houses, Christy listened with pride and felt herself melting into contentment. Why had she ever tried to rush him? Looking at him now and listening as he spoke his keen mind, she decided she would wait for ten years if she had to. Another man like Dan Brockman would not be walking into her life.

"I'd love to see your architectural plans for the project," she said.

He looked at her as though wondering if she really meant it. Had she not shown enough interest in the past?

They reached the small restaurant, located on a spit of land overlooking the Gulf. She took a deep breath of the salty breeze as he opened the door, took her hand, and led her inside.

A piano played in the far end of the dining room, and the glass walls mirrored the candlelight from each table. The hostess led them to a covered veranda with a spectacular view of the Gulf. A light breeze ruffled the palms as the setting sun cast a raspberry glow across the water. Dan pulled out Christy's chair, and she settled in and removed a linen napkin from the water goblet, eager to have it filled with lemon water.

"So," Dan said as he took his seat, "what's going on with Seth?"

"Everything. He's partying every night and chasing women like crazy. But I'm so glad to have him home, Dan. I just hope in time he can patch things up with Mom and Dad."

"Are they still in a standoff?" he asked, as the server filled their water goblets.

"It's not that bad. Seth is very defensive, and Dad doesn't like his open rebellion. Mom's caught in the middle, trying to be the peacemaker."

The server took their orders—grilled grouper—then rushed off to the kitchen.

"So your mother is trying to be the peacemaker." He shook his head. "I've watched my mom walk that tightrope with my brother.

Being caught in the middle is tough."

Christy sipped the ice water, and the server arrived with salads and bread.

"How is Bobbie?" Dan asked. "She seemed fine earlier when I picked you up."

"She's actually doing pretty well. The thing that helps most is that she's found a location for the shop she wants to open, and I'm encouraging her to do that. She was about to sink into a depression, so finding a place to display her 'found treasures,' as she calls them, has boosted her morale."

"That's good."

Neither spoke for a moment, but Christy's mind had zoomed to the pickle barrel, and she suspected Dan had the same thought. That "found treasure" wouldn't be going into the shop.

Their meal was delivered, and they got busy eating the food, the subject of Bobbie momentarily forgotten. A noise in the kitchen interrupted the quiet of the dining room. Soon the kitchen door flew open, and a man charged out.

"Wiley?" Dan called to him.

The man turned, and Christy thought she recognized him but couldn't remember where she had seen him. He was middle-aged and slim except for a round belly protruding over his white pants.

"Hey, Wiley, what's going on?" Dan asked.

Wiley shook his gray head and walked to their table, bringing the smell of fried food with him. "They've got a new, uppity manager, and I don't have to put up with him. I'm filling in for a buddy who's on vacation. Still, nobody's gonna tell me to sit down and peel five dozen shrimp. Unless I'm fixing them for myself," he added with a sly grin. "And he needn't tell me to take the back door on my way out. I'll walk right through here if I want to."

Dan and Christy exchanged an amused glance.

"I'm the janitor at the Blues Club, really. Miss Donna's trying to get her business started, you know, and she's limited on funds. I told her, no bigger than that place is, I'll have it clean enough to pass the codes every time she's checked."

Christy remembered him now. He had appeared at their table to sweep up the pills Bobbie had dropped.

Dan noticed her expression and said, "Oh, sorry I didn't introduce you. Wiley Smith, this is Christy Castleman, Mrs. Bodine's niece."

"I remember seeing you the other night," he said.

Christy nodded. "She stopped you from sweeping up those pills, didn't she? Did you find any later?"

"Nope, never got one in the dustpan before she stopped me." He stroked his short beard. "I hope the police don't go after your aunt over his murder. I know that…well, I can't call him what I'd like in a lady's presence."

"You knew Eddie Bodine?" Christy asked, leaning forward.

"Yep. Didn't recognize him at first because it had been years since I'd seen him. Reckon I was looking more at the brunette, his date. But I'd know that voice anywhere. And once I got a good look at him, I was positive. Fact is, I was ready to call him out myself about the time the ruckus started."

"Call him out for what?" Dan asked, as they both stared at him.

"For years I drove a truck for a good company in south Alabama. Loved my job. At the Florida line, Bodine barreled by in his big truck, cut right in front of me. I grazed his bumper and ran off the road. Lucky for me, the road leveled off to a stretch of grass. He could have killed me. I crawled out of that truck ready to take his head off."

Wiley glanced around the dining room. A couple at the next table stared at him. He lowered his voice. "Anyway, I called him a careless idiot, and he came back with something worse. We got into a brawl down in the grass. Then the state troopers got there. He lied about the wreck, said I was crowding him. Because he flashed papers showing he owned a trucking company, they believed him over me."

"He owned a trucking company?" Dan asked.

"Not much of one. When I got his name, I checked with another driver who knew him. He said Bodine only kept a few trucks, and they didn't run good. Anyway, Bodine got a big fine, but I lost my job." He sighed, staring back in time. "I liked trucking. He put an end to it." He looked down at Christy. "I don't wish your aunt any harm, but whoever did him in made the world a better place, far as I'm concerned."

Christy caught her breath, but Dan seemed to absorb this information without emotion.

"Speaking of the Blues Club, I gotta be there by ten. Nice to meet you," Wiley said, glancing at Christy. "Sorry if what happened to him causes problems for your aunt, but like I said, he had it coming."

Neither spoke until Wiley had left. Dan turned to look out at the parking lot. "He's getting into a gray Chevy, older model."

Christy looked at Dan. "What do you think? Could he still be angry enough to kill Eddie?"

"He's the type who takes out his vengeance with his fists. And what reason does he have to frame your aunt?"

"Maybe it's more a matter of pointing the finger of suspicion in another direction. Anyone who overheard that argument and had a problem with Eddie could have used that scene at the Blues Club to their own advantage."

Dan nodded. "They say it's a small world, but what a coincidence that Wiley once had a run-in with Bodine."

"And still carries a grudge toward him, and happened to be in the same club with him the night he was killed." Christy stared at Dan. "What do you think? I know it's a stretch, but what if Eddie came back, this Wiley was leaving, and they got into it?"

Dan looked at her thoughtfully, then shook his head. "I don't think so. If they met up after hours, and he wanted to hurt Bodine, he wouldn't run the risk of taking him to a storage unit. And he wouldn't waste that much time getting away."

Christy toyed with her food, her appetite gone. "He seems like a hothead who would act first and think later. Let's say the Blues Club was closing down for the night, and Eddie was parked out there waiting. Maybe this guy spotted him, went over and yanked the door open, did him in, then drove the truck a block away and parked it."

Dan nodded. "But that's not where Bodine was found."

Christy laid her fork down on her plate and threw her hands up in frustration. "I know, I know. I'm trying to shove square pegs in a round hole. I guess I'm feeling a little desperate for my aunt."

Dan reached over and touched her hand. "Try not to worry so much. Your aunt seems to have found a way to push this to the back of her mind."

Christy nodded and smiled at him. "Yeah, Jack's helping her do that. I think they're falling for each other."

Dan chuckled. "I know Jack is. That's pretty obvious. I'm glad to see him happy."

Christy nodded. Her gaze locked with his.

"Everyone should have a fair chance to be happy," she said, hoping she had a second chance with Dan. This time she wouldn't mess up.

When he took her home later and held her in his arms, his kisses told her they were entering the second-chance phase of their relationship.

Bobbie had left a light on for her, and Christy peeped into her office–guest room to see her sleeping soundly.

She allowed herself the pleasure of feeling relieved at last. And happy. As she locked up and tiptoed to her room, she kept thinking about the piano player's last love song at the restaurant. She couldn't remember the words, but the melody drifted through her mind, bringing a smile. Despite everything going on, it had been a wonderful evening.

thirteen

Saturday

Tony Panada broke all the speed limits from Atlanta to Panama City Beach. He made a quick stop at the two-story mansion he shared with his Doberman, William, and came out carrying a large gift bag with a lovely pink bow.

Too many celebrations in his life, he thought sardonically, glancing at the bag. He never threw anything away, knowing someday it would be useful. A hard grin jerked the corner of his mouth. Let someone else buy the expensive gifts now. It would not be Tony Panada. He had long ago decided the only person who belonged in his life was William.

He placed the gift bag on the front seat of his car, then backed out of his driveway and cut across to a back road leading to the storage units.

He slowed down his white Rolls-Royce as he pulled through the gate and parked in front of Hornsby's office. As he did, another thought struck him: Bobbie Bodine could be quite useful to him.

It was barely eight o'clock, and Hornsby had just unlocked his office and put on the coffee.

"Did you do as I asked you?" Panada demanded.

"I told them I didn't have the combination to that fancy lock but that you'd be back first thing this morning to open up the unit. They'll be here soon, I expect."

"Thank you, Hornsby." Tony dropped a hundred dollar bill on Hornsby's desk, then hurried back to his car and retrieved the lovely gift bag. At the door to his unit, he set down the gift bag, glancing absently into the wads of tissue paper that held nothing. He punched in the code on his expensive lock. The lock snapped open, and he rolled the metal door high enough to accommodate his height. He ducked under, gift bag in hand. The door rolled down. In less than five minutes, he ducked back out, leaving the door half-open. The gift bag looked a bit different. It bulged on all sides, the contents so heavy the fancy pink bow almost toppled when he walked.

Tony walked back to his car, opened the back door, and placed the gift bag on the floorboard. Slamming the door, he yelled to Hornsby, "I left the unit unlocked."

He slid behind the wheel, and the engine purred to life. He drove slowly out of the gate, waving to Deputy Arnold and a strange man in the front seat beside him as they drove into the storage facility.

⟨≈⟩

The sound of a door closing woke Christy. She sat up in bed and glanced at the clock. Nine fifteen.

She heard her aunt's truck starting up and backing out of the drive. She tossed back the covers and hurried to the kitchen to see if she'd left a message.

Bobbie's bold script covered the page of the message pad on the counter. "Meeting Jack for breakfast. Then he's going with me to sign the lease and put down money on the building. I'll talk to you later on today."

"Okay," Christy said, walking over to the coffee maker and the half-full carafe. She poured coffee in her mug and added cream. With a sigh of relief, she sat down and reached for her journal.

When she replayed the day before in her mind, she remembered her promise to J.T. about talking with Cora Lee Wilson. She took another sip of coffee, then returned to her bedroom. After pulling on her drawstring cotton pants and a T-shirt advertising Miz B's place, she thrust her feet into sandals and hurried out.

Just as J.T. had predicted, Cora Lee stood in the produce section of the supermarket, carefully inspecting a stalk of bananas. Her grocery cart held enough food for twenty people, three of which could be accounted for by Cora Lee's size. She wore a floral housedress and comfortable flip-flops that showed off plain, big feet with varicose veins circling her ankles. Her sun hat sat low on her forehead, covering most of her short brown hair.

As Christy approached, Cora Lee's brown eyes widened in surprise. "Hi, Miss Christy," she said. "You out doing your shopping?"

Christy shook her head. "I need to talk with you if you've got a minute."

Cora Lee's brown eyebrows shot up toward her wide-brimmed hat. "Of course. Did you need my recipe for banana pudding? J.T."—her bright smile faded—"says you like banana pudding."

"I'd love your recipe another time, but I wanted to talk to you about J.T." Christy lowered her voice as other shoppers pushed carts past them.

Cora Lee looked at her, and suddenly a big tear filled one brown eye, though she tried to blink it aside. So Cora Lee was smitten too!

Christy put her hand on Cora Lee's arm. "I know you heard about J.T. being in that bar, but he was only trying to help his best friend. He would never have gone there if Jack hadn't asked him. I've never seen or heard of J.T. being in that bar."

Cora Lee faced her squarely, the hurt obvious in her face. "That's what I thought. It was one reason I loved him. I thought I'd finally found a good man."

"You have." Christy leaned closer, looking her straight in the eye. "I've known him all my life. If you heard about the scene at the Blues Club…"

Cora Lee nodded. "Which was why he should've gone straight home and steered clear of any trouble."

"You're right," Christy agreed gently, "but when he met Jack at the stoplight, Jack was really upset and waved J.T. down. You see, Jack was trying to help. He was keeping an eye on the man who threatened my aunt—"

"Way I heard it, Jack was the one threatening people!" Cora Lee rallied back.

"Eddie Bodine mistreated my aunt for years," Christy continued. "The stress she suffered from years of marriage to him contributed to the angina she now suffers."

Cora Lee cocked her head, a look of sympathy creeping back. "What a shame."

"I was at the Blues Club to hear my aunt sing, along with Dan Brockman and Jack, when Eddie and his girlfriend showed up. He said some awful things to Aunt Bobbie, and Jack and Dan asked him to leave. Everyone thought Bodine had left town, but Jack saw his truck parked in front of the Last Chance Bar. He didn't want to go in alone and persuaded J.T. to go with him. But J.T. wouldn't stay," she added quickly.

"He stayed long enough for my cousin to catch him there."

Christy nodded. "Well, he left Jack there by himself, just so you wouldn't hear about it and get mad. When Jack was sure Bodine and his girlfriend had gone to the motel and wouldn't cause any more trouble, he went home."

Cora Lee took it all in, rocking back and forth on her feet, then shook her head. "The Good Book says we're to help a friend in need. J.T. claims that's all he was doing. And now, since you've explained it so clearly, Miss Christy—"

"Please call me Christy."

"Well," Cora Lee said, a wide smile lighting her face, "I reckon I'll go on down to the meat department and see if they got in some fresh fryers. J.T. loves my fried chicken."

"So...you'll call him?" Christy asked.

"Yeah, I'll call the little stinker and tell him I'm not gonna waste this chicken, so he better come over."

Christy reached forward to hug Cora Lee's big, round shoulders. "Thank you. J.T.'s really crazy about you, you know."

Her sun hat dipped, and Christy caught the flush of embarrassment on her round cheeks. "Yeah, I guess so."

"Well, I'd better get going. God bless you for being so forgiving."

Christy dashed across the front of the checkout and out the door. Once she was back in her car and headed home, she picked up her cell to call Jack at home, then remembered he was helping her aunt. And of course he didn't waste his money on cell phone service.

Turning into her driveway, mission accomplished, Christy decided to accommodate her growling stomach and then work on her book.

Later, as she sat at her computer waiting to get online, her gaze rose to the pictures of Shipwreck Island, pirates' chests, and memorabilia that inspired her series. Then her eyes slipped to a shelf on her desk that held a case of CDs. She opened the case and pulled out a disk containing a downloaded database, one that gave her background information on people who'd been arrested at some point.

She typed in *Eddie Bodine*. Several names appeared on her screen, but it was easy to match Eddie with Memphis. She leaned back in her chair and studied his details. Arrested for DUI in 1994 and 1996. Christy suspected Bobbie's drinking became heavier and more consistent while married to Eddie. She read an account of a 2005 domestic situation between Eddie and Bobbie Bodine. Bobbie had filed an injunction to keep him away from her during the time they were divorcing.

Nothing else. She searched for other information and saw he still owned a trucking company called Bodine Trucking. Small business, she imagined. He or his drivers had acquired a few tickets over the years, and leaning closer, she saw he had once paid a big fine for hauling too much freight for the size of his truck.

She thought about Wiley Smith. She wouldn't put it past Eddie to cut in front of him and cause the wreck. And it was obvious to her that Wiley still hated Eddie for ending the life he enjoyed.

She typed in Wiley Smith and a half-dozen names rolled down the screen. One date of birth fit Wiley, the address a street in Panama City. His arrests made Eddie look like a saint.

Christy read accounts of street fights, barroom brawls, drug deals, and time spent in prison for drugs. While in prison, he had knifed a man in a hassle over who got the last serving of meatloaf, earning extra jail time. If he had been in other fights, maybe he was as hot-tempered as Eddie. She checked the date of his prison term, an old one back in the nineties. She assumed he had tried to behave himself the last few years, but his hard eyes and down-turned mouth gave the impression he could get down and dirty.

When the phone rang, Joy McCall's name and number showed on the caller ID. "Good morning, Joy," Christy answered.

"Hey, Christy. I hope I'm not calling you too early."

"Not at all."

"Good. I have some information for you that may help the investigation."

"Really? What have you heard?"

"My son Mark manages the marina in Panama City. I told him about the guys in the black Mercedes from Tennessee. Last night, he stopped by the house to tell me that two guys from Memphis made a scene at the marina yesterday. And they were driving a black Mercedes."

"Really?" Christy bolted upright in her chair.

"Yeah. They'd been out deep-sea fishing," Joy said, "and when the captain brought them back in, they were yelling about not catching any big fish. Mark tried to calm them down, but they just got worse. They said his place was a ripoff. He didn't like that, and to prove he wasn't trying to rip anybody off, he offered them another trip. They're coming back today. Mark checked the forms they filled out, and they're staying at Summer Place Condominiums. So they haven't left town yet."

"And Mark thinks they're the same guys we've been talking about?"

"He doesn't see that many black Mercedes from Memphis at the marina. And he rarely has clients who behave that way. These are two middle-aged, unfriendly types. Said they looked like the Mafia to him. I don't know about that, but if they're the bookies who were after Eddie, maybe they wanted to get rid of him and blame the murder on your aunt."

Christy wished she could prove they had concocted that plan.

"If they've been trailing him, as the rumor goes, maybe they caught him picking the lock on Bobbie's storage unit and followed him in," Joy said.

"Joy, you're beginning to sound like a real detective. You may have helped the case."

"I hope so. Well, Christy, I gotta run."

The minute she replaced the phone, it rang again. Aunt Dianna's number showed up. "Mornin', Aunt Dianna," Christy said.

"Hi, hon. I'm so sorry about all that's going on in your family. Just try to stay positive."

"I'm trying."

"Listen, my hubby is out of town, and…"

"What do you need?" Why did everyone think writers didn't have a real job and could be called on day or night?

"I have to take the Lincoln over to Panama City to have new brake pads installed. The service department is backed up with jobs, so I'm just gonna leave it. If you can drive me back, I'll take you to lunch and—"

"How far is the dealership from the marina?"

"The marina? I don't know. The marina is on this side of town. The dealership is downtown. Why?"

Christy told her about the guys in the black Mercedes and that she wanted to get a look at them.

There was a momentary pause. "Honey, I'm willing to stretch a theory for Bobbie's sake, but this one doesn't quite fit."

"It may seem like a stretch, as you say, but I need to personally check these guys out."

Her aunt laughed. "Well, I guess it won't hurt to play detective this morning. I've got nothing else to do."

fourteen

An hour later, Christy entered the office of the marina while Dianna stayed outside to look at the boats.

Christy knocked on the door frame to get the attention of the tall, nice-looking man sitting behind the desk. "Mark, got a minute to talk?" she asked.

"Sure. What's up?" Mark flashed a quick smile and pushed his dark hair away from his eyes.

"Your mom called me about those two guys from Tennessee. Are they here?" Christy looked through the office window at a group of men near the boats who were talking with the captain.

"No, they just called to move their time back to one o'clock."

"Describe them to me, Mark."

"That's easy. They look like a before-and-after commercial for some kind of miracle tonic. One guy is about five foot eight, skinny, and losing his brown hair. The other one is about six feet and mus- cled, with a thick head of brown hair. Looks like he spends a lot of time with the weights. I'd guess both of them are somewhere in their forties. They're staying at Summer Place. In fact, they mentioned grabbing lunch, so they're probably in the restaurant now."

"The restaurant at Summer Place?"

"Yeah. I heard the big guy say it's the only thing he likes about this beach."

"Thanks, Mark," Christy said. "I owe you one."

She went outside and waved to her aunt, who was deep in conversation with one of the fishermen. She was a striking woman, and all the men had taken notice.

Dianna glanced at Christy, then turned back to the man. "Hope you catch some big ones."

As they hurried to the car, Dianna studied Christy. "I thought you wanted to find out something about those guys. We weren't there three minutes."

"That's because the men in question are still at the restaurant at the condos. So now I'll take you up on that offer for lunch."

Dianna laughed. "You're a trip, Christy. But since I'm riding back with you, I guess I have to concede that you're the boss." She reached for the cell phone clipped to her white capris. "I'd better call Valerie and tell her I'll be late for my hair appointment."

Summer Place Condominiums towered fourteen stories above the Gulf of Mexico. One could sit on any of the balconies facing the Gulf and see all the way to the horizon. An outdoor pool twice the size of Christy's house offered a place to play, along with whirlpools, a cabana bar, and a vast stretch of sugar beach for sunbathing.

Christy and Dianna sauntered across the lobby, heads high, as confident as any paying guest. They entered the garden-style restaurant and looked around. Seated by the glass wall facing the

Gulf, Christy spotted the two men who matched Mark's description. They were digging into oysters on the half shell.

An attractive hostess smiled at Dianna and Christy. "Two? Just follow me." She led them to a table on the opposite side of the room.

As soon as they were seated, Christy leaned across the crisp linen and nodded toward the men. She whispered, "We're a mile away from them. I've got to get closer."

Dianna turned and looked at them. "What do you suggest? Should we go over and pull up a chair?"

"This is no time to be funny," Christy hissed.

"I thought I was being practical. Maybe the couple behind them will leave, and we can—"

A pretty server appeared at their table. She introduced herself as Elisha and began an enthusiastic speech about the catch of the day and the chef's suggestion.

Christy listened to the food choices, wondering how she could eat without choking, as the nerves in her stomach had invented a new dance.

"Sounds delicious," Dianna responded. "I'll have the special with raspberry tea. What about you, Christy?"

Christy went blank. What were the choices again? "Just a cobb salad. And raspberry tea."

"Coming right up." Elisha flashed a brilliant white smile and hurried off.

Christy turned to stare at the men again.

"Christy, they're going to notice you staring." Dianna spoke in a low voice, her lips barely moving. "Try pretending we're here to eat."

"I'm not centered on food at the moment."

"I can see that. I need to make a trip to the ladies' room," she said, grabbing her handbag. "Maybe I can overhear something as I pass their table."

Christy shot another glance toward her suspects. The short man, who seemed to be doing most of the talking, suddenly paused and turned to look across the room at her. His ability to sense when he was being watched fueled her suspicions.

Her aunt stepped into his line of vision as she passed their table en route to the ladies' room, saving Christy from getting caught while staring. As Dianna walked by, the men looked her over with an evident approval. Dianna seemed unaware of them.

Christy suppressed a grin of satisfaction. Dianna knew how to handle all situations.

Elisha placed their drinks on the table. Christy returned a smile, then took a sip of tea to wet her dry throat. The men were engaged in conversation again, both wearing grim expressions.

Christy stood, focusing her gaze on the path her aunt had taken to the ladies' room. She never looked at the men as she strolled near their table, but she strained her ears to pick up a word or two.

Four words spoken in a husky, unpleasant voice vibrated in her ears. "Bodine knew better than…"

Christy bit her tongue, tasting blood, in an effort to stifle a gasp as she reached for the brass-handled door of the ladies' room.

Her aunt was in a stall, and two older women stood at the sink, washing their hands. She forced herself to wait a couple of minutes before returning to her table.

She prepared to casually stroll past the men again, but when she reentered the dining room, she saw their table was empty. Looking around, she spotted them at the cash register, paying their bill. She hurried to her table, wondering whether they had become suspicious of her stares or had simply finished their food. She sat down and darted a glance in their direction.

They walked quickly out the door.

As soon as Dianna returned to the table, Christy leaned forward and lowered her voice. "Aunt Dianna, I walked by those guys and heard them say, 'Bodine knew better than' something."

Dianna's eyes widened. "Really? That should help Bobbie's case."

"I hope so." Christy fought the urge to follow them. If they were as dangerous as she suspected, this was a matter for the authorities.

The car clock read ten past two when she dropped her aunt off. She debated how best to use the information she had overheard in the restaurant. As she pulled into her driveway, she consoled herself with the fact that she had seen the guys and could identify them.

Bobbie's truck was still gone. She hoped that meant that she and Jack were successfully completing details for her lease and getting her ready to move in. Bobbie would be safe with Jack.

Her mind buzzed as she unlocked the back door and hurried into the kitchen, trying to think how best to approach Deputy Arnold. She began to shape her words, the exact way she would tell him about the two men from Memphis, Tennessee, obviously the bookies, and what she had overheard. *"Bodine knew better than…"* The phone rang, but she let it go to the answering machine.

To her astonishment, the caller was Deputy Arnold. There was no mistaking the booming voice on her answering machine. She ran over and grabbed the phone.

"Hi, Bob…Deputy Arnold," she said breathlessly. "I was about to call you. I have something to tell you about those guys in the black Mercedes who—"

"And I have something to tell you," he cut in. "Where's your aunt?"

"She's not here, but—"

"Well, you'd better find her."

"Why? What's happened?"

"I'm not at liberty to say."

"Listen, Aunt Dianna and I were at the Summer Place restaurant. Those guys in the black Mercedes were there, and I overheard one say, 'Bodine knew better than…'"

"Forget about them."

"What? You mean you don't—"

"The reports on Eddie Bodine's death are in now."

"Well, I wouldn't think a blow to the back of the head would be that complicated to analyze. I mean—"

"That wasn't what killed him," Deputy Arnold said bluntly.

Christy sank onto the barstool and waited, her heart hammering. When there was only silence on the other end of the line, she knew her aunt was in trouble. She also knew Bob had said all he could afford to tell her without jeopardizing his job.

"You'd better find your aunt and bring her to your house. I'm offering an opportunity to handle this with dignity."

Christy swallowed around the lump in her throat. "She'll be here."

"I'll be waiting at your house. With Detective Johanson. And Christy," he said, lowering his voice, "find her a good lawyer."

Stunned, Christy hung up the phone. She walked in circles around the kitchen floor, thinking about who to call first.

Seth. She needed Seth. She was amazed when he answered his cell on the first ring.

"Seth, I don't know where you are, but you've got to get to my house fast. And call Mom and Dad to come too. Deputy Arnold and Detective Johanson are on their way here. I think they're about to arrest Aunt Bobbie."

"Why?"

"He said the reports from the autopsy have come in. Apparently, something incriminated Bobbie."

Seth's voice sounded calm and controlled. "We can handle this."

Could they? "I have to go get Bobbie. She and Jack are leasing a shop."

She hung up and grabbed her cell phone and car keys. As she ran to her car and hopped in, she tried to calm down. There was a mistake. There had to be.

She cut down the back streets, her heart hammering faster. In less than five minutes, she reached the boutique that had gone out of business and spotted both Bobbie's red truck and Jack's SUV. She wheeled in at the curb and ran into the vacant building. Her aunt's laughter resounded from in the back room as she entered.

Bobbie's gold head popped around the door. Smiling from ear to ear, she was obviously in a very happy state, even if her hair was a bit tousled and her lipstick smeared.

"Christy! I'm so glad you came down to see—"

"Bobbie, we have to go to my house. Now."

Jack's head leaned around the door, and even from a distance, she could see the lipstick on his face.

"And Jack, you'd better go home."

Their faces drooped, melting from happiness to dismay in unison. Christy felt like she was watching a cartoon, only this wasn't a comedy. It was a tragedy.

Bobbie and Jack walked slowly into the front room, staring wide-eyed at Christy.

Christy's voice trembled when she spoke. "Bobbie, we have to go to the house. Deputy Arnold and that Detective Johanson are coming to see you."

"Oh." Bobbie squared her shoulders and tried to smile. "Well, if that's all it is, I can handle them." She looked at Jack. "Like she said, honey, you'd better go home."

"I'll come with you," he said, slipping an arm around her waist.

"No, Jack." Christy shook her head.

"You've turned into a real sassy little gal lately," Jack said, glaring at her. "I don't know what's gotten into you."

Bobbie slipped out of Jack's grasp and reached for her purse. "I'll call you later," she said to Jack, giving him a wink.

Christy said nothing more to Jack; she merely led Bobbie out to her car. Once they got inside, Bobbie's cheerful countenance faded.

"Is it that bad?" she asked, looking at Christy as they drove off.

"I guess we'll find out," Christy replied.

When she turned down her street, she could see her parents' car parked at the curb and Deputy Arnold's SUV parked farther down. As she approached her driveway, she saw Seth in the backseat of their parents' car. Everyone looked grim. As soon as Christy's car turned into the driveway, car doors flew open. Beth and Grant hurried across the yard. The slam of more doors signaled the approach of Deputy Arnold and Detective Johanson.

The expression on Johanson's face froze everyone in place.

"Mrs. Bodine," he said, "you are being charged with the murder of Eddie Bodine." He produced a pair of handcuffs and began to read Bobbie her rights. "You have the right to remain silent…" His voice droned on as Christy fought tears.

Beth stood beside Bobbie, her arm around her sister's waist.

Christy thought her mother's face looked as though she had used chalk for foundation, and her eyes held the sheen of tears. In contrast, Bobbie looked devoid of emotion, as though she had gone into shock.

Seth whirled on Deputy Arnold. "What proof—"

"Calm down, little brother," Deputy Arnold warned. "You'll only make things worse."

"Detective Johanson," Grant said, "I believe we have the right to know the cause of Mr. Bodine's death."

"The medical examiner and the toxicologist have determined that the blow to Mr. Bodine's head was not severe enough to cause his death. The main cause of death was the mixture of certain poisons in his system." Detective Johanson delivered this speech coldly, then gripped Bobbie's arm and led her toward the SUV, her hands cuffed behind her back.

Bobbie looked over her shoulder at Beth. "I didn't do it. I swear I didn't."

"We'll be down to get you out as soon as bail is set," Beth called after her. "And Bobbie, we're going to get the best lawyer around."

As the car pulled away from the curb, Bobbie was still staring at Beth from the back window, looking small and frail. The car disappeared around the corner.

For a moment, no one spoke. Christy was the first to break the silence as she glanced at her watch. It was five minutes past three. "Why don't we go inside and have some tea or coffee while we put our heads together?"

"I gotta go home and feed Atticus," Seth mumbled, his head lowered.

Christy could see how upset he was by what had just taken place. Seth being Seth, he would bottle up his feelings, if permitted.

"First, come in the kitchen and grab a bottle of water or juice," she said, stalling him. She unlocked the door, and everyone entered.

"I can't believe this is happening," Beth said, slumping down in a dining room chair.

"Seth, before you go, join us at the table," Grant said. "We need to say a prayer for Bobbie."

Seth pulled back a chair and sat down. The old habit felt natural as everyone clasped hands and Grant spoke a prayer. Christy thought he always found the right words, whatever the circumstance.

"God, we don't know what has happened or what to do, so we ask for your guidance. We trust you to lead the police to the person who killed Mr. Bodine. Most of all, we pray that you will surround Bobbie with your love and healing so that she will be strong enough to face what is ahead. And we thank you for answering our prayer."

After the prayer, Christy's mother turned to face her. "Christy, please forgive me. I've been pompous and judgmental. I've never thought of myself as perfect." She looked from Christy to Seth. "Maybe if I hadn't been so shy growing up, I would have done some of the things Bobbie did. And I know if Grant had not come into my life, well..." She shrugged. "I could be a very different woman."

Grant spoke up. "Beth, nobody gets the easy, perfect life. It's the choices we make that shape our lives." His eyes moved to Seth. "Son, we want you to have the freedom to make your own choices, but we need to be a family again."

Seth stood up. "It's not that easy, Dad, when I know the conditions you're attaching. My faith is as strong as ever, but you have to understand that I may choose to go a different direction."

Christy reached for his hand. "Seth, let's not get into that now. We have to think about Bobbie."

"I don't expect you to come hear me preach every Sunday," Grant said. "I'd be happy just knowing you're worshiping someplace in your own way."

Seth's eyes, hard with defiance moments before, held a brightness that usually preceded tears. He turned quickly. "I'm just not ready yet, Dad," he said, walking out the back door.

"Seth, I have your favorite chocolate cake in the freezer whenever you want to stop by," Beth called after him.

He didn't look back but merely nodded. Christy knew there were tears on his face, and when she glanced at the anguished faces of her parents, she realized they knew it too. They were desperate to mend the break in their relationship, but it wasn't going to be easy or quick.

Beth and Grant both stared at the back door, listening to the sound of Seth's engine as he drove away. Then Beth turned to her husband.

"Did you get someone to replace you in the pulpit tomorrow?" Grant nodded. He seemed stunned by Seth's reaction.

Christy took a deep breath and tried to think. "Want to go downtown in one car?"

Her parents seemed to return from a long journey as their gazes shifted to her.

Grant sighed. "Why don't you ride with us?"

"Fine."

fifteen

I t was a long afternoon and evening for everyone, but by midnight, Bobbie had been released on bail to the Reverend Grant Castleman. Christy knew the "reverend" part, in addition to the huge sum of money her father had put up, accounted for Bobbie's release.

Harry Stephens, a top defensive lawyer from Tallahassee, drove down to Panama City as soon as Grant called him. Harry was a tall, striking man with silver hair and vivid hazel eyes behind small, wire-rimmed glasses. He looked imposing and distinguished in an expertly tailored, dark suit. Christy could see her reflection in the shine of his dark shoes. His voice matched his appearance—smooth and authoritative—and the news he delivered added to the Castleman family's distress even more, something Christy hadn't thought possible.

At the jail, they were given a small room with a table and several chairs for a meeting. Harry sat at the end of the table, looking from Beth and Grant to Christy. Then his gaze settled on Bobbie, who huddled in a chair beside Beth. Her skin had turned gray, and her golden hair had lost its sheen and lay flat against her face.

"The medical examiner has determined that Mr. Bodine died between one and two o'clock Tuesday morning," Mr. Stephens said. "The toxicologist found nitroglycerin, Viagra, and alcohol in his system."

He paused, noting their confused faces. "Apparently, Mr. Bodine had a healthy heart, so he wouldn't be taking nitroglycerin. My understanding is that it's dangerous to give this heart medication to someone who doesn't need it. Add Viagra and alcohol, and the combination is lethal," he explained.

"Now the case against Mrs. Bodine is based on her known use of nitroglycerin for her heart and the fact that the body was found in her locked unit. They're saying the motive was the money. Bodine claimed he came here to collect money Bobbie stole, and they'll argue she refused to give it back." Stephens paused and looked at Bobbie. "Do you wish to say anything to me privately, Mrs. Bodine?"

Bobbie swallowed. "No. This is my family." She looked from Beth to Grant to Christy. "I have nothing to hide. I don't know who gave him the pills or how he got in my storage unit. I did not steal money from him. And Beth and Grant know I was home by eleven thirty."

Christy glanced at her parents, who said nothing.

Stephens said, "Although the approximate time of death is between one and two o'clock, with this type of poisoning, death may not be immediate. On the other hand, the blow to the head would expedite the death."

Bobbie seemed too exhausted to say any more, and no one else seemed to have an answer. Then Christy remembered something.

"Bobbie, you spilled those pills at the club. People were helping you pick them up..." Her voice trailed off as she thought of Jack and Dan. "The pills could have rolled under other tables."

Stephens nodded. "So we can argue that several people in the club could have picked up the pills." He turned to Bobbie. "I need you to count the pills left in your bottle and try to figure how many you've taken and how many are missing."

Bobbie came alive for a moment. "The bottle was almost full. I refilled the prescription right before I left Memphis."

"Count the number you have now," Stephens said, "and write down each time and occasion you took one. We'll need verification from the pharmacist as to the number of pills in the bottle."

"Mr. Stephens," Christy said, "the janitor at the Blues Club, Wiley Smith, swept up that night. He admitted to Dan Brockman and me that he had a longstanding grudge against Bodine. Bodine cost him a job he loved."

Stephens scribbled on his pad. "We'll go into more detail on this in the morning."

She thought of something else. "Mr. Bodine's girlfriend claims he had incurred a huge gambling debt and feared someone was after him. Monday night at the Blues Club, when he made a scene, two strangers were observed at a back table, watching Bobbie and Eddie. A witness saw them leave in a black Mercedes with Tennessee plates. They're staying at Summer Place Condos, and yesterday my Aunt

Dianna and I had lunch there. When I passed their table, I heard one of them say, 'Bodine knew better than...'" She ignored the strange expression on her parents' faces.

"You heard them say that?" Bobbie asked.

"I did."

Stephens nodded. "That's good news." He scribbled on his pad again. "I'll look into that. Obviously everyone is exhausted, so let's get some rest. I'll be staying at my cottage in Seaside. Bobbie, I'd like to meet with you in the morning."

"You can come to our house," Beth offered. She glanced at Bobbie. "She'll be staying with us."

"Is ten o'clock too early?" he asked.

Bobbie shook her head. "No, that's fine with me."

"Then I'll see you at ten. And Mrs. Bodine, try to get some rest. Remember—the burden of proof is on the prosecution."

She nodded, and they all walked down the hall and out the back door to the parking lot. When they reached Grant and Beth's car, Christy climbed into the backseat with Bobbie. She grasped her aunt's cold hand. "Try not to worry," she said.

Bobbie's voice sounded weak and tired as she spoke. "I have money because I sold my shop in Memphis. I'm drawing on the bank account from that sale. I haven't taken anything from Eddie." Her voice grew stronger in her defense.

"We believe you, Bobbie," Grant said as they drove back to Summer Breeze. "Try to let your attorney handle this. I'm confident he'll do a great job."

"I owe you all so much," Bobbie said, her voice trembling. "I don't know how to thank you."

Beth turned in the passenger seat and looked at her sister. "We want to help. That's what families do. And," she added, "we love you, Bobbie."

When her parents dropped her off, Christy retrieved Bobbie's overnight bag from the bathroom and took it out to the car. Since Bobbie had been released to Grant and Beth's custody, there was no question where she would be staying.

Christy said good night and went inside to lock up. As she headed back to her bedroom to put on her pajamas, her body ached from long hours of sitting in a straight chair, waiting for Bobbie's release. She knew her parents and Bobbie, older and tiring more easily than she, must ache from head to toe.

Before she collapsed in bed, Christy grabbed her Bible and turned on the lamp on the nightstand. The Bible fell open to the verses Bobbie had said didn't work for her. She might be more willing to listen now.

"Do not fear; I will help you."

The verse blurred as tears filled Christy's eyes, and she closed the Bible and placed it on the nightstand. She sniffed, turned out the light, and began to pray.

sixteen

Sunday

Roseann Cole decided she'd had all she could take of Summer Breeze. She packed her bags and paid the desk clerk the balance of her bill for the room. Today she was going home! Like the country song said, she was ready to see this town in her rearview mirror.

Two deputies had delivered Eddie's truck to her, waking her from a deep sleep. Quickly she showered and dressed, eager to leave. She climbed into the truck and slammed the door, then picked up her cell phone and punched in her mother's number. While the phone rang on the other end, she pulled down the visor and opened the mirror, plumping up her mass of curls.

"Momma, I'm leaving Summer Breeze," she said as soon as her mother answered. "It's a long drive back, so I'm staying over in Birmingham tonight. Got a friend there. I'll be home tomorrow. I'll give you the details when I get home, so don't start asking questions. I'm a little upset right now."

Loud chatter filled her ears for the next few seconds.

"Yeah, well, don't believe everything you read in that rag of a paper. Eddie was hanging around the wrong people. I just didn't know it. I guess they caught up with him. Now don't you worry about me. I always have a plan. And you take care of Millie. I want my doll in the middle of my bed when I come home. She always makes me feel better."

She paused, listening again. "Maybe you're reading those tarot cards right, about a woman killing him. I'll call you later. Now I gotta hang up."

Roseann took a deep breath and released it slowly. Nobody got to her like Momma.

As soon as she hung up, the phone rang. Maybe it had something to do with Eddie.

"Yes?" she said, not bothering to conceal her irritation. "Oh really, Deputy Arnold?" Her tone changed completely. "You're sure Eddie's body has been taken to the funeral home already? Well, thank you, sir. I appreciate all you've done for me."

Christy tossed and turned throughout the night, getting only a few hours of deep sleep. Her head rolled on the pillow, and sleepy eyes focused on the clock on the nightstand. It was two minutes before eight.

With great effort, she pulled herself out of bed and peeled off her pajamas, heading for her bathroom. She opened the shower door, turned the faucet on hot, and adjusted the spray to hit her shoulders and neck, which felt twisted in knots.

She stood under the shower spray, letting the water pelt down on her neck and shoulders. She luxuriated in the smell of the shampoo as her fingers pressed all the tense points on her scalp. She rinsed, then stepped out of the shower. Thickly toweled, head and body, she walked into her bedroom and opened the closet door to gaze at her choices. What do you wear on the morning you meet with an attorney hired by your father to save a lovable aunt from prison? She decided on tan slacks and a matching tan shirt with wedge sandals. She wandered over to the closed drapes and lifted a tiny corner. A gray, thoroughly depressing day greeted her, promising rain. She dropped the curtain and hurried to the kitchen.

As she made coffee, her mind replayed the events of the past few days, looking for a solution. Could someone have paid off Hornsby to get into Bobbie's storage unit? Who and why? What about the mysterious Panada, whose unit backed up to Bobbie's? She had overheard Hornsby on the phone, his voice urgent, as he related how he had stalled the police on getting into a unit because of the special dial lock. She had sensed he couldn't stall much longer. And what was the point of stalling anyway?

Christy reached for her coffee mug, and her mind wandered to the night at the Blues Club. A thought struck her like a bolt of lightning, and she almost dropped her mug. She'd had to open that pill bottle twice for Bobbie. Why had it been so easy to open that night at the club? Had someone been in the pill bottle and stolen pills? Then, being in a rush, carelessly replaced the top?

Who? Jack and Dan would never try to frame Bobbie.

Who else had access to the pill bottle? Roseann had been at the table. She'd check with Dan to see if Roseann had had a chance to go through Bobbie's purse.

Christy poured her coffee, then called her parents' home. Her mother answered on the first ring. "Hi, Mom. How are you?"

"We're okay. We're having coffee. Your father is glad he asked someone to fill in for him today, since Mr. Stephens will be here at ten."

"Did you get any sleep?" Christy asked with concern. She had seen a different side to her mother yesterday, and now she regretted their argument.

"Enough. What about you?"

"Enough. And Bobbie?"

"She says she slept okay, but of course she was exhausted when she went to bed. I'm trying to coax some oatmeal into her now. I keep telling her she has to keep up her strength."

Christy nodded. "You're right. Tell her hello for me."

"By the way, last night when we passed the Starlight Motel, we saw Eddie's white truck parked there. Is Roseann Cole still in town?" her mother asked.

"She was waiting for the release of the body after the autopsy. And she came with Eddie, so I guess she had to wait until they released the truck to her."

"She must be in awful shape to drive. Maybe we could get someone in the congregation—"

"Mom, you've got your hands full," Christy said. She had seen Beth work herself into exhaustion trying to help someone, and then Beth would wonder why she was so susceptible to bronchitis or a cold.

"You're right," Beth agreed, sighing.

"I'll be over there at ten." Christy said. "I promise to stay in the background, but I want to hear what the attorney has to say."

"We'll be glad to have you here. Seth just called to check on everyone."

"Late-sleeper Seth has already called?" Christy teased.

"He probably didn't sleep well either."

They said their good-byes and hung up. Christy noticed she had several messages. She checked the caller ID on all of them, and to her irritation, Roy Thornberry's number showed up. Angrily, she deleted it. If Roy was calling her, he wanted the scoop on Bobbie for his newspaper. How dare he think she would give him any information after their last squabble, which ended in her resignation? She'd be writing no more weekly columns for him.

Now he had the audacity to call. She was certain he intended to quiz her about her aunt. He was ruthless when it came to a hot news story. During the murder investigation last year, he had driven everyone nuts with his obsessive snooping and endless questions. She couldn't begin to imagine what he might do to scoop this story: "Man Found Dead in Pickle Barrel in Locked Storage Unit of Ex-Wife. Thoroughly Pickled."

She winced. No, even Roy wouldn't add that sarcastic remark.

Christy remembered how Bobbie had bet her line-dancing boots that Hornsby was the nosy type. If she thought Hornsby was nosy, she should meet Roy. She sensed that Hornsby had a few secrets, and she knew he wasn't above taking bribes, but he had not come off to Christy as being anything more than curious.

Christy refilled her mug. With her mind miles away, she took a big gulp of hot coffee, burning her mouth. She set the mug down and ran water over a dishtowel to press to her lips. Now she was awake.

Thoughts zipped back and forth through her brain like paper airplanes. Roseann Cole—what was going on with her? Had she meant what she said when she vowed to wait for Eddie's body and the truck?

Christy stared at the phone, wondering how to shape the words she wanted to ask. She walked over and dialed Roseann's cell phone.

The voice that answered was cool and formal.

"Hi, Roseann. It's Christy Castleman. I understand you got the truck, and…I guess the funeral home is working with you on…" She couldn't seem to finish a sentence. She gripped the phone tightly and squeezed her eyes shut, wishing for words.

When Roseann spoke up, she bit off each word. "I hear your aunt's been charged with Eddie's murder. I don't want to talk with you or anyone in your family! I'm on my way back to Memphis!"

"Wait!" Christy pleaded, knowing Roseann was about to hang up. "There's something else." What else? She had no idea what to say, but she couldn't let Roseann leave without getting her address in Memphis. She still wasn't sure if Roseann knew more than she was telling. "Listen, something might turn up here that you'd want to know about. Can you give me your address?"

There was a pause. "I don't think you'll need it."

"Roseann, Bobbie has been framed. She didn't kill him."

"Oh really?"

She longed to rally back in Bobbie's defense, but her gut feeling was to be nice and keep communication open with Roseann. She gritted her teeth and kept quiet.

Roseann spoke up again. "Then you tell me how the nitroglycerin got in his system. Eddie just had a checkup last week. His heart was fine. He had no reason to take nitroglycerin, so don't give me your excuses."

"Those pills were spilled on the floor of the club, remember?" Christy said. "Other people were picking them up."

"Yeah, like the boyfriend, Jack. Honey, you better face the facts. Your aunt did it, and she may have had some help. I'm done talking to you."

The phone line clicked. Roseann had said all she intended to say.

For several minutes after she hung up the phone, Christy stared out the window. It looked as though someone had hung sheet metal over the yard. She walked into the living room and sat on the couch, picking up the remote. She turned on the Weather Channel, wondering how long the rain would last. According to the ridiculously cheerful announcer, the rain would pass through by noon. She turned him off and walked back to the kitchen, looking through the window again. The palm branches swayed beneath a mounting breeze. The birds were smart enough to avoid her bird feeder, and her favorite little redbird, which usually perched on her windowsill, was nowhere in sight.

The day seemed to match the gloom that had overtaken their world. How she wished all this was a nightmare. She turned from the sink, trying to calm her muddled thoughts. She had to keep a clear head.

Eddie's truck had been held for three days. Had Eddie hidden drugs there, or had they found fingerprints not belonging to the occupants? Fingerprints that implicated her aunt?

Christy glanced at the clock and dialed Dan's number.

"Hi," she said, feeling better at the sound of his hello.

"Christy, I came to your house yesterday, but your neighbor told me you'd left with your parents. He also told me about Bobbie's arrest. I don't know what to say. I'm so sorry."

"Thanks." Christy swallowed hard, trying not to get emotional. "Bobbie was released on bail to my parents late last night. Dad found a good attorney for her, Harry Stephens from Tallahassee. We're meeting with him at ten."

"That's good. I've seen Harry Stephens interviewed on television. He's one of the best attorneys in the state. And remember, it's up to the prosecution to prove anything."

"Yeah, but Dan, I think the prosecution feels they have plenty of proof. Apparently, the blow to Eddie's head knocked him out, but he might have come to and staggered out of the unit or called for help. The cause of death is a mixture of poisons in his system, one of them being nitroglycerin. Eddie Bodine has a healthy heart, so there was no reason for him to take nitroglycerin."

Dan was silent for several seconds, absorbing this information. After a moment, he said, "Christy, can I come over later? We'll drive over to Shipwreck Island. I know that place always relaxes you."

Christy smiled, grateful for a good memory now. "Sounds great. Thanks for being available for me."

"I want to help however I can."

His kindness reached deep into her heart, and she looked forward to spending some time with him. "I'm going by my parents' house at ten to hear what the attorney has to say and to see if there's anything I need to tell him. After that, I'm free."

"I'll grab a picnic lunch. I know it's raining, but we've sat in the car with lunch and watched it rain before."

She smiled into the mouthpiece, as though he could see her. "That's nice of you. How about one o'clock? And I don't care if it's raining."

"Neither do I."

After she hung up, she felt as though someone had removed a twenty-pound backpack from her shoulders. She hadn't realized what a burden she'd been carrying for her aunt and her mom and all the family. Dan had lifted that burden by listening and by offering to take her away from prying eyes and telephone calls.

She took a deep breath, feeling a new surge of strength. Glancing at the clock, she saw she had half an hour before she had to leave for her parents' house.

She turned on her computer and pulled up her e-mail. She carefully worded a letter to her editor, requesting an extension on her deadline. She explained that she had a family emergency. She'd never been late with a manuscript, and since this one had plenty of leeway before the publication date, she felt justified in asking and felt confident her editor would agree.

Before she shut down the computer, she reached for the database program. The Web portal contained on the disk wasn't widely available to the public, but had become invaluable to Christy when she used it the year before as a tool for catching a killer.

The program powered up for her, and she was ready to do a search. Who could be a suspect that she hadn't checked on?

⌒⫍⊙⫎⌒

As Christy drove to her parents' home, the wind picked up, and a fine mist began to fall on her windshield. Not a day for picnics, but Dan knew she loved them. Once, they had driven to a park and sat in his car, feasting on fried chicken, watching the raindrops cascade down the windshield. It had been a different kind of outing, but as she had pointed out, there was more than one way to enjoy a picnic.

She turned in the driveway of her parents' home and saw a gray Lexus with Tallahassee license plates parked in the driveway.

She slipped quietly in the back door and saw everyone seated around the cherry dining table. A huge pot of coffee sat on the counter next to an assortment of pastries on a tray. Christy grabbed a danish from the tray, placed it on a small, white plate, and headed into the dining room where her parents and Bobbie faced Harry Stephens, who sat at the end of the table.

Everyone turned to Christy and smiled as she slipped into a chair. Then all eyes returned to Bobbie, who was describing her medications and explaining why she took nitroglycerin.

"Excuse me," Christy said, "but her pill bottle was difficult to open. Bobbie, if you remember, I had to open it twice for you. But that night, the top came right off, didn't it?"

Bobbie nodded, looking at Stephens, who had dressed more casually today. Every silver hair was in place, and his hazel eyes looked bright and alert behind his wire-rimmed glasses.

"The bottle was new," Bobbie said. "It has one of those child-proof caps. Every time I get a refill, the cap is hard for me to pry off."

Stephens nodded. "That'll work to our advantage in creating suspicion. And you've counted and made notes, and you believe four pills are missing." He frowned.

Christy wondered how many pills it took to mix with Viagra and alcohol for a lethal dose.

"When I opened the bottle at the Blues Club, "Bobbie went on," the pills exploded all over the place. I think someone had already been in that bottle," Christy said.

Stephens leaned forward, a bloodhound treeing new quarry. "Think hard. You didn't have to twist and turn as you normally did?"

Bobbie hesitated. "I was so nervous, maybe I was twisting harder."

Christy pressed her point. "No, she hadn't pushed that hard. I'm sure Jack and Dan would agree with me that the cap came off as though it had already been loosened, or opened and not recapped tightly."

Stephens began to write. "This is important." He looked at Bobbie. "Where did you keep the pills from the last time you opened them until that night at the club?"

"I always keep them in the zipped compartment on the right side of my purse. My doctor in Memphis—"

"What's his name?" Stephens interrupted.

"Goldman. Dr. Jonathan Goldman."

Christy appraised Bobbie as she sat at the table, carefully answering each question. She had obviously shampooed her hair, for it held its usual golden sheen again, and her navy suit and white linen blouse added a new touch of class. The conservative clothes looked out of character for Bobbie, who normally dressed with a colorful flair. Christy thought the clothes looked more like something her mother would wear.

Christy glanced at Beth, whose attention was focused on the attorney. She wore a tense, serious expression. Her father looked equally serious. It was as though everyone had been wearing a pleasant mask but had lifted it to catch a breath.

Beth got out of her chair. "Why don't I bring in more coffee? Mr. Stephens, how about another danish?"

"No, thank you. Folks, I have my work cut out for me," he said. "We all do. I need the exact time Bobbie returned home."

Grant frowned. "We were asleep. I don't know. You'll have to ask Beth. She's a light sleeper, and I think she may have heard Bobbie come in."

Stephens studied his notes. "Bobbie and Jack both claim she got home at eleven fifteen."

Beth entered the dining room with a silver tray, coffeepot, and condiments. "I heard Jack's SUV in the driveway around eleven fifteen, but after that, I'm not sure. I went back to sleep. I know she passed our bedroom door sometime later, but I couldn't say for sure what time it was." She set the tray down on the table and looked around. "Anyone want their coffee freshened?"

Christy stared at her mother. Was she really unsure what time Bobbie had passed their bedroom? When Christy overheard the argument between her mother and Bobbie, she was certain Beth had said, *"Almost one o'clock."*

"I'm sorry," Grant said, studying his wife carefully. "I thought you told me after midnight, closer to one."

"Well, I think I heard something later on, around one, but Bobbie could have gotten up and gone to the bathroom. I don't know." Beth shrugged and poured coffee for everyone.

After a moment, Bobbie said, "So we know some of my pills are missing. As for the Viagra, Eddie took it the last two years I was married to him."

Everyone stared at her. Her statement proved Eddie could have unknowingly aided in his demise, but it also proved she knew he took Viagra.

Stephens grimaced. "Bobbie, don't volunteer that information to anyone else. You'll be asked by the prosecution, of course. So you know he took Viagra when you were married to him, but you don't know about now, do you?"

Bobbie shook her head. "No. By the way, the doctor Eddie saw in Memphis was named William Sommers, I believe. He's an internist."

Stephens wrote down the name.

"What do you think about Roseann Cole, Mr. Stephens?" Christy asked.

He paused, tapping his silver pen. "If the girlfriend is telling the truth, that he left the motel again, then it's crucial to know whom he saw or where he went." He checked his notes. "The truck was found on the street that runs south behind the Blues Club. It's possible he parked there and waited for someone to come out of the club."

Christy thought of Jack and Dan, and her heart sank. She realized Stephens was looking at her.

"I understand that both Jack Watson and Dan Brockman are friends of yours, Christy," he said, "but to be frank, both men made threats, and this Jack threatened to kill him. In addition to his statement, witnesses said he looked mad enough to carry out his threat. I'll have to argue that he may have been furious enough to find Eddie later and obliterate him from Bobbie's life."

Bobbie gasped. "No, don't incriminate Jack. Please."

"If you want to theorize that Jack harmed him, why would he put him in Bobbie's unit to make it look like she did it?" Christy asked.

Stephens' mouth tightened. "The unit may have only been a

temporary holding place. The assailant no doubt planned to move the body when the time was right. The fact that Hornsby's office is next door to the unit makes him more likely to notice the smell than the assailant might realize."

Christy's mind went into overdrive, focusing on Tony Panada. "Mr. Stephens, do you happen to know anything about the man who rents the unit that backs up to Bobbie's unit?"

He consulted his notes. "As a matter of fact, I do. His name is Tony Panada, and he owns a printing business in town. He uses the unit to store extra product. I don't think we can look in his direction for a suspect."

She nodded. Panada had been reluctant to have his unit searched. That wouldn't sound unusual to anyone. It was just her instinct about the whole thing that bothered her, and Mr. Stephens wouldn't be too interested in hearing about her instinct.

"Where was Hornsby that night?" Bobbie asked curiously.

"According to Deputy Arnold, Hornsby claims to have been at home with his girlfriend."

"That man has a girlfriend?" Bobbie blurted and then bit her lip. "Sorry."

"Look," Stephens said as he rose from the table and glanced at his watch, "two hours is enough for all of us. We're just getting started with this." He looked down at Bobbie. "I know you won't be leaving town, but avoid discussing the case with anyone. That goes for all of you. Go on with your lives as best you can, and leave the work to me." He placed his legal pad and pen back in his monogrammed briefcase.

"What life?" Bobbie said. "How can I open a shop with Summer Breeze thinking I'm a murderer?"

"You're not," Christy said. "And maybe for now I'm the one who's opening I Saw It First. Everyone is very excited about your shop." Christy took a deep breath, forgetting the novel she was writing. "Yep, I think we'll be pretty busy getting that shop open."

Her gaze moved to her parents, who smiled. Her dad stood and walked around the table, collecting empty plates. As he reached for hers, he leaned down and whispered, "I didn't realize you were so much like your mother."

seventeen

W hen Christy opened her back door to Dan, he held an umbrella over his head and smiled. Looking past him, she saw the rain had stopped.

"You're joking," she laughed.

He closed the umbrella and placed it beside her door. "Well, you know what they say—take an umbrella and it won't rain; forget your umbrella, you're sure to get a downpour."

"Do they really say that?" she asked, as he closed the door behind him and took her in his arms.

"It sounded good," he said, leaning down to kiss her.

And what a kiss. He was a delicious blend of an autumn morning rain and a subtle shaving lotion. As she melted into his kiss, she knew it would be so easy to let herself go completely. But from the back of her mind, her conscience rushed forth, reminding her that this was a new beginning and she had to keep her head.

She broke the embrace and stepped back from him. "Wow, how you turn a girl's head."

"Not to mention what you do to mine." He rubbed his hands together and looked at the coffeepot. "Is that coffee still warm?"

"No, but I can make some fresh."

"Nah, just let me fill a mug and stick it in the microwave."

"Help yourself. I need to shut down the computer."

When she returned to the kitchen, Dan sat at the eating bar, sipping his warmed-over coffee and reading the morning newspaper. When she entered, he quit reading, folded the paper in half, and stuffed it in his back pocket.

"Is it that bad?" she asked, suspecting he was trying to hide the front-page story from her.

"Not worth reading," he said, standing up. "Ready to go?"

She nodded. "Roy Thornberry's number showed up on my caller ID. I'm so glad I don't write a column for him anymore."

"So am I. Everywhere we went, he just happened to pop up in the parking lot. He always reminded me of someone who had an itch he couldn't scratch."

Christy laughed. "You're stealing my line. Remember, I told you that when you first met him. You said it was the most accurate description of a person you'd ever heard."

"Yeah, it was."

They walked out to his car, and when he opened the door for her, the smell of lemon-roasted chicken wafted from the picnic basket in the backseat.

"Ah, what delights await us in that basket?" Christy asked.

"Not gonna tell," Dan said, backing out of the driveway. "On second thought, maybe I will boast a bit. My mom used to have oatmeal raisin cookies waiting for my brother and me when we got home from school. We were living in Germany then. Dad had been transferred to an army base there. I guess Mom wanted to give us a sense of permanence, so she tried to stick to a routine. Well, I'm off track with my story. I got hooked on oatmeal raisin, and this morning…" He paused, glancing at her.

She studied his face, liking that he wasn't picture-perfect handsome, but handsome in a rugged way. When she looked at him from the side, his nose was slightly crooked, and one eye was just a fraction larger than the other. But she suspected no one but she would notice, and it pleased her that he wasn't perfect.

"This morning you called her and asked her to make oatmeal raisin cookies?" she guessed.

"Nope." At the stoplight, he reached into the backseat, fumbled around in the basket, and brought forth an odd-shaped cookie that smelled warm and inviting. "I got the recipe and made the cookies myself."

"You're kidding! You can't cook." Christy grabbed the cookie, tasted it, and gave a murmur of appreciation. "You can bake cookies," she said, winking at him.

"You don't care if they're lopsided, do you?"

She started to reply but spit crumbs, giggled at her blunder, then almost choked.

Dan patted her on the back and handed her a bottle of water. "You okay?"

She nodded, took a sip, and waited until her throat was clear enough to speak. "These are fabulous, and they're even better knowing you went to the trouble."

He shrugged. "I enjoyed it. Ate half the dough. It brought back a lot of good memories." He reached for her hand. "I just want you to relax and forget your problems today."

As they drove toward Shipwreck Island, she turned to face him. "Let me share something with you. This morning I went on the Internet using a special search engine, just like last year when I found evidence that led to a killer. I'm going to run down the names of everyone connected to Eddie. I started with Roseann Cole, and nothing showed up. But guess what?"

"What?" He steered the car across the bridge to the island.

"There was a Juanita Cole in West Memphis, age sixty-two, who had an interesting background. It seems her line of work is telling fortunes. Over the years, she's been arrested for theft, forging checks, and bilking money out of her clients."

Dan glanced from her to the road and back. "Really?"

"Yeah, though she never spent time in jail. But there was an interesting account of a woman who took Juanita to court, claiming she stole two hundred dollars out of her handbag when the woman closed her eyes to envision her late husband so that Juanita could connect them."

"You've got to be kidding."

"I'm quoting the report. The woman lost the case because there wasn't enough evidence to support her story."

"Well, it makes you wonder if Roseann has inherited some of her mother's traits when it comes to acquiring money," Dan replied, pulling into the shell-and-gravel parking area above the beach.

"I realize she can't help what her mother did," Christy said, "but I found the report very interesting." She looked around. "I'm glad we came here."

She studied the woods in the distance. This area had given her much inspiration and lore, providing the subject for books that had earned praise and monetary rewards. To the east, Lost Lagoon encircled the high ground. To the west, a hundred-acre marsh provided a wetland refuge for seabirds. In some ways, this was a typical Gulf Coast swamp, and yet Shipwreck Island, due to its fabled history, was like no other place in Florida.

"I chose it because you like it here, and so do I. But if you remember, right over there," he said, pointing to a deserted strip of beach, "is where we first met."

She nodded, recalling the day she had come here, worried about the disappearance of Marty McAllister, the local Realtor.

Dan cut the engine and looked at her. "You were very cautious about me when I first walked down from the ship house," he said.

"Yes, I was." Her eyes drifted to the unusual two-story house on the hill. Because of railings and portholes designed by a ship captain, it had been dubbed the ship house. It had recently been sold to a family. Christy could see a kids' swing set in the backyard. "I didn't know you had come here to study the house for your architecture class. In fact, I had no idea what you were doing here."

"I know. You looked like a frightened little creature of the woods, ready to bolt. And I didn't miss the fact that you had your cell phone open as though you might need to call for help."

She laughed. "You're right, I did."

She looked at an indention in the shoreline. "That's where I found the bottle." In her mind's eye, she could see the green bottle with the note tucked inside, a desperate plea for help. She looked around and saw the sea gulls and a few sandpipers, but not the special little sandpiper that had led her to the bottle. She had always believed she'd recognize it again, even though most of them look alike.

She looked back at Dan. "The day I met you, I was looking for a killer. Then you appeared—a tall, handsome stranger who looked out of place in my world." She sighed and looked into his eyes. "And yet you fit into my world just fine."

He cupped her cheek in his hand and leaned in to touch his lips to hers in a soft kiss. Then he pulled back and smiled into her eyes. "And you fit into mine just fine." Their eyes locked for a moment, and then he turned and glanced into the backseat. "Well, good food waits. Are you hungry?"

"As a matter of fact, I am." The sun had found its way through the clouds, its heat absorbing the dampness of the sand. "Want to walk over to the picnic table?" she asked.

"Sure."

A picnic area had been installed over the summer on government property. The rest of the area had once belonged to Buster Greenwood's family, but it had been sold off as home sites. Buster had kept his acreage and an old house, though. "His digs," he called it. Everyone knew it would take dynamite to uproot him.

They got out of the car and walked toward the picnic table,

the basket swinging from Dan's broad hand. A light breeze rustled through the tall oaks in the woods, but the day was neither too cold nor too hot.

When they reached the table, Christy leaned down and felt the damp wood of the bench.

"Oh, I forgot," he said. "There's a tarp in the backseat we can sit on."

"I'll get it while you lay out the goodies." She jogged back to the car and reached into the backseat for the plastic. Something on the floor caught her eye.

A woman's brown compact. Not hers.

Christy took a deep breath, trying not to let this ruin the day. Still, it nagged like a July fly buzzing around a picnic table. Lowering her eyes to the ground as she walked back to the table, plastic in hand, she vowed to keep her jealousy shoved in a corner. *Forget the compact,* she told herself.

She smiled at Dan, hoping her expression revealed nothing. She spread the tarp across the bench, and he sat beside her. With obvious pride, he lifted containers from the picnic basket, placing them on the table. He had brought silverware, china plates, and linen napkins—a surprise. Finally, he pulled out a container of roasted chicken. "Straight from the market," he admitted, "along with the potato salad and fruit salad."

"Perfect," she said.

He completed the meal by pulling out a loaf of french bread and two small bottles of sweet tea. As a final gesture, he reached deep in the basket and then laid a single rose in front of her plate.

She picked up the rose and inhaled its sweet aroma. "You've thought of everything," she said. Then she closed her eyes, offered grace, and added a silent prayer that she wouldn't behave in a jealous or possessive way. She needed to forget about the compact.

Dan sliced a chunk of chicken breast. "Let's partake," he said, carefully moving the neat slice to her plate.

They dug in and enjoyed the food. Neither spoke until they had eaten everything on their plates. The island was quiet, blessing them with gentle breezes and the exotic swish of water on sand.

"Ready for cookies?" Dan asked.

"As special as they are, we should wait until our tummies have had a rest."

He laughed. "I agree. Want to talk about the meeting with the attorney? A shadow has slipped over your face, and I'm guessing that's what it is."

Was she that transparent? At least he had given her an excuse.

She nodded. "I'd like your opinion on some of the things that came to light recently."

"Such as?"

"Bobbie says Eddie could have picked the lock on her unit and gone in, thinking she had stored the vacuum cleaner there."

Dan frowned. "The only thing wrong with that theory is that she wouldn't have left the money in a vacuum cleaner in a storage unit, either here or in Memphis. At least, that's what I think."

"What better place to keep it safe?" Christy pointed out. "But she swears she didn't take it."

"I guess the strength of her argument will depend on the vacuum cleaner bag, which I'm sure they're thoroughly dusting for finger-prints in Memphis."

"But her fingerprints would be on there from before."

"Unless the bag was changed," he said.

"From what Bobbie says, Eddie was no housekeeper. If Roseann stayed with him, she might want things neat and in place. Maybe she got industrious, decided to vacuum, found a filthy bag, and opened it up to change it. Maybe she found the money and took it."

Dan shook his head. "Christy, I don't think Roseann's smart enough to pull off a caper like that, and she's too smart to cross Eddie."

Christy sighed, feeling that theory collapse. "True. Eddie wouldn't have trusted her that much. Bobbie was married to him for years, and he never told her where he kept his winnings. If Roseann wanted his money, she could have cleaned out his billfold and credit cards while he slept."

"Yeah, it sounds like she's been led to believe he owned a big trucking company and had money coming in all the time. Other-wise, I don't know what she saw in him. He was a lot older than she is."

Christy nodded. "You know what she told me when I gave her a ride the other day? She said her mother had a vision of Roseann meeting someone shorter than her and older, who owned his own company and would make her rich. She said when Eddie walked into the restaurant where she waited tables, he kept staring at her. When she went to his table to take his order, he asked her out.

According to Roseann, they fell in love right away." She realized her words sounded mocking of anyone who claimed to fall in love right away. And yet that's what had happened to her when she met Dan.

He sat close to her, listening to everything she said. He stared thoughtfully at the beach. "Her mother predicted that? Or do you think Roseann embellished the story a bit?"

Christy shook her head. "I have no idea."

Dan looked into her face and reached for her hand. "Christy, how well do you know Bobbie? I mean *really* know her?"

Christy entwined her fingers in his. "I've seen her half a dozen times in my life. Over Christmas holidays or when she came through with one of her husbands. But I know her well enough to know she wouldn't kill anyone. Why do you ask? And why do you suddenly look worried?"

He closed his hand over hers. "I hate to say this, but when the authorities charge someone with murder, there has to be strong evidence against that person. They've either got fingerprints on something crucial, or a secret witness or two, or..." He shrugged. "I don't know. I just know that the investigative unit for Bay County has an excellent reputation for playing fair and a high rate of indictments. Most of the cases they're involved in prove they arrested the right person."

Christy listened, feeling sad and knowing she looked it. She sighed. "But she didn't kill him, and somehow, someway, I'm going to prove it."

He didn't comment, and this scared her. She tried another approach.

"When can I see the plans for your new project so I can visualize exactly what you've been telling me about it?"

"When are you not busy?" he asked, picking up the empty containers and returning them to the basket.

"Tonight?" she asked.

For a moment, he seemed occupied with getting everything back in the picnic basket. "I can't," he said, avoiding her eyes.

She waited, but he didn't elaborate.

"Can I keep the rose?" she asked, holding it under her nose. He'd said he wanted to help her, and he had spent the afternoon with her. The afternoon but not the evening. She thought of the compact and stood up, determined to keep her thoughts to herself.

"Thanks for a wonderful picnic," she said as they walked back to the car. She was standing beside him when he opened the door to the backseat and returned the picnic hamper and tarp. His gaze fell to the floorboard, to the compact, and he casually slammed the door, his gaze sliding to hers.

She looked him in the eye for a moment, letting him wonder if she had seen the compact. Then she turned and went around to the passenger side to open the door and get in.

He slid behind the wheel, glancing at her again, as though trying to read her expression.

"I love this island," she said, looking around her. "Did you know that J.T. is crazy about Cora Lee Wilson, Buster's cousin?"

"Really?"

"Yep. And I guess she's crazy about him." She met his curious gaze but said nothing. Let him wonder about her for a while. From now on, maybe she'd start holding things back. She'd always been a private person, and it served her well now.

"There's something I should tell you," he said, after they had crossed the bridge and driven in silence for several seconds.

"Oh?" She looked at him, gently waving the rose in front of her face.

"I can't see you tonight because I made other plans a week ago."

She put up a hand. "You don't have to tell me anything. We agreed that you and I are both free to live our own lives. I know freedom is very important to you. And you know what? It's important to me as well."

He looked at her, and she guessed he was trying to read her thoughts. She wanted to give him his freedom and take back her own, if necessary. She wanted a balanced attitude, not a jealous, possessive one.

Her eyes followed a sea gull lifting from its perch at the top of a small tree, soaring like a free spirit out over the water. Freedom was important, she supposed. But when she felt lonely at night, freedom didn't feel so good.

They approached the turnoff to her street, and she tried to focus her thoughts on opening a shop. What color of paint for the walls?

"When the moving van arrives with Bobbie's furniture," Dan said, "would you like me to round up some of my workers and come lend a hand?"

"I think we're covered. Thanks anyway."

"I'll call you," he said, watching her closely.

"Fine. Thanks again for the picnic, Dan." She smiled, then got out of the car and hurried up to her back door. As she unlocked it, she heard him backing out of her driveway.

Once she stepped inside, she closed the door and leaned against it, fighting the disappointment creeping through her. Tears sprang to her eyes as conflicting emotions battled within her. Did he really love her? Or had he come back to her out of pity? Had he planned the picnic, complete with homemade cookies, to cheer her through this ordeal? And what about his plans for the evening? She knew it was a date. The compact might have been a water moccasin, rearing its ugly head at both of them.

She took a deep breath, brushed a tear from her cheek, and went over to sit at the eating bar. She opened the drawer and pulled out her prayer journal and Bible. She intended to find the strength she needed here. She found the passage that had helped her through other ordeals: "Trust in the LORD with all your heart and lean not on your own understanding."

Christy sighed. *Okay, God, you know I love Dan, but if he isn't right for me, then tell me now. Or are you telling me now? Is Dan trying to tell me too?* She felt confused again, so she reread the verse. *Okay, I won't lean on my own understanding; I will trust you to work things out.*

To everyone else, she seemed so capable, so independent, a got-it-together kind of girl. But when it came to romance, she didn't know how to handle herself. There had only been Chad in her life for so long, and she'd let herself love him and need him. After he died, she had felt like half a person for a long time.

She'd rebuilt that part of her heart and had begun to feel whole again when Dan came along. And now she was becoming needy again, and she had to stop before it took hold. Even if it meant avoiding Dan for a while.

She had to complete herself with God's help. She couldn't depend on another human being to do that.

eighteen

Sunday Evening

Grant Castleman stood in the pulpit looking at a scattered crowd. The evening services were usually much lower in attendance than the morning. Tonight, however, the gleaming oak pews held a record few, as though a flu epidemic had hit Summer Breeze.

Christy slipped into the family pew—right side, third from the front—and sat beside her mother. Beth gave her a tired smile and reached over to squeeze her hand, her eyes too bright. She wore an expression Christy recognized as forced pleasantness.

Christy glanced at one of the six stained-glass windows in the church. Each window depicted a stage in the life of Christ. Miz B had donated the money for the windows in memory of her husband, who had died the previous year.

She sneaked a glance around the sanctuary. Miz B was missing, but it wouldn't be because of Bobbie. She suspected Miz B had driven up to Montgomery to visit her son and his family. Miz B adored her grandchildren.

Determined to ignore the empty pews, Christy looked up at her father, whose face held the weariness the family felt. Her eyes wandered to the organ, where a rose bouquet paid tribute to the death of Mrs. Hayward. Sheila Abernathy had been trying to replace her, but at least once a Sunday, she hit a sour note. Sheila then practiced harder the next week.

"I will be reading from 1 Corinthians, chapter 13," her father said. He began with the part Christy's class had memorized in Bible school one year. "'If I speak in the tongues of men and of angels, but have not love, I am only a resounding gong or a clanging cymbal.'"

As he read on, Christy's eyes inched around the congregation. Dad had chosen the "love chapter" to try to reach the hearts of those who would judge Bobbie—a woman charged with murder—as well as the Castlemans for siding with her and protecting her.

"'Love does not delight in evil but rejoices with the truth...'"

She felt like giving her dad a thumbs-up. She had a sudden impulse to stand up, face the crowd, and yell, *Did you hear that? Love does not judge! Do not judge my parents and my aunt!*

Christy fought a grin of satisfaction as she pictured herself shouting at the congregation. She studied her hands. Obviously everyone in Summer Breeze had heard about Bobbie's situation and her parents' involvement. And Roy Thornberry was the town crier with his front-page news.

A typical Nan Atkins remark slithered through Christy's brain. *Paid a high price to get her out of jail, then hired a fancy lawyer to get her off.* Nan had a personal axe to grind where hotshot lawyers were concerned. Such a lawyer had made a laughingstock of her when she took her accountant to court for mishandling her funds. How many other people in Summer Breeze were reading Roy's front-page story, which Christy refused to do, and talking about Bobbie and her parents?

She must not judge everyone by a few doubting Thomases. Her mom had said some of the church members had offered to deliver meals. *So maybe they're at home cooking,* Christy thought with a cynical half smile.

Hearing her father's voice, strong and firm, Christy glanced at her mother, who sat in rapt attention. She looked back at her father. She knew most of the people who attended this church were not gossipy and judgmental like Mrs. Atkins, but there had obviously been some judgment and speculation. Otherwise, the attendance would not be an embarrassment to her father tonight.

Camp Honeywood, she remembered, glancing quickly around. The half-dozen chaperons had not returned with the group, so of course they would not be in attendance, and neither would the youth. Her mother had returned early, appointing someone else to fulfill her duties because of her family emergency. Beth had remained at Bobbie's side since her return.

Why couldn't people understand that her mother couldn't ostracize her only sister? Or that her dad practiced his beliefs of love and tolerance by putting up a huge bail? She suspected her parents had placed a sizable mortgage on their home to pay Bobbie's bail and Harry Stephens's retainer. Why weren't folks thinking about that?

Well, some of them were, she conceded, hearing the strength of the voices around her singing a well-loved hymn. As she stood beside her mother, sharing the hymnal, the family love that had bound them together through the years rose inside her. She wished Seth were here. They needed him.

As the service ended and people flowed from the pews, she watched the smiles and friendly handshakes offered to her father at the door as he bade them good night. He paused occasionally to listen to a problem and nod in understanding. Looking as though nothing had shattered his family's world, he held himself tall and erect and refused to feel belittled by the possibility that some people disagreed with what he had done.

Beth began to talk with a group of ladies about Camp Honeywood, so Christy slipped out the side door into the soft twilight and headed for her car. One tiny cluster of people lingered, their faces serious, their voices low. *Let them talk,* she thought, unlocking her car and sliding behind the wheel. *Only God can judge a heart.*

nineteen

Monday

Roseann Cole spent half the day in bed after an exhausting drive home in Eddie's truck. The overnight stay in Birmingham had not rested her, because her friend Jodie had gossiped until after midnight. As for the truck—she sighed. She hated stick shifts, even if they saved gas, as Eddie had claimed. She sprawled on her sofa and pulled Millie close to her.

Beautiful Millie. She studied the porcelain doll with its flaming red hair and eyes the blue of a robin's egg. She'd always wished she looked like Millie.

Roseann dressed Millie well. The doll still wore the frilly, yellow, chiffon dress with rosettes on the bodice, just as Roseann had dressed her before she left town. She tightened the tiny pearl choker around the crack at Millie's neck. Millie fell years ago and injured her neck, but this only endeared her to Roseann. Now Millie had a flaw, which made her more real.

Roseann heard a car pulling into the narrow drive, and she jumped up from the sofa to peer through the drapes. Her mother was getting out of her worn Buick Century. Juanita balanced a load of groceries as she walked up the cracked sidewalk to the tiny front porch. As always, she looked tired.

Roseann unlocked the door.

"I hate standing in line," Juanita said in greeting.

She aired her complaints as she walked down the hall to the kitchen, and Roseann trailed after her, shutting out the incessant talking. While Juanita unloaded the sack of groceries, Roseann stared at her, thinking her flushed face meant another rise in her blood pressure.

Juanita was sixty-two years old, and every year showed in the lines and jowls of her face. Her features were large and harsh, and Roseann doubted there had ever been beauty or even softness in that face. Without hair dye and the special hot oil treatment she doted on, her mother's hair would be the color and texture of steel wool rather than a dull auburn. A floral pantsuit covered her lumpy body and its extra fifteen pounds, though she carried it well due to her height. She missed being as tall as Roseann by a couple of inches.

The man who fathered me must have been tall, Roseann thought.

Juanita wore her auburn hair twisted into a thick pile on top of her head and secured with a giant tortoise-shell comb. The only bright spots in Juanita's face were her piercing eyes, so clear and green that when she focused them on something or someone, she seemed to look straight through to the core. Those clairvoyant-looking eyes and her curious way of studying people convinced her clients she could read their futures. Roseann felt the intensity of those green eyes focused on her.

"We need to have a talk," Juanita said, pushing sandwich meats and a half-gallon of milk past the plastic containers in the refrigerator.

"A talk about what? Momma, I'm dead tired," Roseann snapped.

"Yeah, well, so am I," Juanita snarled.

An only child, Roseann tended to get her way with her mother most of the time. Today, however, Juanita seemed ready to fight back.

"Did you work last night?" Roseann asked, hoping to change the subject.

"I work every night." Juanita spoke in a hoarse, throaty voice brought on by years of smoking. The beginning stages of emphysema had motivated her to give up the cigarettes, and these days she did a lot of useless fumbling around in her pocket or her purse.

"How many palms did you read?" Roseann asked, yawning.

"I told you, Roseann. I don't read palms unless my clients nag me into it. I read my tarot cards and look in my crystal ball. That's where I really see things."

"So, Kountess Krystal, did you see anything interesting last night?"

Juanita slammed the refrigerator door and turned to Roseann.

"Unfortunately, I did. Right in the middle of an important reading with a good-paying client, I saw Eddie's face in the crystal ball. Scared the willies out of me."

At the mention of Eddie's name, Roseann's heart sank. "Is that what you want to talk about? Don't you think I've got enough to do, making the funeral arrangements, being hostess to the brother and his wife?" She paused. "Did I make them a hotel reservation? I can't remember."

"I need to tell you something before you talk to anyone." Juanita faced her with her hands on her hips. "Something came to me loud and clear last night. In fact, I stumbled through the reading so badly I didn't even get a tip."

"What are you talking about?"

"Someone is out to get you," Juanita warned. "I couldn't make out the face, but when I laid out the tarot cards, I read trouble again and again. Danger lies in your path, Roseann. I'm gonna brew my special tea to ward off the evil spirits around you."

Roseann stared at her mother and clutched Millie tighter.

Christy told herself it was time to get down to business on the investigation. She had been sidetracked first by the trauma of the arrest and the idea that Harry Stephens would handle things. Then she'd had to deal with her own frustrations about Dan and the sudden, startling plan of becoming a partner in I Saw It First.

But now she was fired up and ready to act.

This grisly murder and ensuing investigation had taken its toll. It was bad enough that her aunt was the prime suspect, but the entire sordid mess was a direct hit on her family. She'd already witnessed the effect of the rumor mill. She could handle herself, but she wouldn't abide people treating her parents shoddily when all they'd tried to do was help Bobbie. Her parents were good, decent people who lived their beliefs.

Last night she had tried to shut out the world by watching a romantic comedy on television. Then she'd surrendered to exhaustion and deep sleep.

Today, however, she felt rested and ready to act. No more escaping into a novel while the real killer—killers?—headed back to Memphis in a black Mercedes. And she wanted to find out what Panada was hiding in the unit behind Bobbie's. No matter what Hornsby said about his reliable printing business, Christy clung to the belief that he had an ulterior motive for renting a unit twenty miles away from his home and work. She always trusted her instincts.

Dressed in white capris and a plaid shirt, she thrust her cell phone in the deep pocket of her pants and grabbed her car keys. She locked the door and hurried to her car.

Cutting across the side streets and hitting the back road to Panama City Beach, on the way to Summer Place Condominiums, she laid out her plans. By the time she turned into the parking lot and squeezed between a white Cadillac and a green Lexus, she felt more determined than ever. Head high, she marched across the parking lot in her three-inch wedge sandals. Height gave her more confidence.

In the lobby, she walked to the reception desk, appraising the young man behind the counter as she approached. Medium height and build, thinning early around his forehead.

"Hi there," she said, tossing a strand of golden brown hair back from her face and giving him a wide smile. "Slow day?"

"Yeah, things slow down after the weekends." His gaze swept over her face. "What can I do for you?"

She considered it a gift from above that she had caught him alone at the counter.

"The two gentlemen from Memphis," she said, speaking in a higher range to sound a bit ditsy. "Can you dial their room, please?"

He frowned, checking the computer. "What are their names?"

Christy giggled. "I don't remember. They asked me to stop by and let them know when we're having the party. Let's see, I'll remember their names in a minute. They're actually friends of my parents." She reached in her pocket and withdrew her cell phone. "I should have checked with my parents, and now I'll get a lecture on not writing down their names." She cast her most innocent smile toward his amused face.

"It's okay," he lowered his voice, grinning at her. "I found them. But they checked out yesterday."

She tried to register disappointment. "You mean they've already gone back to Memphis?"

He looked back at the computer to be certain. "Sure have."

"Oh darn. The party isn't until next weekend. I bet they'd come back if they knew about it. People love the parties my parents host on their yacht."

The young man nodded, and she hoped he had pegged her as a spoiled rich kid with half a brain. That was the part she was going for, at any rate. She stared at the computer. "I don't suppose... Is it possible for me to...kind of peek at their home address or phone number? Daddy wanted me to come over and talk to them on Saturday, but I got sidetracked."

He smiled at that, and his eyes swept as much of her as he could see from behind the tall counter.

She reached over and tapped his hand. "Come on. Make my day and keep me out of trouble."

He glanced around. "I can't do that."

Her face fell, and she cast her eyes downward. "Now I'll have to listen to Daddy rant at me for hours. Tell you what," she said, giving him a pleading look. "Can't you just check on something over there and let me get a peek?" She pointed toward a stack of papers on the counter behind him. "It won't be your fault I broke your rules."

She could see him wavering as he studied her face. "What's your name?" he asked.

"Jennifer Witherspoon," she said instantly. "Want my phone number?"

The grin widened. "You're available?"

She raised and lowered her eyebrows in one of those quick gestures that turned on all the green lights. "Oh yeah. Broke up with my boyfriend this weekend. That's one reason I'm not thinking straight." She grabbed a pen and paper. "I'll write my phone number down while you check on that paperwork behind you."

He gazed at the pen and pad, then turned his back. Christy peered around the computer and saw their names highlighted. She jotted down the home addresses and phone numbers of the men from Memphis. Houston Downey and Joe Panada. *Panada!* Her eyes nearly popped. She wrote as fast as she could, then tore off the slip of paper.

On another sheet, she wrote down the number of her dentist and left it on the counter as he turned back around. She put the other slip in the pocket of her capris and shrugged. "Maybe Daddy won't be so mad after all. And those guys will be glad they came back for Daddy's big shindig. Well," she sighed, as though hating to leave, "see you soon, I hope." She polished off the act with a wide-eyed smile.

He read the phone number again, looked at her, and nodded. "I'll call you tonight."

"That'd be great," she called over her shoulder, quickening her steps across the lobby. At the revolving doors, she stepped aside for a couple pushing through, trailed by a puffing bellboy with an overloaded cart of luggage. She waited for the entourage to get past, then moved through the doors and across the parking lot as fast as she dared.

The weekend gloom had dissipated, and sunshine poured down from the skies with pure gold light. Florida at its best. Christy longed to lower the top of her convertible, but that would be too risky. She had work to do, important work. She thrust her shades over her eyes and grabbed her baseball cap from the glove compartment. After whacking it against the seat a couple of times to get rid of the dust, she set it squarely on her forehead. While guiding her car back into the flow of traffic, she yanked down the visor mirror and surveyed her image. Better tug the cap lower on her forehead. *And* she'd better do more listening and less talking.

Adventures like this brought Chad to mind, but she took a deep breath, knowing Chad was gone, along with her youth. As she headed for Tony Panada's address in an exclusive area of the beach, she thought of Seth. For several seconds, she toyed with the idea of calling him to meet her, then discarded it. If anyone got in trouble for this, it would only be her.

Tony Panada. Joe Panada. She'd bet they called him Joey. There had to be a link. If the same last names were just a coincidence, it would be the first time she had encountered that. In her writing and in her snooping, she didn't fall for coincidences.

Suddenly she thought of Roseann Cole. Those guys were headed back to Memphis. What if they thought Roseann had seen them, could even point them out in a lineup if it came down to it?

She opened her purse and scrambled for the notepad where she kept numbers. A horn beeped, and someone yelled. She was drifting into the oncoming lane of traffic.

"Sorry," she mouthed as the irritated driver weaved past her. She pulled into a parking lot and cut the engine. She didn't need to kill herself or someone else over a hunch.

She opened her cell and dialed Roseann Cole's cell.

"Hello."

"Roseann, it's Christy Castleman. I need to tell you something. I found out those guys in the black Mercedes have left town and are headed back to Memphis."

There was no reply from the other end.

"I don't know if this concerns you, but I just thought you should keep an eye out, in case a black Mercedes with two guys in it starts following you around."

"You mean…" Roseann began to breathe rapidly. "Momma just told me she saw danger in my path. Between you and her, I'm getting the shakes."

"I don't want to upset you, Roseann. I'm just trying to cover every base here. I still think they're involved in Eddie's death."

"You're just trying to get your aunt off," she snapped.

Christy suspected she needed to vent her fear. "Well, you can think whatever you like. I meant well by calling you."

"I can take care of myself," Roseann said. "I may not hang around Memphis anyway."

"Where would you go?" Christy asked, watching an elderly couple walk down the street holding hands. *Does love really last that long?* she wondered, trying not to think of Dan. She realized Roseann had replied. "I'm sorry. I'm in traffic. What did you say?"

"I said I always wanted to live in California, and now I can."

An older woman's voice yapped loudly in the background, and Roseann yelled, "Momma, hush! I gotta go," she said to Christy and hung up.

With a sigh, Christy dropped her cell phone in her purse. What did Roseann mean, *And now I can*? Eddie must have had a life insurance policy, and Roseann must be the beneficiary. Christy wondered how much he had left her. The poor woman probably deserved it after all she'd been through with Eddie Bodine.

Christy concentrated on driving. The snowbirds were out

walking, people her age were running, and the rest of the population was in automobiles heading in one direction or another.

Christy left Front Beach Road at the first cut-through and weaved slowly down several blocks. She had memorized Panada's address, and now she checked the beach map in the passenger seat. She saw she'd reached his neighborhood, and she found his street, so it was just a matter of searching for number 1201.

Midway down the block of impressive homes, she found it. Her gaze scanned the sprawling house and immaculate grounds. Not even a blade of the gardener's perfect grass quivered. The sweeping driveway was lined with decorative urns filled with harsh-looking plants. Cactus? Tony was obviously not a flower man. The door of the double garage on the front of the house stood open, and Christy spotted a white Rolls-Royce. Did Tony Panada skip work on Mondays?

Taking a deep breath, she turned into the driveway. She put her cell phone in her pocket and tugged at her cap again, in the unlikely event he might have seen her around Hornsby's units. She left her purse and all her identification in the car.

Getting into character, she opened the door, swung her legs around, and stood gracefully, in case anyone watched from a window. She planted a wedge heel on each of the three wide steps of his porch and faced the door with false confidence.

A narrow pane of glass flanked each side of the imposing door, which looked as though it had been imported from London. The beveled panes surprised her. She had assumed Mr. Panada wanted complete privacy. But then, the glass served a dual purpose, affording him the opportunity to choose the visitors he admitted to his domain.

She drew a breath and pressed the doorbell.

Somewhere in the depths of the cavernous house, she heard a dog barking. A deep bark that meant business. Soon the wedge-shaped head of a Doberman pinscher appeared in one of the glass panes. His square, muscular body filled the window as he growled at her with rage in his eyes, his lips pulled back to reveal long, sharp teeth.

Christy took a step back, feeling her heightened resolve and false confidence pierced by aggressive teeth. Footsteps resounded on a tile floor, and a man in a lounging jacket appeared from behind the Doberman, his head tilted curiously.

Christy smiled. "Hi, I just need to talk to you for a minute," she called, hoping he could hear her through the door. "I was headed to your office when I saw your car and decided to speak to you per-sonally. We're having a big party." A typical, self-centered airhead—that's how she sounded. He'd probably give her a withering look and walk away.

The lock turned, and the door opened just enough for her to feel the deep penetration of cold, gray eyes on her skin. Flat, expres-sionless eyes behind wire-rimmed glasses. He had probably been checking his stock in the *New York Times* while sipping a martini.

"You want to speak to me about invitations?" His long nose twitched slightly.

Christy nodded, feeling her nerves wind into a square knot in the pit of her stomach. "I know it's rude to show up at your house like this. I mean, I should have called. But I saw your address in the phone book, and...well...I just have one little question to ask." She was the prize airhead, but that was the way she had decided to play it.

His lips were as gray as his face. This was not a guy who sunbathed. "Can't you call my shop and ask the people who handle that sort of thing?"

No, Tony Panada, I cannot.

She decided to stick with the story she'd given his receptionist, although Panada looked anything but gullible. She swallowed. "Daddy's throwing a party at the club for my engagement, and I just need to know the largest number of invitations you can print in the shortest amount of time. And how quickly can we get the invitations? He said I should talk with the owner. I'd be more likely to get the job done."

The Doberman continued to snarl, and Panada looked down in irritation. "Let me take William to the kitchen so we can speak in a calmer atmosphere." His manner seemed to have changed slightly. Christy had found the subject of money to be the quickest and easiest door opener in most circumstances, and this proved no exception.

If Panada invited her inside, should she go? She stuck her hand in her pocket, gripping her cell. Her plans hadn't gone beyond this moment, but she had inched too far out on the tightrope to crawl backward now.

She stood on his stoop for five minutes, long enough for her nerves to start pricking at her skin like mosquitoes. Panada was back, minus the lounging jacket. He wore a chartreuse polo shirt she didn't care for and startlingly white Dockers with European loafers.

"Won't you come in?" he asked. "It must be awfully hot out there."

"My parents are expecting me for lunch," she replied, thinking fast, "but since you're nice enough to answer my questions, I can stay for a few minutes."

Cautiously, she stepped inside the foyer, aware he was looking her over. Just as Eve had faced the snake and regretted biting into the apple, the same apprehension touched Christy now. She swung her head around to look him in the eye.

He stared at her body the way she'd seen men survey an assortment of steaks in the meat department. There was something very sinister about him, so she said nothing. She just waited for him to speak.

"Won't you come into the den?" he asked, motioning to his right.

Said the spider to the fly, she thought, gathering her wits.

"Am I disturbing you?" she asked. "Are you and your wife having lunch?"

He sneered at that. "I've never been married. I suppose I enjoy looking around too much to be tied down to one woman."

"Interesting," she said coolly, cautiously approaching his den, a room that would make a *House Beautiful* living room look shabby. She noticed an open scrapbook on the coffee table. Obscene photographs assaulted her vision, and with a gasp she looked away.

Panada moved around her like a cheetah, grabbing the book and placing it in a drawer and waving absently for her to take a seat. She gritted her teeth and sank into the nearest sofa. Her fingers slid over the smooth leather, soft as a baby's skin. She pretended an interest in the sofa so he would think she hadn't seen his photographs.

Watching him move around the room, she could see his thinness was deceptive. Like his Doberman, he could spring with power and rage, if necessary. How unattractive he was, with his big ears and nose and the sneering smile and offensive eyes. He didn't even bother to conceal his open stares. Every nerve and instinct silently screamed, *Run!*

Instead, she reached deep inside herself for the iron will and competitive nature that had served her in sports, as a star on her high school track team. Her determination had propelled her to the end of the event, even though she sometimes passed out when she crossed the finish line. But she always won.

Recalling those days reinforced her resolve, and she directed her gaze to a grouping of black-and-white photographs on the opposite wall. Other groupings were scattered about, and a painting she immediately recognized as valuable hung above the fireplace.

"Those are wonderful," she said, looking again at the black-and-whites. They were portraits of girls—young girls dressed in skimpy bathing suits, innocently frolicking on the beach below his house. *What a creep.* He must have passed his time sitting in a comfortable lounge chair on a shaded patio, clicking away with his telephoto lens.

"My passion is photography," Panada said, his voice warming to the subject. "My printing business merely supports my passion."

"Oh." She faced him, plunging into another act. "I'd like to take a course in photography. I'm not very good," she said, reminding herself to be Daddy's little girl, out to get her invitations done in record time.

"I have hundreds of phots in my studio, with different people and poses. May I offer you a tour?"

"I don't have time today," she said, standing. "And I've already imposed on you." She watched his eyes narrow, and in her mind, she counted steps to the front door. "What kind of camera do you like?" she asked, hoping to divert his thoughts.

"I have several." He described his favorite, special ordered from New York, where he visited the galleries every year. "Of course, I also have the new digital cameras with all the fancy trappings."

"Do you use a telephoto lens for some of your shots? I've tried to capture the surf rolling in at sunset but can never get in the right position."

"Telephoto lenses are a must if you're trying to pull an object closer." He looked her over. "Do you ever pose?" he asked. "I would love to photograph you."

"Under a sun umbrella?" she asked innocently, knowing that wasn't at all what he meant.

"I see you lying near the surf, having the water spray over you, wearing a tiny bikini or—"

"Oh, look at the time!" she said, indicating the clock. "I'm afraid we've strayed from my reason for bothering you. Daddy's waiting for me to call him. He says your shop does the best work in town, so naturally I want to get my invitations done there. But how many and how long?" she asked, pulling out her cell phone.

His eyes grew cold as he looked at the cell phone in her hand. Then he peered at her, his eyes boring into her, as if trying to read her mind.

She smiled. "Do you think two hundred invitations could be done in, say, three days?"

"Depends on the type of invitation you want," he replied coolly. "You'll need to talk with my office manager about that." His hard exterior cracked a bit, his lips curling at the corners in the semblance of a grin. "But I could tell her I'm photographing you."

She snapped her fingers. "What a great idea! Would you consider—I mean, would it insult you—if I asked you to photograph some of the people at our party?"

The fake grin disappeared. "I don't do parties. I do photographs for my own pleasure."

She nodded. "I understand. Well, may I say again that I think you have extraordinary talent." Thank goodness he wasn't in her path to the door. "Since I've intruded, do you think I can call Daddy and tell him we can depend on your company doing our invitations? I'll keep the design simple. In fact, maybe I'll meet with your office manager and ask for her suggestions."

He shrugged. "That would be best." He followed her to the door. "Her name is Isabella. She knows more about party invitations than I do. But I can assure you that our work will be to your satisfaction."

She reached the door, and with her hand on the golden handle, she looked over her shoulder. "I have no doubt of that," she said. "By the way, where did you study photography? You sound like you're from the East."

"I've lived all over the world," he said, his manner distinctly condescending.

"Then you must have some wonderful photographs. Have you ever been to Italy? I understand the colors are spectacular."

He nodded and seemed to relax for a moment. "Yes, the mellow light in Tuscany is exquisite. Someday, when you have more time, you can visit my studio and see my photographs. My best ones are back there."

I'll bet, she thought.

"Great," she said, pushing the door open. "Thanks so much for reassuring me about the invitations. Now I can tell Daddy to get his money together."

Christy could feel him watching her all the way to her car. She whirled, remembering the reason she had come before becoming totally distracted by the possibility of pornography. "By the way, are you related to Joe Panada? We just met him a few days ago."

"Joe Panada," he repeated, then shook his head. "Afraid not, although it's not a name you hear in Summer Breeze every day."

"He isn't from Summer Breeze," she said and waited.

He shook his head. "Don't know him."

"Just a coincidence, I guess." She hopped in her car and started the engine, then backed into the street. When she glanced at the house, he was still standing in the door, staring after her.

～∞～

The minute she got home, Christy rushed into the office, powered up the computer, and opened her criminal database. She had to find out if Tony Panada had been in trouble over pornography. If he hadn't, it was only a matter of time. The scrapbook of obscene photographs had left her sick to her stomach. It had taken an iron will to remain in his house a second longer, but she knew if she rushed out, it would signal that the scrapbook had bothered her.

She tried three different background approaches, even rearranging his name. Nothing came up.

Leaning back, she slammed her palm against the arm of the chair. Somewhere in the dark caverns of crime, Tony Panada lurked like a black spider.

Joey Panada. Houston Downey. The guys in the black Mercedes from Memphis. Remembering she had their addresses in her pants pocket, she ran checks on both men.

Joey had been arrested in the nineties for assault and battery. She looked at the photo and saw the face of the tall man in the restaurant.

She found nothing on Houston Downey.

She printed out the information on Joe Panada and reached in the bottom drawer of her desk for a file folder. Then she dialed Big Bob's home phone.

A voice she didn't recognize answered. When she asked to speak with Deputy Arnold, the woman introduced herself as Bob's mother. "I'm here from Mobile to housesit for them. Bob needed a few days off after all he's been through with this murder case. Now that an arrest has been made, he took the family down to Disney World for a few days."

"Oh." Christy's hopes sank. She was tired of hitting dead ends everywhere she turned. "Well, thank you very much. Have a nice stay."

Joe Panada's face still filled the computer screen. This Panada didn't resemble the one she'd just left. Was it possible they weren't related after all?

Nah, she said to herself. She wouldn't believe a word Tony Panada said. She did believe the signs she'd read on his face and in his fancy house.

Before she shut down the program, her eyes landed on another heading: "FBI Most Wanted." She double-clicked the link and viewed the list of men and the terrible things they had done. Her eyes inched down the mug shots. Halfway down the screen, a man with a thick, red-brown beard and shaggy brown hair faced her. She frowned and tilted her head, studying the large nose. Then the eyes. She didn't remember the color of Tony Panada's eyes, but they were cold and calculating like the eyes in this man's face. Did he have big ears? She couldn't see his ears through all the shaggy brown hair.

The phone rang. She glanced at the caller ID. A blocked number. She let it ring, but no one spoke on the answering machine. Probably telemarketing.

She read the man's profile. His name was Searcy Jance. The rap sheet listed numerous arrests for child pornography. Born into a wealthy family, he used his money to buy children from poor families. The hideous charges included rape, molestation, and on and on. Considered brilliant, he had escaped prison with two other inmates in September of 1995. The others were shot in the process, but Jance was never caught.

The phone rang again. She read the blocked number and decided to answer. Heavy breathing filled her ears, followed by an obscene comment.

Christy slammed the phone down. The voice sounded like Tony Panada. *Don't jump to conclusions,* she thought. *He didn't know who I was.*

Turning back to the screen, she reread the information about Jance. September 1995. For eleven years this sicko had been on the loose.

The house was too quiet, too still. She jumped at every sound.

Christy got up and looked through her kitchen window. Her backyard was deserted. She went into her living room and lifted the curtain. Aside from the usual traffic, nothing appeared out of order. She dropped the curtain and returned to her computer.

She printed out Jance's information and leaned over to remove the paper from the printer tray. A thud sounded at her front door. She frowned and got up again. She didn't see anyone when she peered out the curtain, so she went to the peephole and looked out. No one in sight.

Resisting the urge to unlock the door, she hurried through the house, looking out every window. No breeze stirred the trees, so the sound hadn't been the wind. When she looked through the pane of her back door, her screen door stood ajar. Hadn't she locked it?

Fear shot through her like an electric shock. Someone was trying to scare her. Panada?

She went to the bedroom and packed an overnight bag. She turned on the fluorescent light over the kitchen sink and grabbed her purse and keys. Then she hesitated. Was someone waiting for her outside?

Opening her cell phone, she put her finger on the 9, ready to hit 11. Looking right and left, she hurried to her car, checking the backseat before she got in. Nothing but a towel from jogging.

Her usual escape was Granny's farm, near Chipley. There she could soak up some fresh country air among wonderful people and, best of all, enjoy her Granny's good cooking and tender-loving care. But Granny had gone on a church trip to Alabama to work on a Habitat for Humanity project.

Her parents had a spacious home. Even with Bobbie installed in the guest bedroom, the room that once belonged to Christy was unoccupied. She drove slowly down the street, looking right to left. It was late afternoon, and down the street two children played in their front yard. Everything looked normal.

What if her imagination was playing tricks on her? But if she felt this anxious in daylight, how would she feel at midnight? She decided it'd be smarter to stay with her parents tonight than lie awake, jumping at every sound.

When she arrived at her parents' home, Christy used a plumbing problem as an excuse to stay overnight. She did have a minor problem she'd been procrastinating about, but the grain of truth served her purpose. Her parents were delighted to have her stay. Her dad had settled into his recliner in the den, but Beth and Bobbie were working in the kitchen. A pot of soup simmered on the stove, and Beth pulled a tossed salad out of the refrigerator. The comfort and security of her parents' home enveloped Christy with loving arms.

"Let's have a glass of iced tea," her mother suggested as Christy and Bobbie sat at the table.

"Christy," Bobbie said, reaching for her hand, "I've been talking to Beth about something, and now I'd like to share it with you."

Christy glanced at her mother and noticed that the end of her nose was red, although her eyes were clear. Unlike J.T., whose nose turned red when his blood pressure climbed, Beth's nose turned red when she cried.

Christy looked back at Bobbie. "I'm glad you feel free to share it with me," she said. She welcomed conversation to ease her nerves. She wouldn't worry her mother and Bobbie about how she felt, but she might speak to her dad when she had the opportunity.

Bobbie was still holding her hand, but she hesitated as though trying to find the right words. "I began drinking when I married Joe Henry and we hung out at the country club. I guess I thought it would make me look sophisticated and important. If I could have seen myself, I'm sure I just looked like the country bumpkin I was. Anyway, the drinking continued over the years. After the second divorce, I lost confidence in myself and felt ugly and unworthy. I had suffered two miscarriages and been told I probably would never have children."

Beth placed the tea before them and patted Bobbie's arm.

"After my second divorce, I met a woman who was into antiques. I became fascinated with old things, or rather seeing and bringing back the beauty in old things. I traveled with her, watching how she bought and sold. She liked her evening cocktails, so of course I joined in.

"On weekends I started going to garage sales and flea markets. For a few bucks, I'd come home with the backseat and trunk of my car loaded down. I spent every spare minute refinishing and touching up my finds. I'd finally discovered a passion, and I didn't care if it made money or not. My neighbor was watching me one Saturday and walked over to buy a couple of things. She suggested I get a booth down at the craft fair.

"I saved my money and made a down payment on a little

building. I worked my fingers to the bone refinishing wood floors, applying varnish, and standing on ladders to paint till I thought I'd drop with exhaustion. A couple of nights I was too tired to drive home, so I slept on a mat in the shop. But I turned that plain building into an adorable shop.

"Then—," she pushed a half-eaten cookie aside. "Then I met Eddie." The sparkle in her blue eyes disappeared as quickly as turning off a light. "I've wished so many times that we'd never met, but I believe people come into our lives for a reason. We should look for the lesson and move on.

"I was never madly in love with Eddie, but he made me laugh and he seemed important. He played the big shot. Then I got pregnant. With my other two pregnancies, I lost the baby in the first six weeks. But I had carried this one for three months, and my obstetrician told me she thought I would go full term. It was the happiest moment of my life. I thought I could love Eddie since he'd given me the baby I always wanted.

"Eddie and I got married and moved into a small house he'd bought the year before. I got busy making the place into a real home. When I painted the walls, I thought of the baby. Soft blues and pinks and pure white. I quit drinking, even though Eddie went out with the guys and came in reeking of liquor. I didn't care. I would lie in the darkness, listening to his heavy snore, and rub my stomach and love the baby inside of me.

"Then," she continued, sighing, "at my next appointment, the doctor couldn't hear the baby's heartbeat. They admitted me to the hospital for tests. I felt certain the baby would be a girl—I'd already named her Angel. But my little angel didn't survive.

"Afterward, I felt as though everything inside me had turned to stone. I went into a depression—couldn't even get out of bed. I felt like I'd died with my baby. Eddie told me I'd better get over it, but I couldn't. I felt like my heart was breaking into a million pieces, and I didn't care."

"That's when you should have called us," Beth said. "No, you should have called us long before that. But then, I didn't call you either." She shook her head and looked sad.

"It's okay," Bobbie said. "At that point, I'm not sure it would have mattered. Eddie started gambling, and I overheard him tell his buddy that he won five hundred bucks on a boxing match. I knew he'd been hiding money in a pair of boots in the closet. I saw him, but I never touched his money. After a real bad day, though, I went over, reached in his rubber boot, and took the money."

She sighed. "I'll spare you the details, but I drove to a bar and got arrested late that night for drunk driving. When Eddie came to bail me out, he was furious because I'd taken his gambling money. I didn't want to go back to the way I had been, so when a friend told me about AA, I started going to meetings, got a sponsor, and worked hard to start a new life. That was almost five years ago, and I've been sober ever since."

There was a moment of silence, and then Christy squeezed her aunt's hand. "I know it wasn't easy for you to tell me this, but I'm grateful you did."

Bobbie suddenly looked ashamed and lowered her eyes. "You probably think less of me now."

"No, I don't," Christy said firmly. "I think you are one of the bravest people I've ever met. You should tell Seth this story. Neither of us has a problem with alcohol, but we may be able to help someone we meet or one of our friends."

"I'm planning on starting church after things settle down," Bobbie said, studying her hands. "In the meantime, Beth gave me some verses." She looked at Christy. "And unlike my attitude with you, this time I'm grateful."

Christy got out of her chair and went around to hug Bobbie. "I'm so glad to hear that."

Later, Christy went to her old bedroom and crawled into the bed she had slept in for so many years. With unsettled thoughts rolling around in her head, she didn't expect to sleep. But as she snuggled down under one of Granny's quilts and closed her eyes, she slept like a child watched over by loving parents.

twenty-one

Tuesday

Christy sat at the kitchen table, facing her father. The coffee mug that warmed her palms failed to offset the chill crawling over her as she told him everything that had happened the day before.

After hearing the story, her father said nothing for several seconds, a deep frown rumpling his forehead. "Christy, I think you should stay with us for a while."

"I'll consider it," she said, knowing she would go back to her house.

"And while I don't approve of your lies and the act you pulled, for your own safety, I have a suggestion. Make that phone call to Panada's office manager. I'm sure you can carry off your act again." He shook his head, anger flaring in his eyes.

"I know what to do, Dad. I'll give the name I used yesterday and a false address. I'll say I'm coming in to look at invitation samples, then find an excuse not to go."

Her father sighed. "In the meantime, I'll call Harry Stephens.

I'll relate all the information you've given me about Panada and ask him to look into it. He's coming down here tomorrow. Maybe he can stop by the printing company on some excuse concerning Bobbie and her unit. That way he can get a close look at Panada."

"Oh, Dad, I don't know what I'd do without you," Christy said, reaching for his hand.

"I'll do this for you on one condition: you don't ever again in your life take such a foolish chance. You've got to quit snooping around and let the police do their job."

Christy sat back and crossed her arms. "Well, they've done a poor job. I don't think they ever took seriously the information about the guys in the black Mercedes."

Grant was quiet for several seconds. "I'm afraid that lethal combination of poisons really incriminated Bobbie. And yet I believe the police have something else. They seem so confident."

Christy's heartbeat accelerated. "The detectives seemed awfully eager to get into Panada's unit."

He nodded. "That's one of the things that concerns me. If Harry learns that Panada's a witness for the prosecution, it means Panada happened to be in his unit—maybe unloading stuff from his shop—and heard noises or saw something. If so, Harry can use Panada's past against them—if this is the same guy."

As Christy listened, she studied her father. His brown eyes looked worried, and dark stubble shadowed the lower part of his face. He had missed his morning shave. Guilt stabbed her for worrying him, but she had to share this information with him.

She pushed her coffee aside. "Dad, I promise to be a good girl.

But what about those party invitations? I can't go down there and go through with my dumb act."

He sighed. "It might be worth the investment to convince him you're whoever you said you were. And you might consider it a lesson to never again take the chance you took yesterday."

"But Dad, what if Panada turns out to be Searcy Jance? Wouldn't you agree I've done the world a favor?"

A reluctant grin relaxed the tension on his face. "I would agree, but we haven't yet crossed that bridge. As soon as Deputy Arnold gets back in town, I'll go down and meet with him privately."

Christy nodded. "He has a lot of respect for Pastor Grant Castleman." She smiled. "As for his daughter, I'm like a pesky little fly he'd love to swat."

Christy slipped quietly out of the house before her mother and Bobbie got up. After all, the plumber was coming early.

As she drove home, most of Summer Breeze was still asleep. Very little traffic stirred along the main road, but soon the little town would come to life.

She decided to take the long way home, driving past the beach. The emerald water lay smooth as glass, lightly teased by gentle waves silver-tipped under the sun. The little sand creatures were free to roam their world undisturbed, and on the horizon a boat bobbed lazily. Christy felt an intense longing to be on that boat going nowhere in particular. Just enjoying nature.

An older woman walked along the beach in a wide-brimmed

hat and a sheer white shirt billowing over her cotton sundress. She strolled barefoot, delighted by the little sandpiper running ahead of her. The world belonged to her this morning, from the sparkling white sand to the blue horizon.

Christy slowed down, easing past so as not to interrupt her thoughts. She watched the woman bend down, lift a large shell and study it carefully, then place it back in the sand. The white beach stretched for a mile, touched only by her footprints.

Christy wondered if she would be like this woman someday, enjoying the autumn of her life here in Summer Breeze. Would she stroll the beach alone as the woman did now? Would she have grown children, or would she say good-bye to Dan and remain single? Maybe it was her destiny, the divine plan for her, to live life on her own. She preferred the words "on her own" to "alone." She would treasure her world, write her books, and be kind to others. It seemed like a good, simple life. Why complicate it?

She thought of Seth, wishing he could mend the break with her parents. Maybe she'd invite him over to spend the night. It would be good to have him there the first night back in her house, and her father wouldn't worry so much.

She guided her car onto a narrow paved road, where flowering shrubs and strewn seashells led away from the beach, and drove toward her neighborhood. The smell of bacon wafted through an open window, as front doors slammed and garage doors rolled up. Another world unfolded, reminding her she had left behind the serenity of the seascape and the otherworld feel she cherished.

Here was reality. Women herding children with schoolbooks

and lunchboxes into cars. A frantic-looking man dropping his briefcase in his race to the car. Newspapers at the curb.

Newspapers that told of the murder, the arrest, the prime suspect living here—right here—in Summer Breeze, where barbecues and ice cream socials dominated the town talk. People enjoyed their front porches, their picnics at the beach, and the backyard get-togethers with neighbors they knew and trusted, and they resented anyone who intruded on their peaceful existence. After all, many were transplants from cities full of crime and traffic. Didn't they bring their children here to protect them from all the atrocities "out there"? And now the silky fabric of their new existence had been torn, the tear threatening to rip apart all they had worked so hard to create, all they wanted to believe could exist for them here.

She sighed. She could relate to their feelings. The tear in their silk sheet of contentment had interrupted her life as well. The work facing her now was not her passion—writing her novel. It was the work of picking apart each fact in this gruesome murder, just as she would pick apart the flaws in the stories she wrote.

Bobbie. Guilty or innocent? One thing nagged at Christy, and she knew she'd have to ask about it before long. There was a gap in the time sequence. If Jack went to the Last Chance Bar at eleven thirty, he had already left Bobbie. Her mother had originally thought Bobbie went to her room around one o'clock. That left ninety minutes unaccounted for. Not a big thing, but in a trial, the prosecution might pounce on it.

Her mother claimed she couldn't say for sure, that she may have heard Bobbie up in the bathroom at one. And of course Bobbie would say, *"Oh honey, that's right. I got up to use the bathroom, and I looked at the clock and it was one, but then I went right back to sleep."*

Christy thought of Dan's question: *"How well do you really know her?"*

She was learning more about her aunt all the time. The fact that Bobbie had admitted she was a recovering alcoholic and then told the sordid story of her past made Christy respect her honesty. Did that honesty reach to all areas of Bobbie's world?

If Bobbie was innocent, someone had better prove it in a hurry.

Christy parked the car, then got out and scanned her yard. A light rain during the night had softened the ground around her shrubs enough to reveal any footprints in the yard or tracks on the porch, but she saw none. Everything seemed in order. Nevertheless, she reached for her cell phone and called her dad as she unlocked her door. He stayed on the line while she inspected every room and closet in her house.

"Everything's fine," she said, "but I think I'll call Seth to come over and spend a couple of nights."

Her father agreed, and she said good-bye. She locked the door behind her, picked up the phone, and called Seth, getting his voice mail. "Hey, brother. Call me when you get this message. I'd like you to come over tonight." He was probably still asleep after a late night.

She hung up and hit the button on her message machine. Jack's gravelly voice vibrated through the first message: "Hey, little gal. Give me a call. I'd like us to talk."

"Okay, Jack. We'll talk," she said, reaching into the fruit bowl for a banana.

The other message was from Dan, left at six thirty last night. "Hi, Christy. Sorry I missed you. Could you call me when you get in? We need to talk."

Since she hadn't come in, she hadn't called. She wondered what he thought of that. She wasn't ready to talk with him yet. She needed to work through her feelings so she would be okay if they broke up for good.

She sank down at the kitchen bar and reached for the phone to dial Jack's number. As she did, she opened the drawer and pulled out her journal. She studied the first page where she had written down favorite proverbs, favorite lines of poetry, books she wanted to read again. She read a favorite poem while the phone rang, and she felt the lovely words replenishing her soul.

"Hey there," she said when Jack answered.

"I don't eat hay. Where were you last night?"

"At my parents' home, drinking tea and eating cookies with your favorite girl."

"You're my favorite girl."

She finished the banana and aimed the peel at the open trash can. Missed. "I don't think I'm your favorite girl anymore, and I have to tell you, I'm a teeny bit jealous."

Jack's hearty chuckle filled the wires, lifting her spirits. "Is that what's got your nose out of joint? You've been acting like I forgot to brush my teeth or use my deodorant."

She laughed. "No, I still love you, Jack. I just got upset about..."

"My white lie."

"That was a black one."

Jack made a disgruntled noise. "You asked if I ran into Bodine or talked to him. I didn't do either. Just watched him. And I didn't want Cora Lee beating up on J.T. I just wanted to be sure Bobbie was safe, Christy. How would it have sounded if I'd said, 'Yeah, sure, I followed that little punk to the bar. Then I sat there figuring out the best way to kill him. Being a reasonable kind of guy, naturally I kicked him in the head and stuffed him in my girlfriend's storage unit.' Does that make sense to you?"

"The part about you trying to protect J.T. and Bobbie makes perfect sense. The rest is a joke, and we're past joking here, which you already know."

"I know. But the wise guys downtown have already been out here to hammer me. They said, 'Mr. Watson,'—with a lot of sarcastic emphasis on the *Mr.*—'you must have forgotten to tell us you happened to stop off at the same bar as the guy you threatened.' I snapped my fingers and said, 'You're right. That did slip my mind.'"

"Jack, I hope you didn't play with them on this." She frowned, afraid he had.

"Nah, they wouldn't appreciate my jokes. I told them the truth, and I want you to know that. Also, I guess you're still praying for me. I didn't remember seeing Goober Fields, my neighbor down the road, but he was coming back from his barn, having suffered through labor pains with his prize mare. He saw me drive by at ten minutes past twelve. Says he'll swear I passed his house then because he looked at the kitchen clock."

Christy digested that information, her hopes rising. "How did he happen to tell the police about this?" Christy asked.

"Two detectives came to his door, asking questions about me. He told them what a charming, lovable guy I am."

"Sure, he did. I don't even know Goober Fields." She laughed at the name in spite of herself.

"You wouldn't. He and his wife bought the farm next to mine this summer. He had a peanut farm up in Alabama but got sick of peanuts. Came down here to fool with horses. I never see him much, because we don't exactly live the same lifestyle."

As she listened, she reached into the fridge for juice, the cordless phone propped between her head and shoulder. "What do you mean?"

"He's a real nice guy. In fact, he and his wife, Ann, are the money behind the building project on that little church down the road."

She smiled at that. "Good. Maybe one Sunday he'll drag you down there." She thought back to the other things he had told her. "So the detectives established he was a reliable witness and believed that you were home when he said. That way your time is pretty much accounted for from the time you left the Blues Club."

"Yeah, and I told them if they'd witnessed the kind of scene Bodine made, they wouldn't go straight home without being sure he went home too. I mean, if they cared about their woman."

She wanted to reach out and give Jack a hug. Maybe she'd bake up a batch of his favorite brownies. "So…you aren't in trouble for lying to them?"

"Don't know. Don't really care." He yawned. "When are you gonna come see me?"

"When are you ever home?"

"Well, your aunt wants me to come into town and help her with her shop. She wants my expert opinion before the moving van hauls in her valuables. So that's where I'll be in about an hour, if you wanna drop by."

She had been sipping the juice as he spoke, and now she sank back down on the barstool and smiled, pleased with the way he had handled everything. "Okay. And Jack…I've missed you."

"I've missed you too, little gal. And I swear never to lie to you again."

She laughed. "Be careful! Don't make promises you can't keep."

"Then you'd better be careful what you ask."

They were both laughing now as they said their good-byes and hung up. Jack's evening had been accounted for, as he had left Bobbie between eleven fifteen and eleven thirty.

What had Bobbie done from eleven thirty until one o'clock? Or had her mother been mistaken about the time? She took a deep breath and again considered the words she had overheard when she stood on the porch, listening to the sisters argue. Was her mom referring to the time she heard her in the hall or the time she came through the door? The gap in time haunted her, a question she generally managed to push to the back of her mind until something popped up to drag it front and center again. Her mother wasn't likely to get her times mixed up after watching the clock for so many late nights when her children did or did not keep curfew.

Christy sighed. She wasn't ready to deal with that just yet. Right now, she was just glad she could put to rest any suspicions about Jack. She reached for her pen, grateful she had a praise report for her journal.

She gasped. The phone call to the printing company! Tony Panada would be after her for sure if she didn't follow through. He would not take being lied to without retaliation.

She took a deep breath and closed her eyes, forcing herself back into yesterday's no-brain Jennifer Witherspoon. She reached in the drawer, withdrew the phone book, and wrote the number for the printing company on the front of the book. She dialed the code to block her number, then dialed the printing company. A split second before the receptionist answered, she remembered to ask for Isabella.

"Yes, may I help you?" Isabella sounded all business.

"Hi, my name is Jennifer Witherspoon, and I was told by Mr. Panada that you're great with party invitations."

"Yes, he told me to expect your call."

So he was checking to see whether she would call. "Well, I meant to call first thing, but I overslept. Anyway, my parents are throwing an engagement party for me at the club next weekend, and I need about two hundred invitations fast."

"I see," Isabella replied, rustling pages. "As I explained to Mr. Panada, this would depend on the type of invitation you want." She launched into a long speech about card stock, type style, and so on, until Christy was ready to scream. "And, of course, with so little time, we may have a problem with engraving addresses on the envelopes."

"Oh, I see. Well, I'm not fussy, but Momma says I should be. Maybe I should have her call you later on. She would understand all this better than I do. Oh, could you please hold on, Miss Isabella?" She put her hand over the mouthpiece and counted to ten. She knew businesslady Isabella had written her off as a complete airhead, but she didn't care.

"Momma says she's flying to Atlanta today and thinks she can get it done there. Truth is, I think she just wants to be in charge. She's a very controlling person," Christy said. "I'm sorry, but I do appreciate your help. And Daddy says he'll use your company for something else."

"Well, we hope so. Have a good day."

After she hung up, Christy sighed and shook her head. She hated to lie, but she had promised her dad she'd finish this charade and then stay out of other people's lives. Remembering the obscene phone call from last night, she shuddered. She'd learned her lesson.

The phone rang again. Christy looked at the caller ID and shook her head. "Guess who," she answered, using her cutesy voice.

Bobbie laughed. "Yes, it's me, your worrisome aunt. Oh, honey, I'm so excited I don't know what to do. I'm down at my new shop. I have a painter-slash-artist designing 'I Saw It First' in just the right twirl. Can you come down in a little while?"

"Be right there," Christy trilled back, matching Bobbie's breathless tone.

"Thanks, hon." The phone clicked, and Christy imagined Bobbie line dancing down the center of her shop, thrilled to have found a home for her treasures. Come to think of it, she might be line dancing with Jack.

⸙

Tony Panada looked up from his desk as Isabella entered his office.

He had always thought her unattractive. Her severe haircut was spiked and cut shorter than his, and her dull pantsuits did nothing to flatter her figure. If she had one. Looking at her face, void of makeup, Tony wondered if she was really a woman.

"I'm afraid that young lady who pestered you yesterday just wasted your time."

"Oh?" He laid down his pen and appraised her coolly. He really should replace Isabella with someone more appealing to the public.

"After I took the time to give her details on party invitations and prices and even committed to getting the job done in a hurry, she checked with her mother, who said she'd get it done in Atlanta today. Frankly, she sounded like a total airhead."

He nodded slowly, not at all surprised by this news.

"She's not as dumb as she appears," he said, picking up his pen and focusing on the letter before him. "Thank you, Isabella."

When the door closed, he lifted his eyes from the letter and swiveled his chair around to stare out at the busy traffic along the beach highway. Bombshell, Hornsby had called her. She was a looker, all right, but she was no airhead. She was in for an unpleasant surprise, though, if she thought for one moment she had fooled him.

He had known from the minute she stepped into his house exactly who she was. He had only gone along with her silly game to try to figure out what she wanted from him. Or how much she knew.

It hadn't taken long. She was there to check him out, and he was pretty sure she'd seen his scrapbook before he managed to hide it. He was still cursing himself for forgetting he'd left it there the night before.

His thoughts drifted back to Monday night when he and one of his little friends had been making a movie. It was after eleven when he left his storage unit, but he hadn't missed the real show. He sneered at the memory of that little guy stuffed in the barrel.

On top of everything else, Roseann Cole was still a loose canon rolling around out there somewhere.

He steepled his hands before him, then thought of something and glanced at the phone. He lifted the receiver and dialed a number.

"Let me to speak to Joe," he said.

twenty-two

Christy drove through Summer Breeze and found a parking space several doors down from Bobbie's new shop. She thought being a partner in the shop would be an interesting adventure. Maybe she'd take a course in antiques at the college in Panama City. She needed to expand her horizons. She pulled over to the curb, got out, and fed the meter.

From behind her, she heard a man and woman talking.

"It's a disgrace letting a murderer open a shop three doors down."

"What will it do to our business?"

Irma and Stanley Lee were opening their ice cream shop for the day and had paused in the door, their eyes focused on Bobbie's red truck parked at the curb. Christy frowned as she dropped her keys in her purse and prepared a response. Why hadn't it occurred to her sooner that the neighboring merchants would consider the new shop an ugly reminder of the dead man in the pickle barrel?

"Hi, Mr. and Mrs. Lee," she said, stepping onto the sidewalk. The middle-aged couple exchanged quick glances, each wondering how much Christy had heard. "Still have some of that good praline ice cream?" she asked.

"Er, yes. We do." Irma Lee looked dumbstruck, as though ice cream, their livelihood, was the last thing on her mind.

"Great. Nobody makes ice cream like you do." Christy looked at Mr. Lee, who shoved his hands in the pockets of his chambray pants and followed them through the doorway. "It is homemade, isn't it?" she asked, giving him a friendly smile.

"Why, yes. We make all of our ice cream," he replied.

They walked past the empty tables and chairs to the ice cream container, where Irma loaded up a sugar cone.

"Just one scoop," Christy said, fishing in her pocket for a couple of bills. "But I'll be coming back for more."

Irma handed her the cone and took the money.

"I'll need a couple of those as soon as I find out what flavors Bobbie and Jack want," Christy continued. "Did you know I'm opening a shop just three doors down?"

"You are?" Irma's countenance changed from reserve to total confusion.

"Well, my aunt, Bobbie Bodine, is a partner. She's famous for her designs. She's been written about in magazines and has done workshops all over the country. She can restore antiques, take family heirlooms that have been trashed and make them lovely again, and...well, she can do anything. Except murder someone," Christy said, looking from Irma to Stanley. "In case anyone in Summer Breeze is interested, some very bad guys who take care of people who don't pay gambling debts tracked Eddie Bodine to a storage unit here, which happened to be Bobbie's. This will be proven in a court of law. Until that time, don't you agree that a person is innocent until proven guilty?"

The ice cream dripped down her cone, across her hand, and onto her blue jeans, but Christy was scarcely aware of it. She was too busy watching the faces of two people guilty of convicting her aunt without just cause.

Stanley came around the front of the counter. "You're right, Christy. I've seen that little woman come and go, and from what I've heard about the…er…incident, she isn't big enough or strong enough to…do what was done."

"Thank you, Mr. Lee." Christy looked at his wife. "I told Bobbie that folks in Summer Breeze were good, understanding people, and that we have no room for Mafia types who want to come into town, pull off a gruesome murder, and lay the blame on an innocent woman."

Irma slowly shook her head, convinced now. "That's right, Christy. And if there's any way we can help with your shop—"

"There is. Just keep repeating what I've told you. And by the way, the church youth will be returning from Camp Honeywood late Wednesday afternoon. We'd like to have treats for them. Could you handle an ice cream order for, say, fifty people?"

Pleasure spread over both faces like melting cream. The Palace of Sweets thrived while the spring breakers and summer tourists were in town, but the business suffered after Labor Day.

"Yes, we'll be happy to supply ice cream for the church youth," Stanley said. "Just let us know what flavors."

"To keep it simple, why don't you do chocolate, strawberry, and vanilla," Christy suggested. "More chocolate, perhaps. I'll pick the order up around five o'clock tomorrow, if that's okay."

"That's fine." The couple nodded, grinning.

Christy smiled. They looked like a different couple from the one she had first seen, all deep frowns and angry eyes as they stared at the new shop down the street.

"And if you'll let us know what kind of ice cream your...aunt and Jack want...," Irma said.

"Yes, I'll let you know right away."

Christy hurried out of the shop, wondering if she had told the truth. Actually, she had repeated a universal truth. A person was innocent until proven guilty. Her aunt might take advantage of people here and there, and she had faults like everyone else. But she was not a murderer.

"Christy!"

Christy stopped and looked across the street. Donna Whit-ford, owner of the Blues Club, hurried out of the dry cleaners, a red linen jacket showing through the plastic flapping against her arm.

"Could you wait up a minute?" Donna called.

"Sure," Christy said. She watched Donna cross the street, her blond head lowered to gauge her steps. The morning sun touched the highlights in her hair, adding to her sophistication. She wore a smart blue pantsuit with matching sandals. Again, Christy con-ceded she was an attractive woman. Maybe she had a few years on

Christy and even Dan, but who noticed when she looked up and smiled, showing off her dimpled cheeks?

"Christy, I'd like to talk with you if you're not in a hurry," Donna said once she'd reached Christy.

Christy shrugged. "I'm not, but if it's about my aunt, she's in the shop on the corner. We're opening I Saw It First. Found treasures restored, that type of thing."

"Sounds fascinating," Donna said, "but it's you I need to speak with, and it concerns Dan."

Christy stared at her for a moment. "Oh?"

Donna indicated the bench in front of the Palace of Sweets. "Could we sit down for a minute?"

"Sure." Christy suddenly became very aware of her appearance: no makeup, maybe a smear of lip gloss. And she had dressed for remodeling a dusty shop.

"Dan and I went out after you two broke up," Donna said, "but he was never interested in me. I could tell. And then when I met you, I saw why."

"Donna, you don't have to say anything," Christy said, uncomfortable with the conversation.

"Yes, I do. I know he started seeing you again, but he had already obligated himself to escort me to a Chamber of Commerce dinner Sunday night. I invited him, by the way."

Christy had been avoiding eye contact, but now she turned and looked directly into Donna's pale blue eyes.

"He was gentleman enough not to break the date, but he told

me Sunday night that he was hoping the two of you could get back together again." Donna looked down. "He said he probably wouldn't be seeing me again. But he wished me 'all the luck in the world,' to quote him."

A spark of hope ignited in Christy's heart, but she tried not to feel it.

"I want to explain about the compact," Donna continued. "On that first date, I'd put my purse on the floor, and when Dan braked suddenly, several things fell out. I thought I had picked up everything, but I guess the compact rolled under the seat. It must have slid through to the back when he bounced over the rough roads at his building site. In any case, he didn't even know it was in his vehicle. When he asked about it, I told him it was mine."

Christy smiled. "I appreciate you telling me this. I saw the compact. I knew he had been seeing someone, and he even started to explain, but at that point, I didn't want to hear it. We'd both decided to give each other plenty of space."

"Yeah, well," Donna sighed, studying her rose-colored acrylic nails, "I don't think he wants that space. He's quite a guy." She looked up at Christy. "If he weren't so honest, and if you weren't so nice, I might work a little harder to hang on to him. I don't know how you feel, but there's no room in his heart for anyone but you." She stood up. "I gotta go. I just wanted to say this to you, and now I feel better."

"Thanks, Donna," Christy said. "I really appreciate it. Maybe I can do something for you sometime."

"Just get your aunt through this nightmare, and send her back to the club. Nobody sings the blues like her. Oh, and another thing. Dan told me about Wiley and asked about that night when the pills were spilled. After we closed up, I turned the lights on bright and walked around. I didn't see any little white pills anywhere. And when Wiley swept around that table and a few tables back, I watched him closely. There were papers, bits and pieces of stuff, but he didn't sweep up any pills. I'm sorry. I don't have anything against Wiley, but I'd sure like to have seen something that would help Bobbie. I hope the police find the real killer."

Christy nodded. "I feel the same way. We appreciate your support, Donna."

She watched Donna hurry back across the street and get into her sports car, then tossed the melted glob of ice cream into a street bin. While she walked toward Bobbie's shop, she thought about what Donna had told her.

Wiley could be ruled out as a suspect. Even if he had killed Eddie, he wouldn't have been foolish enough to admit he knew him. He certainly wouldn't have divulged his belief that the world was a better place without Eddie Bodine. Why hadn't she and Dan considered that? Maybe because they were desperate to find someone to blame.

Another ray of hope brightened her dark mood. The more she thought about what Donna had told her about Dan, the better she felt. She smiled, allowing her hopes to build just a bit. He'd left a message saying they needed to talk. Maybe she'd call him tonight.

Bobbie stepped out of the shop and stood, hands on hips, to study the painter's work. At Christy's approach, she turned with a wide smile.

"Honey, come look at this! Right now we just have a plain old building, but I'm going to paint it yellow with red accents. Doesn't that sound unique?"

"Yes, it does." Christy looked at the two large windows on either side of the door. "You have a nice display area too." Her gaze returned to the red calligraphy swirled across the glass: I Saw It First.

"Perfect," Christy said.

"Yes, hasn't he done a nice job? Now come inside so you can get a feel for what the shop will look like."

As they crossed the threshold and entered the large front room, Christy suspected her aunt was keeping busy to avoid thoughts of the murder. She seemed to be totally focused on her shop, and Christy thought this was a good thing.

She looked around. "Those cream-colored walls are in good shape and go nicely with the hardwood floors. Doesn't look like you'll have to worry about painting or floor covering."

"Thank God," Bobbie replied. "And my wreaths and baskets will look great displayed on those walls."

"What kind of wreaths?"

"All kinds—dried flowers, fresh flowers, vines. The room is spacious enough to accommodate large items, and I have quite a few. I do a lot with doors and windows—" A splintering sound from the back room interrupted her. "Come on, I'll give you an idea."

In the back room, Jack sat in a folding chair, an old window on his lap, a garbage can beneath the window. "Stand back," he warned.

Christy backed up as the hammer hit the glass in one of the panes and shards fell into the garbage can. Jack seemed to be enjoying pounding on the glass, and she wondered if he was venting frustration and worries concerning Bodine.

"Jack had that old window out in his shed, and I insisted on bringing it in and reworking it into something lovely."

"What do you plan to do?" Christy asked.

"Remove the glass, chisel out the glazing compound, and special order mirrors to replace the panes." She tilted her head to the side as though visualizing the finished product. "I'll do something interesting with the original wood. Then I'll have a lovely object to hang on the wall." She turned to Christy and sighed. "All of this keeps my mind off Eddie's murder."

Christy nodded. "Good idea. You're going to have something special here, so just hold that thought." She glanced at her watch. "Gotta run. Jack, be careful with that glass," she called. Then she gave Bobbie a hug and headed out the door, pleased that her project was going well.

When she reached her car, she remembered the ice cream. Jack liked maple walnut, and she guessed her aunt would go for chocolate. She headed back down the street.

twenty-three

R oseann Cole was in a cold sweat. The two guys in the black Mercedes were following her, she was sure of it. When she came out of the bank, she saw them parked across the street. Pretending not to notice, she got in Eddie's truck and drove to the car dealership where she had left her 1989 Ford.

She stood in the showroom of the Memphis dealership, her eyes fixed on a creamy white Lincoln Continental. When she came by yesterday, she had told the salesman she would trade in her car, which she left for the mechanic to check out, and Eddie's new white truck on the Lincoln. She thought a white Lincoln spelled class, and from now on, she wanted to be classy.

Today the older salesman seemed as unimpressed as yesterday. She asked to speak with the sales manager. He walked toward her, a fake smile on his face. "Hi, I'm Sam, the manager. You wanted to speak with me?" She could hear that uppity tone in his voice, and she hated it. She'd heard it all her life.

"Yes, Sam. I expect to be treated well," she said. "Just because I look like I don't have any money doesn't mean a person has to act like he's wasting his time."

"Oh, no ma'am," Sam said, pulling at the starched collar of his white shirt. "The problem is, your older car isn't worth much by the book, with the brakes almost gone and the transmission nearly out." He lowered his voice. "But we're pleased to have your business." He looked over his shoulder and said loudly, "Tommy's just a little out of sorts today."

"Well," Roseann said, "just so you'll know I'm serious, I have enough money in the bank to pay cash for this automobile. But unless I'm treated with respect, I'll take my money elsewhere."

Sam perked up. "We don't want you to do that. And, again, I apologize if you've been made to feel…unwelcome." A pleasant smile changed his tone of voice. "Do you want to try the Lincoln out? Be sure you like it?"

"I like it all right. But yeah, I'd like to drive it to be sure."

"Great. I'll tell them I'm leaving for a little while." He hurried inside a glass-walled office. Roseann watched him lean over a desk and speak to the guy seated behind the desk. The guy shot a quick glance at Roseann.

She turned and sauntered around the showroom, returning to the side of her new car and stroking its silky exterior. She peered through the showroom window at the busy street. Were the guys in the black Mercedes still out there? At first she didn't see them, but as she looked farther down the block, she spotted the side of the car. They had pulled in between two other vehicles, trying to be inconspicuous.

Roseann opened her purse, pulled out her cell phone, and dialed home. "Momma, you were right. There's danger in my path, for sure. Now, I don't want you to get upset, but I think we'd better leave town for a few days. You'll have to say we've got a family emergency. Tell them your sister died and we have to catch a plane out tonight. Since you're in poor health, I have to go with you, of course."

Momma started in, but Roseann cut her off. "I've helped Mitford and his boring wife as long as I can stand it. Call the funeral home, and call Mitford at the Holiday Inn. You can say I'm out shopping for clothes for the funeral. You know how to manipulate people, Momma, so do it! Then pack a few things in a shopping bag and drive down to the parking lot of the Piggly Wiggly. I got some cash, and I'm going to the insurance company to see how long it'll take to get the money Eddie left me. You'll get a nice little cut if you just do as I say, okay?" She paused for breath, noticing Sam walking toward her, keys in hand. "Listen, Momma, I gotta go. Eddie had some bad guys after him, and I don't want them to know where I live. I'm trying to protect you, Momma. I'll meet you where I said in half an hour."

She hung up with the words *crystal ball* echoing in her ears.

"All right, Miss Cole," the manager said, all smiles now. "Are you ready to take that drive? I'll pull the Lincoln out to the side lot for you."

When Roseann got in behind the wheel, she leaned back against the soft leather cushions and sighed. She guided the steering wheel and drove carefully, taking the back route to avoid traffic. Once they reached the interstate, at the sales manager's suggestion, she "opened her up."

She felt like she was floating on a cloud. This was the life she was meant to live. Drivers in small, cheap cars stared at her, and she liked that, too.

"I'm sure I want it," she said, slowing at the first exit and driving back to the car lot. She pulled up beside her truck, parked on a side street.

"I'll just be a second. I need to get some things out."

She hopped out of the Lincoln, unlocked the truck, and reached into the front seat. She withdrew her overnight bag and Millie, then opened the back door of the Lincoln and placed them on the seat.

"I, er, don't know that we can get the paperwork completed today," Sam said, craning his neck to see what she was doing. His gaze lingered on Millie.

"With two vehicles and cash for the balance, how much paperwork is involved?" Roseann reached in her purse, pulled out a wad of bills, and stuffed them in his hand. "Here's a little something to keep you happy until I get back in the morning." She hopped behind the wheel again and guided the Lincoln into the back parking lot.

He glanced at her, his eyes widening. "Tell you what, I'll take down your address and phone number and—"

"I already gave that to the other guy when I was in here yesterday." She assumed the same irritated expression she'd worn when Sam came out of his office to soothe her ruffled feathers.

"Oh." He sat for a moment, weighing a decision. Then he looked at the white truck.

Roseann heaved an impatient sigh. "Make up your mind. Do I take the Lincoln with me, or do you want to keep it?"

"Are you leaving the keys to the truck? I don't want it parked on the street."

She reached in her purse, removed the truck keys, and handed them to him.

"I'm running late for my appointment with the *insurance company*," she informed him, hitting the words with emphasis.

Sam nodded, slowly opening the passenger door. Roseann extended her hand to touch Sam's arm through the crisp white shirt.

"I'll be back first thing in the morning." She waved to him and turned the wheel, gliding out of the back parking lot. She laughed, knowing the guys in the Mercedes were waiting for her to come out the front door.

twenty-four

Christy hadn't stopped by the Treasure Chest, her mother's gift shop, in over a week. Recalling how kind and caring Beth had been to Bobbie, and how sincere in her apology to Christy, she felt a deeper respect for her mother. She had never doubted her mother loved her, but when Christy had mutated into a rebellious teenager, tension built a wall between them. After Chad's death, her mother had begun to break down that wall by comforting Christy and being there to help her through the darkest hours of her life. Christy had been strengthened by the love of her family, and over time, most of the tension disappeared. Most, but not all. A few broken stones from the wall still littered their path.

She still felt a twinge of resentment, at times, when she compared herself to her mother. She named the problem: her own guilt. Beth had admitted she wasn't perfect and had never tried to be or thought of herself that way. Yet Christy had cast her in that image and widened the gap between them.

She turned into the parking lot of her mother's store, a small building that truly resembled a treasure chest—brown walls with gold shutters flanking the windows and a brass door whose handle looked like a huge gold key. Her mother had come up with the idea and made her gift shop a success. She carried items native to the area as well as unique items she ordered to complement the inventory, like the antique green bottle Christy had found on the beach at Shipwreck Island, holding the note that had turned Summer Breeze upside down.

She walked up the stone walkway, absorbing the orange-blossom aroma flowing through the half-open windows of Beth's shop. Her mother always had wonderful scented candles that managed to smell delightful without irritating anyone's allergies.

Christy stepped up to the door and pressed the gold-key handle. When the door swung back, an antique bell signaled the entrance of a customer.

"You're a welcome sight," Beth called from her desk at the far end of the counter. She was doing her bookwork, a Tuesday chore, and she peered over her bifocals to smile at Christy.

"Are you busy?" Christy asked.

"Does it look like it?" Beth answered, lifting a hand to gesture at the empty shop. Her quick question with its veiled sarcasm sounded more like Bobbie than Beth. Christy walked around the counter and hugged her tiny mother. She wore casual tan slacks and a navy sweater with a watch-plaid collar.

"You've really gone out on a limb for Bobbie," Christy said, sinking into the nearest chair.

Beth closed the black ledger and leaned back in her Victorian chair. "She's my sister and I love her. What else would you expect me to do?" She removed her bifocals and hooked them onto a clasp on her sweater that kept them within reach.

Christy hesitated. If she were honest, she'd admit she had been surprised by the way her mother stood by the sister with whom she had never shared a loving relationship, but then she should have known her mother's heart was warm and kind. Christy wanted to remove the final remnants of the wall between them, and she shook her head, her gaze slipping over her mother's round face.

"It's exactly what you would have done," she said. "You and Dad are wonderful. Have you heard anything from the lawyer? Or anyone else?"

Beth sighed. "Your father planned to telephone Mr. Stephens first thing, but he hasn't called me yet. I hope and pray we can find the terrible person who did this, who has brought so much suffering to everyone."

The shop's phone rang, and Beth smiled after the hello. "Christy just stopped by, and we were wondering if you had talked with the attorney."

Christy could hear her dad's deep voice on the other end, but she couldn't make out his words. She watched her mother's face, trying to read her reaction to her father's news.

"I see. Yes, she's right here. Just a minute."

Christy reached for the phone, hoping her mother wouldn't find out about their early morning conversation concerning Tony Panada—or Searcy Jance. She knew her father would have some information.

"Hi, Dad. What's up?"

"Don't react to this, because I'd rather your mom didn't know about Tony Panada."

"Oh, you're right. I agree," Christy replied.

"When I spoke with Harry about the matter, he informed me it was quite a coincidence I had asked about Searcy Jance. It seems he was arrested in a London suburb late last night. It'll be all over the news today. Harry emphasized they were certain they had the right man."

"Really?" Christy said, feeling an odd disappointment. She looked at her mother, careful to keep her expression bland.

"You see, Christy, this is a lesson in jumping to conclusions. Mr. Panada may be doing some evil things, but he's not Searcy Jance."

"Okay, Dad. You have a nice day too. See you later." She handed the phone back to Beth, who hung up.

Christy shrugged. "No news yet."

"I know," Beth said. "We just have to be patient, I suppose. At least Mr. Stephens has a meeting with someone in the district attorney's office tomorrow. Maybe we'll find out what they claim to have as proof that Bobbie…"

Christy cupped her mother's hand. "Try not to worry. We have to keep our hopes up. And our faith."

Beth leaned forward and kissed Christy's cheek. "Thanks for being a wonderful daughter."

"My pleasure," Christy said. "Well, gotta run. Just thought I'd check on you."

As Christy stood, the bell over the shop door announced the arrival of one of Beth's most loyal customers.

"Hello," Virginia Wallace said as she entered, a friendly smile on her face. "Beth, I'm afraid I have a rather large order. I hope it won't be too much trouble."

"Not at all." Beth stood, smiling at Virginia. "It's good to see you," she added.

"Have a nice day, Mrs. Wallace," Christy said as she left the shop. She hurried down the walkway to her car. There were so many good people in the world. In time, others would realize Beth had done what she had to do, and that her husband had been loving and supportive of his wife by trying to help her sister.

Christy thought about what her father had just told her and decided she didn't have to feel jumpy about Panada or anyone else. The obscene phone call was probably a teenage prank, and the sound she thought she'd heard at her front door could have been a stray ball from the kids playing down the street.

As Christy drove home, her thoughts returned to her conversation with Donna, who had no reason to be anything but honest. Now, more than anything, Christy wanted to be with Dan.

She dialed his number as she turned into her neighborhood. By the time she reached her driveway, he had answered.

"Hi there," she said.

"Hi, Christy," Dan replied warmly. "What're you doing?"

"Oh...kind of wondering what you're doing."

He laughed. "I've been working hard the past two days, and I'm ready for a break. Want to play hooky with me?"

She got out of the car, cradling the phone against her ear as she unlocked her back door. "What'd you have in mind?"

"A boat. Deep water. Feeding the fish."

"You're describing my dreams."

"We could leave out of Destin, take our time, and enjoy the sunset. What do you think?"

"Are you serious?"

"Completely. I think it would be therapeutic for both of us. The truth is, I'm considering buying a slightly used boat from a friend who just found out he's going to be the father of twins. He needs a little cash."

"I can imagine. Are we trying out his boat?"

"No, it's in dry dock for a checkup to be sure everything works like he says. I trust him, and I've been out on it a few times and loved it. I told him if he ever wanted to sell, I wanted first chance. To my surprise, he called me last night, and today that boat is all I can think about. Well, not all."

"Is that what you wanted to talk about when you left me a message?"

"Not really. But I would have gotten around to it, no doubt. Since he called me, I've been thinking that maybe I really should buy it. I love the water, especially the Gulf. When I got out of the service last February, I came here to visit my folks. But the other reason was that I wanted to look at the water for a dozen years to chase away some nightmares. After two weeks, I knew I wanted to stay here, live near the water, build old-fashioned bungalows and

Victorian cottages on the water, and fish, fish, fish. So why not invest in something I enjoy so much?"

Hugging the phone against her shoulder, Christy walked through the house to the bedroom. "I don't believe in coincidences, but it's pretty coincidental that we're having this conversation," she said. "This morning I took a quick drive along the beach, staring out at the Gulf and wishing I could be on a boat I saw bobbing out on the horizon. You know, just leave my cares behind and go play with the dolphins."

"We can do it. I'll call now and book a charter on a small boat. Business is slow on a weekday, now that tourist season is over."

"Terrific," Christy said. "To save time, I could drive over and meet you at the marina. Where are you now?"

"Leaving a building site near Seaside." She heard a door slam and an engine roar to life. Dan lived closer to Destin than Summer Breeze. "You don't mind?" he asked.

"Why should I mind? Sounds like the best plan."

"Okay. Give me an hour to locate a boat, shower, and change, and I'll meet you there. Around four?"

"Sure. Want me to stop by the deli? Or will you have time to bake cookies?"

"Nah," he said. "If I charter a boat, we'll get dinner. That's the object—we do nothing but pamper ourselves or let someone else pamper us."

Christy turned on the shower. "That's the best idea I've heard in a long time. I'll be there."

⸉∽∝∾⸊

An hour later she pulled into a parking space at the marina. Dan stood talking with a captain, who pointed out a boat that looked too big for just the two of them. Dan smiled and nodded.

Christy grabbed her tote bag from the passenger seat. It held a cap, a Windbreaker, sunscreen, and her iPod. She adjusted her sunglasses and tucked a stray hair behind her ear.

He heard her slam the car door and turned. He wore black shorts and a striped shirt, with a black sweater tied around his shoulders. A white cap held his dark hair in place, and although the sunglasses hid his eyes, the smile he wore lit up the dock.

They had dressed as opposites, and Christy almost laughed. She wore a white shirt and shorts, with a white sweater tossed over her arm. Her cap was black.

"How does this one look?" Dan asked, reaching for her hand as she stepped across the boardwalk.

She turned to the gleaming white boat, the *Sea Maiden,* and nodded with approval. "Looks like a lot of fun," she said.

"When can you take us out?" Dan asked the captain.

"Whenever you're ready. She's fueled up and ready to go."

"We're ready," Dan said. He extended a strong arm to Christy, and they stepped down into the boat.

The captain started to give them a tour, but Dan politely waved him aside. "We just want to sit up there and relax."

Hand in hand, they walked to the front of the boat and sank into the deck chairs facing the water. Christy set her tote bag down and reached in for sunscreen. Once she touched up her face and dabbed sunscreen on Dan's nose, she capped the tube and settled into her chair. Soft music floated from the boat's stereo, and the September breezes caressed her skin.

Dan settled into the chair beside her. She rolled her head and looked lazily at him. "You going to fish?" she asked, certain he had arranged for everything he needed.

"Not this time," he said, removing his sunglasses. His blue eyes glowed beneath his white hat. "I just want to spend some time with my girl."

She smiled at the phrase and tucked her hand in his. He squeezed her hand, then turned to look into the distant waters, the lines in his face beginning to relax.

"You look like you belong here," she said. The captain started the engine, and the smell of fuel drifted to them.

"I think I do," he replied lazily, "as long as you're with me."

"Well, it feels like I'm here."

She didn't spoil their lazy contentment with more conversation. The boat pulled out and headed toward deep water.

"Oh, I forgot," Dan said, reaching for the ice chest behind him. "The captain filled it with bottled water, soft drinks, and snacks. He'll serve us dinner below—or out here, if we wish."

"When you said pamper, you meant it, didn't you?"

He grinned at her. "Yeah." He popped a can of Coke, poured it into a chilled glass mug, and handed it to her. He did the same for himself. Then he opened a bag of sun-dried chips. For a while, they were content to feel the sun on their faces and sip their cold drinks, watching sea gulls soar and swoop as though leading the way over the turquoise waters.

Christy turned in her seat and, with the cap shading her eyes, looked back at the small seaside town they were leaving behind. She allowed herself to believe she had abandoned her worries back at the marina and was sailing into the wild blue yonder without a care.

"I want to ask you something," Dan said when the engine throttled down. A quiet peace settled over them as the sun climbed westward.

"Don't get personal," she teased, looking at the trail of gold across the water.

"It's personal. You didn't appear jealous or upset when you got to the Blues Club and saw me sitting beside another woman."

Glad I fooled you, she thought, grinning at him. "She didn't look like your type."

He rolled his eyes. "I hope not. And then, when we went on the picnic, I know you saw the compact, but you never said anything. You just hopped out without a good-bye kiss."

"Your point being?"

"That maybe you just don't care anymore."

How should she answer that? "I'm showing respect for your freedom."

He crushed the Coke can in reply and tossed it into the trash bin. "What I'm trying to say is that you've changed. Was it a conscious change or...do you not care? Well, maybe you just don't care as much."

She removed her sunglasses and looked into his eyes. "I don't know if I can afford to care as much," she answered. "You need your freedom, but I need my sanity. I've told you it took me years to get over Chad's death and build a new life for myself. Once I did, I vowed to protect myself against another heartbreak. That's what I'm doing, Dan. Until we're more sure if our relationship is right for both of us, I'm trying to keep a level head."

He nodded. "Okay, fair enough. I like that you're not so tense anymore or acting like you need something from me that I can't give. At least, I thought I wasn't ready to give it."

"You're not," she said, pushing her sunglasses back over her eyes and staring ahead. "Look! I see a dolphin!"

She jumped up too suddenly and lost her balance, but he was right behind her, his strong arms clasping her waist as they leaned out over the deck. They stood close together, waiting, their eyes straining for the dolphin.

In the next moment, the dolphin came out of the water in a graceful leap, water glistening on its gray back. Then, with a simple elegant twist, it dove under again.

Christy and Dan watched in awe.

"There's another one swimming close by," he whispered, pointing.

She smiled.

The dolphins engaged in a playful, twisting dance before disappearing into the blue depths.

"Usually they travel in pods," Dan said, "but I don't see any others." He shaded his eyes and scanned the water.

"We don't need to see more," Christy said, feeling the magic spin around her. "That was perfect. Dan, thank you for renting the boat. I'm having a wonderful time."

"So am I," he said, leaning down to kiss her.

In the next hour, a wind kicked up out in the Gulf, and Christy pulled on her sweater.

The captain appeared. "Excuse me. May I suggest you have dinner below? I think it'll be more comfortable down there."

"Good idea," Dan said. He wrapped his arm around Christy's shoulders as they went below deck to the private dining room, where a table had been set for them.

A young man appeared dressed neatly in a server's uniform. "We've prepared lobster. I believe the captain said he spoke with you about the meal, sir?"

Dan nodded. "I told him we'd enjoy lobster." He looked across the cozy table at Christy. "That okay with you?"

"More than okay. This is a fantastic treat."

As expensive as lobster had become, she rarely dined on it. As the server delivered their meal, Christy knew this would be the one of the best meals of her life because the afternoon had been so special.

Goblets of lemon water were placed before them, followed by salad and bread.

"You did a wonderful job ordering this meal," Christy said, looking at Dan.

"Thanks. I met the captain last week when I was over here wandering around."

"My compliments to the chef—and to you. But Dan, you must

have spent a fortune renting the boat and ordering a lobster dinner! I really do appreciate it." She squeezed his hand.

"My pleasure. I consider it a very good investment."

The server appeared again, holding huge blue plates, and gently placed one before her. Slices of lemon, parsley, and drawn butter graced the plate of lobster.

"A meal like this deserves grace," Christy said, and offered a quick one.

Their appetite had been whetted by fresh Gulf breezes and long spaces of quiet serenity as they lost themselves in the seascape surrounding them. The boat rocked lightly but not enough to affect their dinner. When they had finished and the dishes were removed from the table, the captain sent word that he had headed back to shore since the wind was gaining momentum.

"That's fine with me," Dan said to Christy. "I'm glad you don't get seasick."

"I never have, but that doesn't mean I'm immune to it if a boat got too rocky."

By the time they reached shore, the wind had died down again. Lights twinkled through the velvety darkness as the boat docked, and they climbed back onto the boardwalk. Christy felt weak-kneed. Even Dan needed to pause and stretch.

They walked in silence to her car, their souls bathed in contentment.

"So you'll buy the boat?" she asked.

"Yes, if you come with me."

"When I can," she replied noncommittally. She turned to him.

"Thanks so much, Dan." She didn't tell him what she had learned from Donna. She simply stepped forward, put her arms around his neck, and gave him a kiss he wasn't likely to forget.

For one wonderful evening, they hadn't talked about Bobbie or the blues she had cast upon them.

twenty-five

Wednesday

The phone rang somewhere in the depths of Christy's dream. She rolled over and frowned at the clock. Seven thirty. She fumbled for the phone and breathed a sleepy hello.

"Good morning, Christy." Bobbie's voice sounded too cheerful for this early in the morning. "My moving van left Memphis early this morning, and I called Hornsby late yesterday to ask if he has another unit he'd rent me. I'd like to keep all my things in one place. It's less hassle."

Christy sat up against the pillow and rubbed her eyes, trying to follow the conversation.

"Naturally he's reluctant to rent anything to me, but he said he'd rent to you. So…" Bobbie's voice filled with apology.

"You want me to rent a unit?" Christy asked.

"Hornsby says the guy directly behind me vacated his ten-by-twenty yesterday," Bobbie said. "I can have that one, but we'd have to put it in your name. Is that okay?"

Tony Panada had vacated his unit. *Interesting,* Christy thought.

Bobbie rushed on. "The moving van will come to my shop first, and after they unload here, I can send them out there to store the furniture for my house, as soon as I find one."

"Okay," Christy said. "I'll take care of it."

"Oh, thank you so much, sweetie. Talk to you later."

Christy got dressed, putting on old jeans and a sweatshirt in keeping with renting a dusty storage unit. She dumped out the contents of her leather purse and filled up her tan, fringed slouch bag. She made sure she had her checkbook. Unlike Bobbie, she did not carry hundred dollar bills around.

She heard a car in the driveway and ran to the door. A weary-looking Seth trudged up the driveway. "I listened to your message when I got in, but it was late."

"Glad I wasn't depending on you," she said, although she had completely forgotten the scare of Monday night.

"Hey, watch it. I'm dependable now. For your information, I was working last night."

"Working?" She looked him over. His hair had been pulled into a ponytail, and he wore dark pants and a white shirt with the name of a popular restaurant stitched onto it. "Good for you," she said. She hugged him and got a whiff of fried oil.

"Yeah, I got my old job back. I worked the evening shift last night, but I'm going in for the day shift today. Why'd you call? Anything wrong?" His brown eyes were tired but concerned.

"No. I ended up going on an evening cruise with Dan."

Seth smiled. "Good."

"Listen, I'm on an errand for Bobbie, and I've gotta run."

"Me too."

"Hey, I'm proud of you," she called after him as he trotted back to his car.

She smiled as he roared off, then unlocked her car and hopped in. As she drove toward the storage units, her memory flashed back to the previous evening with Dan. The boat ride had done wonders for her nerves, and his generous gesture of renting the boat and ordering the fancy meal went a long way toward knocking down her resolve to keep a lid on her feelings. She was in love, and it felt good.

Christy slowed down as she reached the storage facility, noticing the freshly spread gravel in the parking area. She eased into the lot and coasted to a stop before the office.

Apprehension crawled over her at being forced back to the scene of the crime. Still, she had promised Bobbie, so she might as well get the job done.

The office door was open so Hornsby could have a clear view of his domain. Christy thought she saw him flinch as she stepped over the threshold. A contract lay atop the desk clutter, and Hornsby shook his dark head as she sat in the uncomfortable chair opposite him.

"I know, you wish you'd never seen us," Christy said, "but just remember, I'm not responsible for other people's actions."

He made a barely audible humph as he glanced from the contract to her. "I understand *you* are renting a unit, and if anybody asks me, this is *your* stuff."

"Okay," she said lightly, making a mental note that Hornsby's arm could be easily twisted. She thought of something. "Who rented my aunt's unit before she did?"

His head jerked up, the question catching him completely off guard. She could see he wasn't a multitasker, in his work or in his thoughts.

"Why do you ask?" he shot back.

"I'm wondering if someone got their units mixed up."

"Like maybe someone just happened to have the right key to your aunt's padlock, and that someone dragged Bodine in there and killed him."

He reached back and yanked open a drawer of his filing cabinet labeled Former Tenants. She could see he was determined to make a point, so she allowed him to sort through his alphabetized list until he found what he wanted.

He yanked a file out and waved it at her. "Miss Theola Winters, resident of Sunny View Nursing Home, stored her furniture here for three years. She died last month, and her daughter cleaned out the unit." He plopped the file on the desk and arched a dark brow at Christy. "Now it's possible that Miss T could have come back to haunt us, floated through the walls and—"

"Never mind," Christy snapped. "Put Miss Theola back in her drawer, and may she rest in peace. It was just a theory. I'm here to pay you for the vacant unit behind Bobbie's."

"Good," he said, heaving a sigh. "The only reason I'm doing this is because this mess has hurt my business and—"

"Hornsby, is this your only vacant unit?"

He hesitated, hating to concede the enjoyment of making his point.

"Then be glad you're renting it quick and easy and that the only tenant you lost was Mr. Panada." She paused. "Why did he move out in such a hurry?"

"It wasn't in 'such a hurry,' as you put it. Mr. Panada got a special price for ordering a truckload of paper. Naturally, he couldn't house it all in his printing office downtown, so he stored the extra boxes of paper here. He has a thriving business, and this week he needed the rest of the paper. Afterward, he had no use for the unit."

She couldn't argue with that, but her instincts told her something was off about Panada and his storage unit. Why didn't he store the paper in a unit closer to his shop?

Hornsby clicked a ballpoint pen and handed her the contract.

"Before I sign, I'd like to see the unit," Christy said.

For a moment, she watched him waver. He wanted to be sarcastic, but the money forced him to be polite.

"The moving van will be here today," she continued, "and I just want to see how to arrange the furniture."

"Fair enough," he said, standing up. "Follow me."

As they walked, Hornsby glanced sideways at her. "What's your aunt planning to do now?" he asked. She noticed he had replaced the torn shorts with navy ones and his shirt looked fresh. He was ready for the press, if necessary, and no doubt he'd already spent countless hours being interviewed by the sheriff's office.

"Bobbie's working with her attorney," she answered. "She's telling him the truth about everything that happened from the time we rented this unit until the day Deputy Arnold interrupted her demonstration at the Red Hat club."

"Demonstration?" he asked.

"She gave a speech, showing how she turns trash into treasure, items of junk into objects of beauty. She turned a back-porch post from my grandparents' farm—paint-chipped and seemingly use-less—into a stunning coatrack. In other words, she makes old things into useful things again."

"Like turning a pickle barrel into a coffin."

Christy stopped in her tracks, which happened to be in a puddle. She glared at him. "That was uncalled for," she said in her meanest tone.

"Sorry." He shook his head. "Couldn't resist. At least I'm not calling the corpse a pretzel. The joke around town is that Bodine looked like a thrown-away pretzel and—"

"That does it!" Christy snapped. "I'm not renting this unit."

He grabbed her arm. "Hey, I'm sorry. Considering all the pain I've been through, let me have the first laugh I've had all day."

Christy looked coolly into his weary eyes, which seemed to have sunk a notch. "I don't mind you having a laugh, but I don't appreciate you having one at our expense."

"I won't do it again."

"I'll accept your apology if you'll answer a question for me."

They reached the backside of the units. "What is it?"

"When you went in that…that foul-smelling unit, did it look

like there had been a struggle?" Christy asked. "That maybe Bodine fought for his life?"

"Nope." He scratched his head. "I could see the jack handle lying in the middle of the floor, but other than that, nothing looked out of place. When I followed the smell to the barrel…there he was."

Christy grimaced at his explanation. "Hornsby." He turned to her, and she faced him with her hands on her hips and a piercing gaze in her blue eyes. "Have you heard the theory that Bobbie was framed?"

He nodded. "I heard it. And I've been thinking about our conversation concerning those bookies being after him. Or some of their errand boys. I'm inclined to agree with you." He sighed, glancing around to see who might be listening. An older man a safe distance away unloaded a couple of patio chairs from his truck. "That little woman just didn't look like she'd do such a thing. I'd bet money she couldn't have done it alone."

Christy frowned, troubled by his words.

"Another thing," Hornsby continued, on a roll now. "I pointed this out to the police. That padlock had a couple of fresh scratches around the lock. I know locks, and if I had to make a guess, I'd say someone either tried to pick the lock or actually did pick it."

She smiled, cheered by the possibility. "Thanks, Hornsby. I'm starting to like you better all the time."

They arrived at the open door of the unit Tony Panada had vacated. At first glance, the unit was clean and neat, identical to the one Bobbie had rented. Christy walked in, looking right and left.

Metal walls enclosed three sides, and the concrete floor looked clean. "He didn't keep this unit long, did he?" she asked. "It looks as though it's hardly been used."

"No, he didn't stay long. But I always sweep and spray the units after every occupant moves out."

She nodded. It soon became clear why he had consented to rent this unit to her. The smell of heavy deodorizers drifted from Bobbie's unit. She realized Hornsby must have worked overtime spraying the unit or had hired a professional outfit to do it.

Trying not to sneeze from the strong deodorizers, she glanced toward the end wall that separated the units. On the other side of that wall, Eddie Bodine had been murdered. If only walls could talk. Christy took a step forward, her mind replaying the horrible scene, and saw a hole. About four feet from the bottom of the wall was an irregular-shaped hole. It was old, she decided, seeing rust stains around it, and it looked as though it had been cut by some sort of instrument or tool.

"I don't remember seeing that hole when we rented the other unit," she said, pointing.

"You two didn't stay in there long enough to see anything except the size," Hornsby countered.

"What happened? Why is the hole there?"

Hornsby glanced at it. "Miss T, the woman who rented the other unit before your aunt, had it piled high with junk. Something poked that hole in the wall, but before I could patch it, Panada rented this one just as it was. Is it a problem now?" He looked at her, a hint of annoyance rising in his sharp gaze.

"No, not a problem," she said. She leaned down to peer through the hole. She had a clear view of Bobbie's other unit, and knowing what had taken place there gave her a chill. She straightened and turned to Hornsby.

He watched her carefully, a wary expression on his face, as though he was trying to read her mind. She decided not to tip her hand.

"The hole won't be a problem. We can just push furniture up against it." She clapped her hands together, ridding them of dust. "Okay, let's sign that contract, and I'll write you a check."

Hornsby nodded. "I'll leave these metal doors open to air it out."

She could almost hear his covert sigh of relief as they walked outside.

Once she'd signed the contract and written the check, she snapped her fingers as though remembering something. "I need to see where to place that king-size bed and dresser. I think there's enough room," she said innocently, "but I don't want to waste time when we're paying those moving guys by the hour."

"Yeah." Hornsby chuckled, sticking the check in a drawer. "They'll want to get in as many hours as they can. It's best to be prepared."

She sauntered back to her newly rented unit and walked straight to the back. She leaned over and peered into the hole again, taking more time to look things over. She had a perfect view into Bobbie's unit. The pickle barrel was gone—she hoped never to see it again, though she would probably see pieces of it in court, if her aunt's case came to trial.

Had Panada made the most of this odd hole? Had he heard the rumor of Bobbie stealing money from Eddie? Was he trying to figure out where she might hide it? Christy straightened, her eyes wide.

Surely the police had seen the hole. While they had checked out all the units, they had shown a particular interest in this one. Now she knew why. She felt certain Panada had been questioned about the mysterious hole.

Then something else occurred to her. Harry Stephens had indicated that he had not yet been through what lawyers call discovery, when the prosecution would have to reveal their witness list. Her hopes sank. Maybe Tony Panada was their secret witness.

She turned and hurried out of the unit, waving good-bye to Hornsby as she walked to her car. All the way home, the idea of Panada as a witness for the prosecution worried her. Harry Stephens had to find out.

❧

By the time she arrived home and walked into the kitchen, a loud growl from her stomach reminded her she hadn't eaten. Pancakes sounded good, so she washed her hands and began to prepare a late breakfast.

She was flipping the second pancake in her iron skillet when a horn blasted from the driveway. A deep, big-boy horn. Frowning, she turned off the burner and laid the spatula on a plate. Then she unlocked the front door and stepped onto the porch.

A moving van had tried to pull into her driveway, driving over in the grass on each side of the concrete drive.

An older man with a sweaty face thrust his round, mostly bald head out the window. "This street is pretty narrow. I don't have enough space to back the truck in."

Christy walked out to the moving van and the two guys perched high within. "You're at the wrong address. Are you looking for Bobbie Bodine?"

"Yes ma'am, and this is the address we was given." He waved a rumpled sheet of paper at her.

"She did live here, but now she's at my parents' home."

"So where do they live?"

Christy shook her head. "The furniture goes to her shop and then her storage unit. But first let me call her."

It had become a habit to stick her cell phone in her pocket—after all, a cell phone in her jeans pocket had once saved her life. She pulled it out and dialed her aunt's number.

"Hello!" Bobbie sounded as excited as a debutante at her first dance. No one could possibly imagine, hearing this happy voice, that she had been arrested for murder and released on bail.

"Bobbie, a moving van is parked in my driveway ready to unload," Christy said, trying to control her irritation.

"Oh, for heaven's sake. They were supposed to call me and meet me at the shop. I'll send them out to the storage units once they're finished at the shop, which should take two or three hours.

Maybe Beth can go out to the storage unit. I don't know if I should be seen out there."

"Mom has to be at the shop today," Christy said. "She's expecting some ladies from Tupelo."

"Oh…well, could I impose on you one more time?"

Christy sighed. "You want me to go out to the unit with those guys and tell them where to put things. Okay. I think I have an extra padlock in my dresser drawer."

"Great. I'll have them stepping fast because I'm paying by the hour. I'd love for you to come by and give me some opinions, but if you're busy, I'll call you when they leave the shop."

"I'll be down later." Christy said good-bye and hung up.

"Well?" The driver looked tired and out of sorts.

"Guys, go back into Summer Breeze—just follow that street north." She pointed to the street that paralleled hers. "Stay on it through town till you reach the corner of Breezeway and Palm. It's the shop on the corner. You'll have plenty of room to turn around since it's on the corner."

He huffed a big sigh and pulled his head back into the cab.

The little guy on the other side, who'd been so quiet she thought he was dozing, leaned forward and stared at her. "Is this the town where Eddie Bodine bought it?"

Christy flinched, drawing herself up to her full five feet three, barefoot. "He died in this area, yes."

"I used to see him down at the gym, working out. Nobody liked him," the little guy said.

Was that supposed to make her feel better? Christy wondered.

The driver leaned back out his window. "Did Bobbie really do him in?"

Christy stepped back from the truck, frowning at both men. "No, she did not. The bookies got him." She watched two sets of jaws drop.

"No…" The little guy mumbled something Christy couldn't hear and probably didn't want to hear.

"She's waiting," she snapped, then turned and marched back up to the house.

As she went inside and locked the door, irritation tugged at her like a puppy yanking on a pant leg. She never seemed to have time to do the things she needed to do for herself. Like eating pancakes for breakfast. Well, today she would.

As she took the pancakes to the eating bar, she realized that her life, and that of her parents, had been consumed with taking care of Bobbie lately. Maybe things would change when Bobbie was settled and Harry Stephens proved she was innocent.

The warm, syrupy pancakes almost made up for Christy's hectic morning. As she finished the last bite and drained her milk, she felt fortified to deal with the rest of the day. She rinsed her dishes and put them in the dishwasher, then turned down the hall to her bedroom.

She slowed at the door to her office and cast a longing glance toward her computer. Ten chapters of her new manuscript lay stacked neatly in a drawer. She sighed. When was she going to get back to work? She needed to have boundaries in her life, for herself and others. People seemed to forget that writing was her job, her income. Her mother hadn't closed her shop, and her father certainly hadn't abandoned his job. While this was a personal investigation involving her aunt, Bobbie had come to expect Christy to be at her beck and call.

Christy walked on, determined to be more assertive. She must start using the word *no*, which had been missing from her conversations with Bobbie.

As she faced her reflection in the dresser mirror, whisking her hair back in a ponytail, she thought she recognized the exasperation in her eyes. She had seen it in her mother's eyes when Christy was growing up. Winding the rubber band around her hair, she began to get a clearer picture of her mother's childhood. She wondered how many little favors Bobbie had asked of sweet Beth. How many times had Beth watched her sister make choices and then find ways to avoid the consequences?

The word *choices* filled the screen of Christy's mind, like huge white letters on a blackboard.

Her bedside phone rang again, and she steeled herself for one more request from her aunt.

"Christy," the voice on the other end said, "it's Roseann Cole. Eddie lied about leaving his insurance money to me. Guess who gets it? Your innocent little aunt. Apparently, he never got around to changing the beneficiary, as much as he claimed to hate her."

"Oh no," Christy said, thinking this was one more strike against Bobbie.

"Oh yes. And those guys in the black Mercedes have been following me for two days. They even parked down the street from my house. Momma and I got away from them and left Memphis yesterday."

"Why didn't you call the police?"

"You don't call the police when those guys are on your tail. You run. Eddie was right. They're dangerous."

"So where are you now?"

"I'm in Summer Breeze, but I'm not staying at the Starlight this time. I'm down the road at the Breezeway Motel, me and Momma. I don't have much money. Your aunt's got a lot of money. She needs to be a little more generous. All this is her fault anyway."

Christy bridled. "No, it isn't. I'm sorry for what's happened to you, but I don't think my aunt needs to give you money."

"If she doesn't, I may be killed," Roseann snapped. "None of this would have happened if Eddie hadn't come here looking for that missing ten grand."

Christy sighed. "Okay, you've made your point. Do you think those guys followed you here?"

"No, I'm traveling in a car they don't recognize. They're still looking for Eddie's truck."

"Why are they after you, Roseann? Do they think you have the money?"

"Yeah, and they think I've got Eddie's little black book with the numbers of all the bookies and who knows what else in it. But I don't have it, and I don't know what he did with it."

Christy bit her lip. "Okay. I'll see what I can do. What room are you in?"

Roseann hesitated.

"I'm trying to help," Christy said.

"Room 118."

"Okay. Be careful."

Christy heard a noise in the background, and Roseann told someone to turn on the television. The phone clicked in her ear.

Christy jumped up and began to pace the floor. As much as she hated to face it, Bobbie looked guiltier every minute. Did she know Eddie's life insurance policy was in her name? Did she take his money and run, bringing down the Mafia and who knew what else on Summer Breeze? On her family?

Christy ran out the door and jumped in her car, watching every vehicle, every side street, for the black Mercedes. No strange cars yet.

She whirled down the street to the shop and double-parked beside Jack's SUV. Grabbing her purse, she ran into the shop, where Bobbie was happily instructing the sweaty movers where to place a huge gilded mirror.

"And be careful," Bobbie warned. "You know the old saying— break a mirror and get seven years of bad luck. With one that size, I'd say twenty-one years!" A laugh rolled from her lips, but the movers did not look amused.

Bobbie noticed Christy and hurried over. "Here, honey." She reached into her pocket and withdrew a key. "I had an extra made for you in case you need to get in the other unit." For a moment her expression saddened as she placed the key in Christy's hand.

Bobbie took a deep breath and glanced at the object nearby. "Look at this," she said, obviously wanting to change the subject.

Christy stared blankly at a teacart Bobbie had loaded with china cups of all sizes and shapes and an assortment of teapots.

"I converted that cart from a rusted, thrown-away baby carriage," Bobbie said proudly.

If Christy had felt more supportive, she might have marveled at Bobbie's talent. In her present state of mind, however, she was in no mood to appreciate talent or humor. She glanced toward the back room, where Jack was putting up shelves to hold cans of paint.

"The people who own the ice cream shop walked down to welcome me. Isn't that nice?" Bobbie asked.

"Very nice," Christy said, wondering how many others she'd have to bribe.

"They were really impressed with my treasures," she said. Then her big blue eyes searched Christy's face. "What's wrong, honey?"

"For starters, Roseann Cole and her momma are in town. The guys in the black Mercedes are after *her* now. They think she has the money along with some information Eddie might have given her."

Bobbie frowned. "But what are we supposed to do?"

Christy sighed. "She needs money. Do you think we should help her out?"

The warmth in Bobbie's blue eyes faded. "I can't believe you're asking me such a question. I don't owe that woman one thing."

Christy glared at her. "Maybe you do. She's been through hell because of Eddie Bodine, and the only reason my parents and I are entangled in this is because he followed you here."

Bobbie stepped back from her, a look of shock and then defiance crossing her features. She walked over to her purse and withdrew several twenty dollar bills. "Give this to her," she said. "Then you needn't bother me with any more suggestions of charity for Roseann Cole."

"I have a question you've never answered," Christy said, Bobbie's cash clenched in her fist.

Bobbie headed for the back room but then stopped. She turned her head and looked over her shoulder at Christy. "What's the question?"

"Where were you from eleven thirty until one o'clock on Monday night?"

twenty-six

B obbie whirled to face Christy, her blue eyes widened in shock. Without a reply, she picked up her bulging purse. She reached inside, and Christy stood motionless for a second, wondering what secret nestled in that purse, a secret that would account for the lapse of an hour and a half.

Bobbie pulled out a small slip of paper folded in a neat square and handed it to Christy. She opened the paper and read *Mary Dixon,* a name she didn't recognize, along with a phone number with a local prefix.

"Ask *her,*" Bobbie said. She turned on her heel and walked away.

Christy stared after her. What if this woman admitted she'd picked Bobbie up and driven her someplace to meet Eddie? Was her aunt that confident Christy wouldn't go to the authorities if Mary Dixon incriminated Bobbie?

Christy had to get out of the shop; she had to breathe fresh air. She folded the paper and shoved it in her pocket, then turned to the movers heading back to the truck for more "treasures."

"How long before you're ready to head out to the storage unit?" she asked.

The big guy looked around the crowded shop. "Thirty minutes."

She nodded. "I'll meet you there. It'll be the first unit on the backside." Bobbie hadn't said thank you or good-bye, and Christy stomped out of the shop, fighting tears. She stuffed Bobbie's money in her purse, then reached in her billfold and added more money to Roseann's pile.

Something began to jell in her mind, something she didn't want to believe. The list of suspects had narrowed, and Bobbie had moved to the top.

⌒∞⌒

Christy sped to the Breezeway Motel, looking in the side- and rearview mirrors of her car for a black Mercedes with a Tennessee tag. She glanced around her little town of colorful shop awnings and hanging baskets of flowers on lampposts. At the park, children played and dogs dozed in the sun. Everything seemed normal in Summer Breeze, but the knowledge Christy carried in her brain and in her pocket burned like a white-hot fire in her stomach.

Five minutes later, she turned into the parking lot of the motel. She didn't recognize any of the cars in the parking lot, so she tried to clear her head and summon a bit of logic. Roseann had said room 118.

She found the room at the far end. She knocked softly on the door, and a woman's harsh voice called out. "Who is it?"

"Christy Castleman. I'm a friend of Roseann's."

The door jerked open, and she faced a dumpy-looking woman with an older, fatigued face and a pile of auburn hair drifting loose from the knot on top of her head. So this was the woman who read tarot cards and warned of danger.

"May I speak to Roseann?" Christy asked politely.

"I'm Juanita, her mother. She's gone for takeout at that hamburger joint down the road. Come on in."

Christy stepped inside the room and closed the door. Purses and overnight bags were piled haphazardly about the room. The long dresser held a carton of Cokes, unopened, and several packs of peanut butter crackers. One bed was turned back, and Juanita sank onto it.

"I'm not feeling well," she said. "We've been driving for hours, and I'm stressed and have a heart condition."

"Oh?" Christy took a step toward her, concerned. On the nightstand beside the bed, a glass of water sat next to a bottle of pills.

"Nitroglycerin is supposed to help certain heart conditions," Christy said on a hunch, squinting to read the prescription bottle.

Juanita turned on her side, her arm crooked around the end of the pillow. "That's what I take. They cost a fortune."

"My aunt misplaces hers all the time."

"Yeah, so do I."

She looked at the other bed. A porcelain doll with red hair and round blue eyes perched against the pillow. Her yellow dress fanned out on the floral bedspread. Black Mary Janes covered her feet. Christy stared at the doll, curious about the world Roseann inhabited. In the center of the bed, the September issue of a popular fashion magazine had been left open.

Christy looked at Juanita, whose eyes were closed as though she were about to doze off, and then at the pill bottle. Was it possible?

She looked at her watch. Thirty minutes had zipped by, and she had to go. Juanita didn't look like she would miss her, and Christy didn't know how long Roseann would be gone. She walked to the door. "I have to meet a moving van out at the storage unit, but will you please tell Roseann I'll come by later?"

Juanita nodded, her eyes still closed. "Are you moving?"

"No, just storing some furniture."

"Mmm."

Christy decided not to leave the cash. Juanita didn't look as though she would remember to tell Roseann. "I hope you feel better," Christy said. She walked out and gently closed the door.

She gave the parking lot one last glance but saw no suspicious cars. Nor did she see Roseann. She got in her car and drove out to the storage units, her mind in a daze.

Roseann had access to nitroglycerin. And last Monday night she believed she was the beneficiary of Eddie's life insurance money. Did she kill him? Christy frowned. Maybe the nitroglycerin was just a coincidence. But then, she reminded herself, she didn't believe in coincidences.

When she pulled into the parking lot, she saw that Hornsby's truck was gone. She parked and got out, spotting the note on his door. "Back in twenty minutes." She smiled, thinking that was a good way to goof off because he didn't say what time he'd left.

She heard the groan of the moving van and got in her car, motioning them to follow her around to the back. She parked three units down so there would be plenty of room for the van to unload, then grabbed the padlock and key she had brought from home.

The movers studied the empty unit, sizing up the space. "We better get busy," the big man said to the little guy lagging behind.

"Listen, you guys," Christy said, walking up to them. "Was there a vacuum cleaner on this van?"

They exchanged glances. The big guy heaved a huge sigh. "It got taken off the van by a couple of Memphis cops. Or so I heard."

She nodded, looking from one man to the other. They both looked exhausted. "How about if I run down to the service station and pick up some Powerade for you guys? That always gives me energy."

"That'd be great, ma'am."

"Want some candy bars or cheese crackers?"

"No ma'am. We'll get a square meal once we're finished here."

"Okay, I'll be right back." Christy hesitated. "Could you guys leave that little peephole in the back wall uncovered?" When they agreed, she walked back to her car and got in, thinking about the vacuum cleaner.

So it had been dusted for fingerprints, thoroughly searched, and kept. Was it more incriminating evidence against her aunt? Did a new vacuum cleaner bag bear her fingerprints?

Christy's eyes narrowed as she turned onto the highway. When she finished at the storage units, she would call a meeting at her parents' home.

The slip of paper with the name lay in her pocket, the missing piece to an important puzzle. She wasn't looking forward to checking out the name and number. Maybe she didn't want to know. The change she had seen in Bobbie this morning reminded her of a question Dan had asked: *"How well do you really know Bobbie?"*

The memory of Dan and their sunset cruise brought a momentary escape from the tension surrounding her like smoke from a forest fire—a fire closing in on her. Whatever happened with Bobbie, Christy intended to have a life again, hopefully with Dan.

She arrived at the service station and rushed inside, gathered up several Powerades, and paid the attendant. When she returned to the storage facility, the office was still locked, and on this Wednesday afternoon, there was little activity around the units. She drove to the back and parked, then carried an armload of energy drinks toward the moving van.

The guys were grateful for the Powerade, and when she saw what they had accomplished, she knew her quick dash for drinks had paid off. They had fitted armoires, tables, a sofa, and chairs into the unit better than she could have advised them.

While they worked, Christy grabbed a bottle of the energy drink for herself and sauntered around to the front of the building. There was no one in sight, so she reached in her pocket for the extra key Bobbie had given her and inserted it into the padlock.

She thought Hornsby had told her the police still didn't want anyone in or out, but glancing about, she decided to take a chance. She unlocked the door and slowly rolled it up. The smell of deodorizers was even stronger here. She stepped inside and, as an afterthought, pulled down the door.

She could see traces of a thorough investigation. Dark spots showed where the area had been dusted for fingerprints. Reluctantly, her eyes moved toward the spot where the sixty-gallon barrel had stood. Where Eddie had died.

At that moment, Christy knew she had to do the right thing, whatever it cost her family emotionally or financially. She tried to live by the commandments instilled in her by her father, and one in particular filled her mind now. You did not take another's life.

Resigned to the task, she pulled out the slip of paper, unfolded it, and punched the number into her cell phone.

When the woman's voice answered, Christy hesitated, then plunged in. "Hi, my name is Christy Castleman."

"You're Bobbie's niece. She talks about you all the time."

Christy swallowed. "Yes. I didn't realize she had friends here."

Mary Dixon sighed. "She doesn't have enough friends at a time like this. I've been so worried about her. We've talked every day. Did she want me to call her now?"

"Actually, no. She just wanted me to ask you about… Did you see her late Monday night?"

"No," Mary said, "but we talked on the phone for a while. She called me from your parents' house."

"Would you tell me about that? I…really need to know so I can understand what Bobbie's trying to…explain."

"First, I have to ask what she's told you about her personal life."

"You mean with Eddie Bodine?" Christy asked.

"No, I mean personal habits, good or bad."

"Oh. Are you referring to alcohol?"

"Yes."

"I know she's a recovering alcoholic and that she attends AA here," Christy said.

"That's right," Mary said. "And I'm her sponsor."

Christy shoved a box aside and sat on one of the planks covering the floor. Mary's words brought tears to her eyes. She realized how much she loved Bobbie and hadn't wanted to believe her own awful suspicions.

"She came in from her date with Jack on Monday night," Mary continued, "and sat in your parents' den, just thinking, I suppose. She called me about eleven forty. I'm a night owl, so she knew I'd still be up. She needed to talk, and I don't betray a confidence."

"That's fine, Ms. Dixon. You don't have to. She called you at eleven forty from my parents' home?" Christy questioned, wanting to be sure of the details.

"That's right," Mary said. "Their number showed up on my caller ID. I was prepared to go to the police and tell them, but she said her sister heard her come in and could testify that she was home if…this darn case goes to trial."

"Thank you so much. And by the way, Jack's a great guy."

"Yes, I knew from the way Bobbie spoke about him that night. Even though she's afraid to love again, she's met someone who gives her hope. I told her one has to be brave in life. My husband is a sailor, and we sail almost every weekend. He once told me the safest place for a boat may be the slip we rent at the marina, but boats weren't built to stay in a slip. We have to keep trying, keep hoping. That's what I told Bobbie that night."

Christy sniffed, suddenly aware of the sounds of the men in the other unit and the fact that she should get back. "Thanks so much," she said. "I have to run now. You sound like a wonderful friend. I'm glad my aunt knows you."

"And it's my pleasure to know her."

Christy slipped the phone back in her pocket, along with the slip of paper with Mary Dixon's name on it. She blinked, realizing she was staring at the boxes she and Bobbie had left here last Monday. The tops were open, the contents searched by the police. She hadn't expected the jack handle to be here, and of course it wasn't. What else had they taken for evidence? She didn't touch anything but walked to the back of the unit, leaned down, and looked through the hole.

The movers had stopped for a minute, taking deep gulps of the drinks she had bought them. It was as easy to see into that unit as it had been to look into this one.

The hole was not freshly drilled but had already been there when Panada took the unit. She visualized him kneeling down, peeking through the hole, taking pictures perhaps. But what was there to photograph? Maybe he'd known there was going to be a murder and he was filming it for someone. If the Mafia had hired the men in the black Mercedes, maybe they wanted proof that their henchmen didn't find the money and pocket it and that Eddie was out of the picture.

It was all that made sense to her, and it led her straight back to Houston Downey and Joe Panada and the comment she had overheard in the restaurant: *"Bodine knew better than…"*

Better than what? Not to pay up? To lie about the money? Both?

She turned around and studied the unit from the back vantage point. The flaps of one of the boxes sagged, and Christy realized some of its contents had been removed.

She peered inside, seeing books and magazines. Why would the police take a book or magazine? She knelt by the box, taking a sip of her energy drink before she capped it. On the top of the box and inside it, she saw more evidence of dusting for fingerprints. Surely they didn't think her aunt would hide money in a cardboard box and leave it in a storage unit.

Curious, she lifted out the three magazines remaining and looked at the books. *Furniture Refinishing*. She held the book up and shook the pages. Nothing fell out but a fringed bookmark. No money. She laid it down and picked up *Making Old Things New* and repeated the process, shaking hard. This time not even a bookmark fell out. She considered the book on the bottom, the heaviest—but what was she thinking? If there had been money in any of these items, the police would have taken it for evidence. Just in case, she shook the heavy book. Nothing fell out. She read the cover. *Hope for Alcoholics*.

Christy stared at the book, longing to talk to Bobbie, to tell her she knew she was innocent, that she had been framed. She replaced the books and magazines, wondering what was missing.

Wait a minute. She had carried this box in herself. She recalled glancing through the flap on top of the box and seeing a glamorous blonde looking back at her from the cover of a fashion magazine.

She frowned. That fashion magazine on Roseann's bed...wasn't there a blonde on the cover? Was she jumping to conclusions? She recalled the lesson she'd learned when she had suspected Tony Panada of being Searcy Jance. Lots of people were buying the new fall fashion magazines, and it made sense Roseann would.

Christy walked back and peered through the hole. The movers were wrestling a cherry armoire against a side wall. The unit was almost full, and she suspected they were finishing up.

She heard Hornsby's truck pulling in next door. She froze, knowing she shouldn't be in here. At least she'd pulled the door down. She heard the office door unlock and then the accompanying slam of doors, and she realized how thin the walls were. If only he had been here that night! But of course, he locked his office at five even though the gates remained open until one.

She could hear him on the phone now. With the door closed, the metal unit would soon feel like an oven if she didn't roll up the door and get some air. She glanced at her watch—ten minutes till five—and wiped away the perspiration gathering on her forehead. Hornsby would leave at five. She'd just have to stay in here until then.

Uncomfortable in the heat, she suddenly thought of Eddie Bodine. What had he gone through before he died? As Hornsby had said, there were no signs of struggle. Eddie must have convinced whoever brought him here that the money was hidden in this unit. And that person had already planned to kill Eddie once the money was located because his system had been filled with the poisonous mixture of drugs. When there was no vacuum cleaner, that person had become angry, struck him in the head with the jack handle, and shoved him in the pickle barrel. The abundance of alcohol he had drunk worked with the drugs to finish him off.

She stared at the empty spot where the barrel had been. How long had he been in there before he died? No matter what Eddie Bodine had done, he didn't deserve to die like that.

The cell phone jangled in her pocket, and she opened it quickly before Hornsby could hear. She slipped to the back of the unit where the guys were making a lot of noise on the other side.

"Yes?" An impatient hello, but she had lost her manners in the heat and stress of hiding.

"Christy, it's Roseann. I thought you were bringing money."

"I did. But your mother was half-asleep, so I told her I'd come back after these guys finished unloading."

"Are you moving?" Roseann asked, just as her mother had.

"Just storing some stuff. Well, I'm not actually in that unit. I'm in…the other one."

"What are you doing there?"

Christy realized Hornsby had stopped talking next door. Had he heard her? "I gotta go. I'll call you later," she whispered and hung up.

Hornsby would be leaving in five more minutes. She didn't want him to catch her here.

"Hey, ma'am."

Christy whirled to see a big eye on the other side of the hole in the wall. "We're ready to go. Could we use your phone? Just got one question for the little lady."

Nodding, she opened her phone and dialed her aunt, then wedged her cell through the irregular-shaped hole.

"Why are you whispering?" he asked.

"I don't want the manager to know I'm in this unit. He's in his office, but he'll be leaving soon," she whispered. "Tell Bobbie I'll be back to the shop in a few minutes."

He nodded, then spoke into the phone. "Miss Bobbie!" Christy watched his broad back lumber toward the front of the unit as he talked. Then the metal door rolled down.

"Wait!" she called after him as loud as she dared. The men were so tired and rushed, they forgot to return her phone. Well, she'd get it from him as soon as she reached Bobbie's shop.

She could hear the moving van's engine fire up and the crunch of gravel as it drove off.

The phone rang in Hornsby's office.

He answered in his usual tone, and then suddenly his voice changed, and he began yelling. "Listen, Panada, I've done enough for you. Don't expect more."

At the mention of Panada, Christy rushed back toward the metal wall. Her foot caught the end of a plank and she tripped, grabbing a box to steady herself. A thud echoed across the metal interior. Had he heard her? Her breath jerked in her chest, but she leaned closer to the section of the wall that she thought paralleled his desk.

"You may be a witness in this frame-up," Hornsby yelled, "but you better plan on getting outta town as soon as they put the noose around the bombshell's neck. Those detectives stayed in your unit too long to be looking at an empty unit. I think they got curious about something you left behind."

There was a momentary silence followed by a loud curse.

"How would I know what it was? You told me you got your stuff out. You never told me to go over and check it out. You must have dropped one of your dirty little videos or one of the props you use filming them."

Christy cupped her palm over her nose and mouth to muffle a gasp and flurry of short breaths. She pressed her ear against the warm metal wall, straining to hear more.

"Don't threaten me. You and Joe may be cousins, but you've dug a hole for yourself by helping them out. I did what I was paid to do. That's it."

She heard the phone slam down, and a string of curses burned her ears. Christy froze against the wall, snatches of his conversation banging in her head. She lined the words up like plot points.

"*A witness in this frame-up.*" She looked at the hole in the back wall. Panada was the DA's ace in the hole.

"*Frame-up… Your dirty little videos… You and Joe may be cousins…*"

And the detectives were on to something. Maybe he filmed pornography back here. Maybe he sold pornography to minors.

But what had Hornsby been paid to do? Was he paid by Panada?

Christy thought back to last Monday when she and her aunt drove up to his office. Bobbie had plopped her purse on the counter and left it there while they went next door to examine the unit. Hornsby had gone back to get the contract while she and Bobbie lingered, sizing up the unit.

Did Hornsby snoop around in Bobbie's purse in those few minutes? Did he find the pills and concoct the perfect frame-up as he dumped some in a drawer?

Why would he do that? Had Joe Panada and Houston Downey followed Bobbie and Christy to this unit Monday morning? Had they called Hornsby just when they spotted Bobbie getting out of her truck? Did they tell him Eddie Bodine was chasing her, and Eddie had to die, so find a way to frame Bobbie for his murder?

A quick yet masterful plan. And Joe had Tony on the payroll to be sure things were handled right.

Or was Eddie looking over his shoulder at Hornsby rather than the guys in the Mercedes? Had Hornsby followed Eddie and Roseann across the street to the motel, knocked on the door, and grabbed Eddie while Roseann was in the shower? It would be a simple matter to offer him a drink and tell him he knew about the stolen money. That Bobbie had hidden it in her storage unit and he could take him to it...for a price. The scene unfolded in Christy's mind like a video on fast forward.

She hunkered down against the wall, gripping the cold drink in her hands.

Would he go around back and see her parked car? Would he come back to this unit and open the door? If he did, she would be trapped. Her eyes flew wildly around the unit. There was nowhere to hide unless she lay behind the boxes. Then she'd have to melt into the concrete floor not to be seen.

Maybe she should just make a break for it, say her aunt had sent her out to retrieve something. But Hornsby had just proven he was sharper than she'd given him credit for. When he heard her come out, he'd suspect she had overheard the conversation. If he was involved with Panada and the others, he wouldn't let her leave.

A drawer slammed—what was in the drawer? Then she counted his steps to the front door. She crawled over to stretch out behind the boxes, her arms flattened against the dirty concrete. Her breath jerked through her chest. She waited. Keys rattled in the lock of his front door.

She lay still, scarcely breathing as the screen door slammed. Silence. What was he thinking now? Which way was he looking? Had he decided to check out this unit again?

twenty-eight

The cool concrete floor dampened with her perspiration as Christy lay still, her ears strained for Hornsby's next movement. She could hear footsteps on gravel, then a truck door opening and closing. When she heard the engine start up, she moaned with relief. She waited until the sound of the truck's engine faded down the street before she moved.

She jumped up, weak-kneed, and wiped her perspiring face. She had to get out of here. She didn't want another close call like that one. Her mouth felt like the Sahara desert, and she looked around for the drink. Hobbling over to pick it up, she guzzled down a long swallow, then recapped it.

Where was her purse? She set the drink down on the floor and looked around.

Tires crunched gravel, a softer crunch. A tenant bringing something to their unit.

Christy let out another deep breath as she located her purse at the back of the unit near the hole. She peered through the hole one last time. The furniture had been neatly placed, honoring her request to leave the peephole free.

The door of the unit rolled up, and Christy whirled. Roseann stepped inside, pulling the door down behind her.

Christy tried to conceal her sudden anxiety. "Leave it open. I'm just walking out," she called.

"You'd better get your purse," Roseann said, pointing to the back wall.

Christy turned and reached down for her purse. Just as she straightened, something cracked against the back of her head, sending an explosion of pain through her. She saw stars, then darkness, as she crumpled.

When she came to, she had been dragged to a corner and set upright against the wall. Her hands were bound behind her, and her mouth was covered with duct tape. She tried to scream, but only a muffled sound came through the heavy tape.

"You lied to me about the money, didn't you?" Roseann asked, towering over her. On the floor at her feet lay one of the two-by-fours, which would account for the throbbing pain in Christy's head. She heard a click. Roseann held a switchblade knife, the blade pointed at Christy. A cry of fear died in her throat as she stared at the sharp blade.

God, help me!

Her mind screamed the plea while her lips moved uselessly beneath the gray duct tape. Behind her back, she twisted her wrists against the heavy binding. She had to break the binding and free her hands, or she would die without a fight.

Roseann moved closer, the switchblade pointed at Christy's neck. The sharp blade pricked her skin, and Christy felt a trickle of blood.

"You lied to me, just like Eddie lied to me about the insurance money. Why do people think they can keep using me and I'll just take it? That I won't fight back?"

Christy tried to reason with her, but the tape reduced her words to incoherent mumbles.

"I have one friend," Roseann said. "Only one friend. I'll let you meet her." Roseann sank to the floor, stretching out her long legs. In her lap, she held the doll Christy had seen in the motel room.

Christy stared at her. *She's crazy. She has to be. Why didn't I see it, or at least get a hint of it?*

"Millie's the only friend I can trust," Roseann said. "Let me show you why."

She removed the pearl choker, and Christy saw the crack in the doll's neck. Roseann twisted the doll's head, and it came off in her hand. Bills sprouted from the doll's neck. Roseann stuffed the money back in the body of the doll. As she did, she pushed down a vial of pills.

Christy felt sick. It all made sense now, but it was too late.

Roseann gave her a sly grin. "Momma and I watched a documentary on deadly combinations of medicines. You don't give nitroglycerin to a healthy heart, and you sure don't combine it with Viagra. I knew Eddie took Viagra."

A look of satisfaction settled over her face. "Momma said, 'If that Eddie ever stands you up again, I guess you'll know what to do.' And she was right. I knew exactly what to do. So I grabbed a handful of Momma's pills and put together my little mix here. Then I hid it in my lingerie drawer in case I needed it.

"I was sick of Eddie within a month, but I kept hoping his trucking company would pay off. And then I found out he lied about that. He was in hock up to his eyeballs. When he insisted on chasing after Bobbie, I left Millie home but brought my little mix along in case he mistreated me. He still loved Bobbie, even though he pretended he hated her. Every time he got drunk, he talked about her. That night at the Last Chance, I'd had it with him. When I told him to shut up about her or I'd leave him, he was just drunk enough to challenge me. 'Go ahead,' he said. 'I don't really love you.'

"I knew then what I would do. We'd already been out here to these units earlier, when he'd picked the lock to go in and snoop. We even left it unlocked so we could get back in later if we needed to. I pretended not to be hurt by what he said about not loving me. I just smiled at him, thinking in my head how much I hated him. 'I just thought of something,' I told him. 'We didn't look in the bottom of one of those boxes.' He said, 'You were supposed to look.' I said, 'Honey, I forgot.' Anyway, we went back to the motel so I could change out of my orange blouse and I wouldn't be so easy to see. After we got in the motel, he made it so easy for me. He wanted more ice cubes in his drink, and I was glad to freshen it up for him. I went in the bathroom, dumped the mix in his drink, reached into the bucket for ice, then stirred it up.

"He took his drink with him, too addled to notice the taste. By the time we got out here, he wasn't too observant. While he got out of the truck, I put on the gloves he kept under his seat. The unit was still unlocked, so I just pushed the metal door up and got him inside. 'Look, Eddie,' I said, pointing, 'there's a box down in the barrel.' When he walked over to look, I grabbed the jack handle and hit him in the back of the head. Then I shoved him in the barrel.

"I meant to wait for him to die, but I heard something and realized somebody was in the unit behind us. I had faith in the poisons, so I left. I drove the truck to the street behind the Blues Club and parked it. Then I walked to the motel."

Roseann sighed. "You want to know why I'm telling you this, don't you? Because in my whole life, I never did anything smart. I mean, I never did anything that other people considered smart. This was my masterpiece, but I couldn't tell anybody. Now I get to tell you, the smart mystery writer. But, sad thing is, you won't get to write about it."

She paused and studied Christy. "You look like you're dying to say something. I'm gonna loosen that tape around your mouth for just a minute. But if you start to scream, I'll cut you. Not enough to kill you right away, just hurt you bad."

She yanked the duct tape down, and Christy gasped for air. "You killed him so my aunt would take the blame, right?"

"Yes, little Christy."

"I do have the money you asked for," Christy said, praying for the right words, "but if you kill me, you'll never get it."

"Oh, I think I will." Roseann leaned forward and put the tip of the blade on Christy's bottom lip. "Where is it?" She removed the blade so Christy could answer.

"In the box." She nodded toward the box of books and magazines she'd gone through earlier.

"I don't believe you," Roseann said.

Christy kept her body still, but behind her back, she worked her hands against the binding. She felt it loosen. "I had some cash when I came to the motel," she said, "but your mother was half-asleep, and I didn't want to just leave the money without talking to you. I did intend to come back to the motel, Roseann, whether you believe me or not. But when I came here and saw some things were missing from that box, I hid the money in the big book on the bottom." The excuse sounded lame to Christy, but maybe Roseann would at least turn her back and check the box.

Outside, the daylight faded, making the unit darker. Roseann became a silhouette of curly hair, dark clothing, and white sneakers. "Well, Millie," she said, looking at the doll sitting primly on the floor, its blue eyes iridescent in the dim unit, "I guess we'll find out if she's lying."

Christy twisted her wrists so hard that she heard something pop. She thought it was a bone, and it might have been, but it was also the tape. She wiggled her hands. They were free.

Roseann went to the boxes, looking to see which one held books. She looked over her shoulder. "Now keep your mouth shut. If you scream, I'll be back in a flash and make mush of that pretty face."

She turned back to the box. Christy slowly brought her hands to her side, wiggling her fingers to pump the circulation. She stared at Roseann's long back.

No matter how smart you think you've been, you're still dumb,
Christy thought. She knew this was her moment to make a move.
Her eyes jumped to the two-by-four. She couldn't pick it up
quickly or quietly, and she dismissed it, her gaze moving to the
thick bottle of energy drink. She could grab the bottle and use
enough force to stun Roseann for a moment.

She stood up slowly, her movement masked by the slam of the
first book on the floor. Roseann reached for the second book.
Christy steeled herself to wait until Roseann dropped the book.
Greed had made Roseann careless. She hadn't bothered to look
over her shoulder again. The book hit the floor.

Christy ran lightly across the floor and grabbed the bottle just
as Roseann turned around. She slammed the bottle against the side
of Roseann's head. The bottle top flew off, and red juice cascaded
down Roseann's face.

The blow stunned her long enough for Christy to knock the
knife out of her hand. It bounced and rattled against the floor, disappearing into a dark corner of the unit.

"Now I really will kill you," Roseann sputtered, trying to stum-
ble to her feet, the red drink filling her eyes. With the loose end of
her shirt, she swabbed her face.

Christy ran toward the door. She yanked it up just enough to
dip under, stalling Roseann, who would have to push the metal
door higher to get out.

Through the mellow light of late afternoon, the white Lincoln
graced the parking space in front of the unit. Christy ran to it,
grateful the door was unlocked. She jumped in the car just as the

metal door flew up and Roseann stumbled outside. She looked like a clown with red streaks on her face and clothes. Her hair hung in a damp mess, red juice dripping from the curls. She gripped the two-by-four like a club.

Christy punched the lock on the doors. She glanced at the ignition, but Roseann had taken the keys.

"Help!" she screamed.

She heard a screech of tires as Jack's SUV roared up the driveway.

Roseann slammed the wood against the window of the Lincoln. Christy scrambled to the passenger side, watching in horror, waiting for the glass to crumble. It didn't. She thanked God for the strength of glass in new cars.

Jack's SUV skidded to a halt behind her, and both doors flew open. Roseann whirled, holding the wood as a weapon.

Jack dove into her, knocking the wood from her hand and wrestling her to the ground. Bobbie yelled into her cell phone. "Get out here now!"

Christy unlocked the door and toppled out of the car.

"Your neck is bleeding," Bobbie cried, tearing off the corner of her T-shirt to press against Christy's neck.

Horrified, Christy watched the wrestling match. Roseann was younger than Jack and almost as strong. They rolled over, and Jack pinned her to the ground, facedown.

Christy stepped into the melee, lifted her foot, and pushed on Roseann's back. "I think you've got her, Jack," she said.

"Not yet," he said, tugging at Roseann's arms, trying to pull them behind her back.

"Jack, be careful!" Bobbie yelled. She shoved her hands into her pocket. "I don't have the hammer," she mumbled, "but I've got the nail." She dropped to her knees beside Roseann and pointed a nail at Roseann's eye. "Be still, if you don't want to lose an eyeball," she snapped.

Roseann stopped wiggling, and Jack gripped her wrists with one hand. He unbuckled his belt and whipped it loose from his pants. Then he circled Roseann's wrists with the thick leather and wound the ends into a knot.

"That should hold her," he called over his shoulder, his breath coming in gasps.

Bobbie jumped up to hug Christy. "Oh honey, when the guys came back without you, the big one remembered he had your cell phone—"

"—and mentioned you were hiding from Hornsby," Jack turned to her, looking pale and shaken. "I couldn't get here fast enough."

"We were scared to death." Tears rolled down Bobbie's cheeks. "If anything had happened to you…"

"But it didn't." Christy hugged her back. "Thanks to you and Jack."

A siren screamed, and everyone looked toward the gate. A fire truck appeared and roared to a stop. Two strong-looking paramedics bounded forward, ready to take charge.

Behind them, the deputy sheriff's car skidded through the entrance. The car shuddered to a halt, and Big Bob leapt out. He lumbered, wide-eyed, toward the crowd and then turned to Christy, slack-jawed with disbelief.

For a split second, no one spoke.

Christy tried to calm herself. Her voice shook, but she couldn't resist asking the question that suddenly popped into her mind. If she didn't make a joke, she was going to burst into tears.

"How was Disney World?" she asked.

twenty-nine

Friday Night, September 29

The Blues Club was packed.

When Bobbie stepped to the microphone, a roar of applause filled the room, but no one moved while she sang. She looked stunning in a red silk dress with silver heels and silver chandelier earrings. Her blond curls dipped around her face, accenting the vivid blue of her eyes. As she sang, her eyes drifted up, seeing her own vision somewhere outside of time.

Christy, Dan, Jack, and Seth sat at the front table. As her aunt's rich voice told of love gone wrong, Christy thought about what they had all gone through and felt a lump swell in her throat. She looked at Dan, who had hardly left her side the past two days.

Wednesday night he had rushed into the emergency room as soon as he'd heard of her ordeal with Roseann. "I'm not letting go of you again," he told her, gently placing his arms around her shoulders as the doctor finished the last stitch on her neck.

She merely winked at him, afraid to move her mouth for fear of disrupting the doctor.

Dan glanced at her now, and as she smiled, he put his arm around her and pulled her closer to his side.

Jack stared up at Bobbie like one in a trance. For the first time in many years, Jack had fallen in love, and Christy knew it was the kind of love that would last because Bobbie loved him just as much.

Seth had surprised them with his appearance when he arrived. His sported a short haircut and wore fresh jeans and a blue polo shirt.

Christy leaned over and whispered to him. "You look great."

Seth made a face and whispered back. "I feel like a nerd, but I had an appointment with financial aid and the dean at Florida State in Tallahassee. Just got back into town and rushed over here. I haven't had time to dirty up yet." He grinned.

Christy waited anxiously. "Good news?"

His brown eyes lit with satisfaction. "My application for a scholarship has been approved."

She squeezed his hand. "Have you told Mom and Dad?"

"Not yet."

They were distracted by the big man who walked up to their table and pulled out a chair. Deputy Arnold greeted them, then turned his attention to Bobbie. She wound down the last notes of her song, and there was a moment of silence. Then the crowd leapt to their feet, clapping and yelling for more.

For a moment, Bobbie hesitated, obviously touched by the warm welcome on her first night back. "Thank you," she said, smiling around the room. Her gaze came to rest on the front table.

"And thanks for believing in me. I love all of you."

Seth leaned toward Deputy Arnold. "I think she means you."

Deputy Arnold shot a gaze at Seth. "I don't think we've met," he said with a wry grin, looking pointedly at Seth's haircut and neat shave.

"Everyone have a good evening," Bobbie called. She blew a kiss to the crowd, then stepped away from the microphone.

The band struck up a happy tune as she walked from the stage down to the table where her fan club waited. As she approached, the men stood, but she waved them back down.

"That makes me uncomfortable," she said. "Beth and Grant want us over for a late-night snack. And Deputy Arnold, you're welcome to join us."

"Thanks, but my wife needs me home with the kids tonight. They're still keyed up from our trip to Disney World. But I wanted to talk to all of you before I head out. I just asked Donna if we could borrow her office for a few minutes so we could have some privacy."

They followed him to the back of the club and entered Donna's neat office. Big Bob leaned against the wall as Jack, Bobbie, and Seth settled into chairs. Dan sat in the last vacant chair and pulled Christy onto his lap.

Deputy Arnold cleared his throat and folded his arms over his broad chest. "I want to give you some information to put your minds at ease. I don't want you looking over your shoulder, worrying about anybody coming after you," he said, looking at Bobbie.

"Roseann Cole is making a full confession," he continued, "hoping it will keep her off death row. She told us her story, beginning with the night Eddie won ten grand on a football game. She knew he hid his money, so she watched him carefully when they got home. Seems he thought she was asleep on the couch when he opened the door to the closet. With his back turned, she couldn't see what he was doing, but she could see an edge of the vacuum cleaner and she heard him unzip something. When he finished and turned around, she closed her eyes again.

"The next day, when he went to gas up the truck for their trip to the football game, Roseann checked out the closet and found nine grand in the bag of the vacuum cleaner. She hid it in that doll of hers.

"Eddie had hoped to win more money that weekend to pay off his debt of fifteen grand. Since he had a thousand on him, he didn't check the hiding place until he returned. The vacuum cleaner was gone, along with some other items, and he knew Bobbie had been there. When they went looking for her, they learned she'd left for Summer Breeze. Eddie told Roseann that enforcers had threatened to break some bones if he didn't pay off his debt."

A deep sigh heaved through Deputy Arnold's chest. "Here's the way we've got it figured, and some of our facts came from Hornsby. Tony Panada paid him to check the unit for money after Bobbie and Christy left on Monday. Hornsby knew about Panada's pornography and that bookies were after Eddie, but he swears he didn't know Eddie had been killed until he found him and that he wasn't sure who'd done it.

"Hornsby volunteered his suspicions to us, which check out with what Roseann told us. He figured the guys from Memphis—

Downey and Joe Panada—followed Eddie here with orders to get the money he'd won. Tony tipped Hornsby that his cousin Joe had called and they should keep an eye out for Eddie Bodine and his white truck. Hornsby said Tony happened to be leaving one of his units when Bobbie and Christy arrived that Monday. Tony made a call on his cell phone when he spotted the red truck with Tennessee license plates. The Memphis guys had learned Eddie was after his ex-wife, who had stolen his money, so they hurried down here. They were staying at the Summer Place Condos, waiting for the right time to nab Eddie.

"But before they did, Roseann killed him. She claims she saw a light in the unit behind her when she shoved Eddie in the barrel. She knew someone was back there, so she got out. It had to be Tony Panada."

"So Panada must have peeked through the hole and witnessed what happened," Christy said.

Deputy Arnold nodded. "Apparently. When Roseann got back to Memphis, she got a call from a blocked number. The caller told her he saw what she did to Eddie, and if she didn't fork over the money to Downey and Panada, he'd tell the police what he knew. He reminded her that enforcers play rough, but she was too greedy to give up the money and took off."

Big Bob paused for breath, thrusting a hand through his thick silver hair. "So there was a witness to the murder after all. Tony Panada. But he's already in big trouble for filming and selling pornography of minors. The FBI was building a case against him before all this happened. Now, with Roseann's information, he's in a lot more trouble. We'll see what happens."

Everyone stared at him, trying to absorb the information. Then a soft whimper filled the room as Bobbie put her hands to her face and began to sob. Jack wrapped his arm around her, holding her close.

"I'm sorry, Mrs. Bodine," Deputy Arnold said, tugging at his long nose the way he often did when frustrated.

"Don't call me Bodine!" Bobbie cried, looking up. "I'm Bobbie, just Bobbie."

"And there'll be a different last name soon," Jack announced.

Deputy Arnold grinned. "Glad to hear that, Jack."

"Hey," Seth spoke up. "Mom and Dad are waiting. I say, let's go."

Bobbie dried her tears and was smiling again as they walked out of the club into the soft September evening.

"Honey, the way you sing the blues…" Jack said, shaking his head in amazement.

"Yeah, well, it's gonna be hard to sing the blues after tonight. I can't put my heart into a sad song anymore."

"You did tonight," Christy said.

"I was saying good-bye to the past. To a world of blues. I know life can't be perfect," Bobbie said, "but I've got a real chance for happiness with you guys. And with my new shop."

Christy nodded, thinking about her own role as a partner in I Saw It First. Her mystery novels had centered on buried treasure, but Bobbie had intrigued her with the treasure-from-trash con-cept. Maybe she'd find an old gold coin or a hidden diary in one of their finds.

Christy and Dan reached the car, but she turned back. "See you guys in a minute," she called.

She looked again at Bobbie, the small, vivacious woman in red, whose soft laughter drifted through the night. Her chandelier ear-rings swung as she dipped her golden head back to look up at the stars.

Christy smiled. Bobbie had burst into their lives, mysterious and intriguing, and upset their comfortable world. She had brought laughter and fun along with heartache and tears, but she had taught them a valuable lesson about courage and hope.

Most of all, she had taught them to look beyond the flaws and find the promise.

Bobbie's Umbrella Lamp

The purpose of this project is to take a lamp you already have and perk it up by covering the lamp shade with a unique umbrella shade.

Supplies:

- Umbrella (a small lady's or child's umbrella), preferably one with stripes, plaid, or an eye-catching design (even a schoool logo). Bobbie used her grandmother's parasol.
- A lamp with a "tired" shade
- Hot glue
- Wire cutters or tin snips
- Paints and paintbrush
- Saw or pipe cutter

Instructions:

1. Detach the support spines from the ribs of the umbrella by cutting with wire cutters or tin snips.
2. Remove the umbrella pole by sawing (if wood) or cutting with a pipe cutter (if metal).
3. Position the umbrella over the present shade, adjust height where you like, and use hot glue to tack in place.
4. Paint the base of lamp in colors to match the umbrella.

To see a picture of this idea, along with other do-it-yourself projects, visit www.PeggyDarty.com.

Thanks to Carmie and Diana at Pieces Unique Décor for advice on this project.

Acknowledgments

I wish to thank the following people for their advice and con-
tributions to this novel:

The Florida Department of Law Enforcement and former
Alabama coroner Dell Green for setting me straight on technicalities.
Joyce Holland, thanks for your expertise and advice on the Emerald
Coast, and thanks and a hug to Dorothy Sanders, my authority on
"found treasures," who opened my eyes to a new world of antiques,
flea markets, and "curbside treasures." Without Dorothy, I would
never have thought of the pickle barrel! Thanks to Lori O'Callaghan
at Junk Warehouse in Lake Barrington, Illinois, who looks beyond
the flaws and finds the promise, providing my theme for *When Bobbie Sang the Blues*. And finally, thanks to Carmie and Diana at Pieces
Unique Décor, a shop in Polson, Montana. They gave me valuable
advice on restoring special pieces and allowed me to poke around
among their things.

Special thanks to Judi McNair, a great friend and Queen
Mother of A Lotta Dazzling Divas. You've helped in many ways,
and I owe you a red luncheon! Hugs to all the other great Red Hat
sisters across the country who bring fun and laughter to my life
and my stories. That includes you, Denise!

For all the gang at WaterBrook Press, I can't name everyone
who has helped me for fear of leaving someone out, but you are all

very much appreciated. Thank you, Shannon, for vision and gentle suggestions that sharpened the mystery. Steve, Dudley, and Ginia, thanks for your commitment to my work and your constant encouragement. You're truly the best in the business.

Finally, love and hugs to my family: Steve and Lucy; Darla; Lan, Susan, David, and Drew; and my husband, Landon. You strengthen my life with your encouragement and your love.

Most of all, I thank you, the faithful reader, for without your loyalty, there would be no books. I sincerely appreciate and thank all the wonderful booksellers across the country who buy, stock, and point out my books when a shopper strolls by. God bless you!

About the Author

I have been writing off and on for twenty years while raising a family and living in different parts of the United States. Writing is my passion, and nothing is more fun for me than stepping into a brand-new world, filling it with characters, and planning a life for these characters. I've written romances, historicals, romantic suspense, and mystery. The cozy mystery is, by far, my favorite, because this genre allows the reader to participate in solving the mystery.

My faith has been a fundamental part of my life, and I thank God for being richly blessed. One of the greatest blessings is the opportunity to write. I hope to show in my writing how God works in miraculous ways through the lives of people. I want my stories to portray themes of hope and forgiveness through his love. In this story, Bobbie Bodine offered us a valuable lesson: look beyond the flaws and find the promise.

My husband and I have reached a point in our lives where we can now pursue the dream of spending our summers in Colorado and our winters in Florida. I draw inspiration from both places.

I love hearing from my readers, so please stop by my Web page, www.PeggyDarty.com.

Since my readers are my friends, I'll end this little note with a favorite Irish blessing: May the road rise to meet you, may the wind be always at your back, may the sun shine warm upon your face, may the rain fall soft upon your fields, and until we meet again, may the Lord hold you in the palm of his hand.

More Mischief and Mayhem on the Florida Coast!

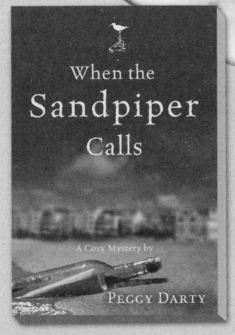

When the
Sandpiper
Calls

A Cozy Mystery by

PEGGY DARTY

A message in a bottle and the ladies of the Sassy Snowbirds help mystery writer Christy Castleman solve a real life crime while finding romance and deepening her faith.

Available in bookstores and from online retailers.

WATERBROOK PRESS
www.waterbrookpress.com

To learn more about WaterBrook Press and view
our catalog of products, log on to our Web site:
www.waterbrookpress.com

WATERBROOK
PRESS